A CORNISH ROSE

Recent Titles by Linda Sole from Severn House

THE TIES THAT BIND
THE BONDS THAT BREAK
THE HEARTS THAT HOLD

FLAME CHILD

THE ROSE ARCH
A CORNISH ROSE

A CORNISH ROSE

Linda Sole

This first world edition published in Great Britain 2001 by
SEVERN HOUSE PUBLISHERS LTD of
9–15 High Street, Sutton, Surrey SM1 1DF.
This first world edition published in the USA 2002 by
SEVERN HOUSE PUBLISHERS INC of
595 Madison Avenue, New York, N.Y. 10022.

British Library Cataloguing in Publication Data

Sole, Linda
   A Cornish rose
   I. Title
   823.9'14 [F]

ISBN 0-7278-5652-9

Typeset by Palimpsest Book Production Ltd.,
Polmont, Stirlingshire, Scotland.
Printed and bound in Great Britain by
MPG Books Ltd., Bodmin, Cornwall.

Prologue

*G*érard is dead and my heart is turned to stone. As I sit looking out at the streets of Paris, I know that I shall leave this place soon and I do not believe I shall ever return. Without Gérard, my life seems empty, meaningless.

Our time together was so brief and yet so glorious, a golden moment of perfect love, enshrined in my memory forever. Perhaps happiness such as ours was never meant to last – perhaps we made the gods jealous and so they took him. He was so beautiful, so sure . . . so reckless. And now he is gone and I am left alone with my heart of jade.

Sometimes I look at the pendant of green jade Gérard bought for me at the fair. I think it must have been an omen – just as the gypsy's warning that day. She told me that my destiny lay across the water and that I would know grief and despair. How true were her words!

Why am I not dead, too? Why can I not die so that they could bury us together, to lie side by side for all eternity? I have longed to die, but the nuns taught me too well. It would be a sin to take my own life.

Besides, Gérard's child is growing in my womb. How could I destroy the life of an innocent child?

I must learn to live with my grief and the fear that dwells always in my mind. For Laurent has condemned me to suffer the torments of hell until I can discover the truth.

If Laurent is truly my father, then Gérard was my half-brother – and our child is the fruit of a forbidden love.

How can I bear to go on living? And yet I must. Tomorrow

1

a ship will take me to England, the land of my birth. Perhaps there I shall finally discover the truth. Perhaps in time I shall be able to untangle the web of lies my mother wove to protect me, and in doing so I may find a measure of peace.

One

'Take care of yourself, my dearest Jenny.' Kate clung to me emotionally. She was my one real friend, the only person with whom I could share my darkest secrets, and she had come to say goodbye before I left France. We both knew it might be a long time before we met again. 'I shall miss you so much.'

I glanced at our reflections in the wall mirror: Kate so neat, plainly dressed with her dark hair swept up into a coronet about her head, and me, my wild red curls escaping from the ribbon that held them, my face pale, gown black but elegant and of the finest cloth. We were so different, and yet in many ways so alike.

'You will write to me?' I asked. I was feeling lost and lonely, afraid of the unknown future waiting for me in London. 'And you won't tell Laurent – or Henriette – my secret?'

Kate was going to live at the Comte de Arnay's chateau. She was taking my place as a companion to Madame Henriette Rossi's son Charles, a rather naughty little boy of whom I had become fond during my months as his unofficial governess.

Henriette was the comte's wife's cousin, and a widow. She had chosen to live at the comte's chateau for reasons of her own. I thought she was a little in love with him, though he seemed not to think of her in that way.

Although I felt nothing but hatred for the comte now, and had left the chateau vowing never to return, I was pleased for Kate. I believed she would be able to make a

3

new life for herself there – and life had not always been kind to her.

'You know the answer to both those questions, Jenny Heron,' Kate said and hugged me. 'I shall never forget that you accepted me without question after . . . after all that I told you. You are my friend, and I shall always care for you.' She smiled at me, reaching out to touch my cheek. 'Be happy, Jenny – and don't worry too much over things you can't change.'

She was referring to the child I carried, of course. Kate knew all my secrets, just as I knew hers. We had suffered much the same fate, both conceiving a child out of wedlock – though her lover had abandoned her, leaving her penniless and forced to do things she would rather forget. My mother had helped her, but Kate had disappeared afterwards, ashamed and afraid that I would not be able to accept what had happened to her. Gérard had brought us together again a few weeks before the riding accident that had caused his sudden death. Neither of us would ever forget that. And now that I was in trouble, Kate was proving herself a staunch friend.

'We should be leaving.' The sound of Marie's voice made us both turn our heads. She was standing in the doorway, watching us, a rather odd expression in her eyes that made me wonder if she had been listening to our conversation. I suspected that she was a little jealous of my friend, though I did not see why she should be. 'The cab is here, mademoiselle.'

'Ask him to wait,' I said. 'I shan't be long, Marie. I want to say goodbye to Kate.'

Marie was a pert, pretty young woman, who had once been my mother's maid and was now to be my companion. She went without a word, but I sensed her silent disapproval and wondered at it.

'I wish I could come with you,' Kate said, after the door had closed behind Marie. 'I know Marie was your mother's maid – we met once when Adele invited me to her house –

but I do not like the idea of your going to London with her as your only companion.'

'You had no one,' I reminded Kate. 'When you were deserted, alone in that inn without a penny, you had nothing and no one to help you. I am much luckier. Laurent has given me the house in London – and an income for life. I would prefer not to take his money . . . but I shall do so for the sake of my child.'

'It is because of the child that I am worried for you,' Kate said. 'I know you, Jenny . . . I know you will be tormented by doubts. I wish I could be with you – but I scarcely escaped arrest the last time I was in London. We had chained ourselves to the railings outside the Palace of Westminster and the police were dragging us away one by one. I hit one of them and knocked his helmet off. And they put posters out all over the city, offering a reward of fifty pounds for my arrest.'

My friend was a staunch supporter of Women's Suffrage, and I smiled as I thought of Kate knocking off the policeman's helmet. She had always been a little reckless, and fierce in defence of her beliefs.

'It's all right, Kate,' I said. 'Please do not worry about me. I shall be fine.'

She nodded, an answering smile in her eyes. 'Of course you will, Jenny. It's just that I shall miss you.'

'And I shall miss you,' I said. I turned to the child hiding behind Kate's skirts, her dark eyes peeping out at me curiously. 'And now I want to say goodbye to Louise. Come, give me a kiss, my darling.'

Kate's daughter held out her arms to me, and I swept her up to kiss her and inhale the sweet baby smell.

'She's so beautiful,' I said to Kate as I set the child down again. 'So perfect.'

'As your child will be,' Kate promised. 'Even if Gérard was your half-brother – and there is no proof, Jenny – it doesn't necessarily mean your child will suffer.'

'No, of course not.' I hugged Kate once more. Her words were meant to comfort me, but even she could not banish the nightmares that came to haunt me when I was alone at night. 'I must go now. I'll write when I'm settled.'

She nodded and let me go. In the hall, Madame Leconte was hovering to say goodbye before she set out to visit her sick brother. It had been her intention to accompany me to London as a chaperone, but fate had intervened.

'You will be all right, Jenny?' she asked, glancing at the wedding ring I was wearing – a ring to which I had no right. 'Are you sure you do not want to wait until I can come with you?'

'No, madame,' I said, and kissed her cheek. 'I want to thank you for all you have done for me – but my mind is made up. I shall call myself Madame Heron, as Mama did. No one in London will know that I am not married.'

Madame Leconte looked at me doubtfully. She had been a good friend to me since I left the chateau, and to my mother before me. They had been friends all the years Mama worked as a seamstress in Paris – the years when she had also, unbeknown to me, been the Comte de Arnay's mistress.

If only she had told me the truth!

It was useless to look back, or to apportion blame. Gérard and I had been reckless in our love. If we had obeyed the laws of society, if we had waited to wed before succumbing to our passion, I should not now find myself in this precarious situation.

And yet I should never forgive Laurent. Believing himself my father, he had, after my mother's sudden death, taken me to his chateau – the house where his invalid wife still lived! – without telling me that there was a blood tie between us. How could he have been so careless? How could he have over-looked the possibility that Gérard and I might fall in love?

When he discovered we were lovers, he had revealed the secret that had led Gérard to ride off in anger – a tormented, terrible passion that had resulted in his death.

Laurent was the murderer of his own son. Because of him, I felt that my heart had turned to stone – and I hated him. Nothing he could do would soften my heart towards him. Even his generosity towards me after the tragedy of Gérard's death could not ease the hatred I felt.

The cab was waiting to carry me on the first stage of my journey – a journey that would take me across the water to a new life. I was nervous as I stepped into it that day, fearful of what I might find – and yet it was also a relief.

Perhaps in England the nightmares would cease and I would be able to find some peace.

I stood on deck of the ship carrying me to England, looking back as we left the shores of France far behind, watching the foaming wake as it broke over the waves. I could taste salt on my lips but did not know whether it was the tang of the sea or my tears.

Everyone I had ever loved was left behind. I was abandoning all that was dear and familiar to go to a strange land, where I should know no one, and I was apprehensive.

Perhaps in England, I should discover the truth of my birth. Mama had spoken of my father as an English gentleman, and I had seen him as a kindly, bewhiskered, rather scholarly man.

But Laurent believed he was my father, and my mother had allowed him to believe it. How could that be – and why had she lied to me all those years?

It was very strange, very hurtful that she should have lied to me this way. I was nervous of what I would discover. Yet I had to know the truth . . . for my child's sake.

Somehow, when I was ready, I would find my mother's family. Gérard and I had planned to search for them together, but now I would have to do so alone. But perhaps not just yet – not until my grief was less raw, until my child was born. Perhaps then I might find the strength to face up to the secret Mama had hidden from me for so long.

*   *   *

'A man has called to see you,' Marie said as she entered the parlour where I was standing at a window, looking out at a large but unattractive garden. 'He says he is Monsieur de Arnay's lawyer here in London and wants to know if *Miss* Heron will see him.'

She handed me a white card with plain lettering in black ink. I glanced at it for a moment, feeling a flutter of nerves as I caught the flash of gold on my left hand. We had been in town only three days and I had not expected to hear from Laurent's lawyer just yet. I was not sure how to explain the situation – but there was nothing to be gained by putting the meeting off.

'Tell Mr . . .' I looked at the card again and sighed. It was useless to wish myself back in France; that part of my life was over and I could not go back. 'Tell Mr Walters he may come in.'

Marie went away and I returned to my contemplation of the garden. It was very neat and dull with a large area of uninteresting lawn, but could be made pretty if I decided to stay here. I could have more shrubs planted. Pretty flowers that would remind me of home. Perhaps a pergola covered with white roses . . . the thought stirred a memory of the gardens at the chateau where I had walked with Gérard, and I felt the sting of tears in my eyes.

It was so foolish to let myself remember!

'Miss Heron?' I blinked hard and turned as a man spoke. 'Forgive me for disturbing you but the Comte de Arnay asked me to call as soon as possible . . .'

'I prefer to be called Madame Heron,' I said, giving him my hand, which he held briefly. I had decided that I must be frank with him. 'It is my intention to live here alone with my personal companion and the servants. Therefore, I shall let it be known that I am a widow and still in mourning.'

He looked startled for a moment, then nodded. 'I see . . .

then I must open your account at the bank in that name. Mrs Jennifer Heron – is that correct?'

'My friends call me Jenny, but I was christened as Jennifer, I believe. Will you have some tea with me, Mr Walters?'

'Thank you, madame. I believe I will.'

He was smiling at me. He had rather an attractive smile, though he was not a handsome man. His face was a little too fleshy, his hair thinning at the temples. I judged him to be in his mid-thirties, successful, fond of his food and good-natured.

'Please sit down, Mr Walters.'

'Thank you.' He flapped out his coat-tails and sat on a hard, brocade-covered chair by the fireplace. 'Monsieur de Arnay has instructed me to help you in any way possible, madame. If you need anything you have only to contact me and I shall do whatever I can to assist.'

'You are very kind, sir – but I believe my needs will be quite insignificant. I shall live very quietly and I am sure you have more important calls on your time.'

'You are telling me you wish for privacy?' His eyes were intent on my face. 'You need not fear interference from me, madame. I am here only to serve you.'

I felt I had been rude and blushed. In the grate, the fire crackled and spat little sparks of burning wood at the guard. I lifted my head, looking at him proudly.

'You are perhaps surprised at my desire to live alone – without a proper chaperone?'

'I dare say many young women would do so if they were able. My wife is a strong supporter of the Suffragette movement. You might like to meet her? She did ask me to offer an invitation to dinner one evening, though I warned her you would probably refuse. We entertain only a few friends and no doubt you have been used to society of a very different order . . .'

'No, indeed I have not,' I said. 'I met a few friends of my guardian – and of my mother when I stayed with her in Paris.

9

I attended one small dance, but no grand balls or assemblies, nothing like that.'

'Your mother died some months ago, I believe?'

'Yes; it is about a year since her death. I still miss her.' I blinked and looked away. Gazing into the fire, I watched one of the logs burn out and crumble into ash. And I was thinking of my mother, of Gérard – both of whom I had loved, both gone now. *Ashes to ashes . . . dust to dust.* 'I loved her very much.'

'Of course.'

Perhaps he was wondering why I was still wearing black. I did not tell him that I was mourning the death of my lover. He would have been shocked, especially if he had known the whole truth – that I was carrying a child. I doubted that he would have been so eager to introduce me to his wife then; I should be a social outcast, a fallen woman.

Marie brought in the tea, gave me a quizzing glance behind his back, and then left again. I poured tea, offered milk and sugar and a fresh seed cake baked by my housekeeper, all of which he accepted.

'I should like to meet Mrs Walters. Would you give me a few days to settle in and then ask her if she will call, please? Although I intend to live quietly, I have no wish to be a hermit. I hope to make friends – with people I like and trust.'

'You will like Susanna,' he assured me and helped himself to another slice of the cake. 'She is a little outspoken perhaps – but honest like yourself. We have a son of twenty months who leads her a merry dance, but she has never-ending patience with him.'

'I am already looking forward to meeting her and your son. For the past few months I was in charge of a rather boisterous boy of some five years. He was a little difficult at times but . . .' I sighed as I recalled the look on Charles's face when I'd told him I was leaving. He had been angry, sulky, resentful . . . and unhappy. It was his unhappiness that hurt me. I knew he was lonely, because Henriette did not have enough time for him, and felt I had let him down. 'I shall miss him. And I fear he will miss me.'

'You will be seeing him on your return to France, perhaps?'

'It is not my intention to return to France. I shall make my home in this country – though I am not certain I wish to live in London . . . '

'You have been used to the country?' I nodded and he looked understanding. 'London can seem noisy and dirty at first – though you will discover there are several parks where you can find peace and quiet.'

'But if I wished to live in the country? I am not sure . . .'

'Of your financial position?'

'My guardian said something about the house . . .' I looked at him uncertainly.

'The house is yours. The deeds are in my safe. You are at liberty to sell or lease if you wish – though I would not advise the sale of such a valuable property. As for your income – you are to receive five thousand pounds each year and a sum equal to twice that has already been placed at your disposal.'

'Ten thousand pounds!' I gasped. 'Surely that cannot be right? It is a fortune!'

'A small one,' he agreed. 'Used sensibly it could give you security for life. Your income is respectable, madame – though you are not wealthy by the standards of some of your neighbours. This part of town is one of the better areas, you know. Houses in most of these squares fetch a pretty penny these days.'

'You have shocked me, sir.'

I fought for calm but my mind was whirling in confusion. When Laurent had spoken of an income I had not dreamed he meant to settle a fortune on me, nor had I expected a house of this importance and size. It was far too much! My first instinct was to refuse his blood money, but I had to be sensible. I had to think of the future. I was carrying Gérard's child; our child

11

must have security. My pride could not be allowed to put that security at risk.

Mr Walters sensed my unease.

'Monsieur de Arnay is an extremely wealthy man, madame. He would not expect his ward to live on less than five thousand a year. You may not find it as much as you think. The upkeep of a house like this does not come cheaply. You could live for far less in a smaller but adequate house in the country.'

I nodded thoughtfully. 'I may decide to look for a house somewhere else. Would you be able to advise me – on values and legal matters?'

'Of course. That is my business – and my pleasure.'

He had finished his tea. I lifted the silver teapot to offer a refill. 'Would you care for another cup, sir?'

'No, thank you, madame. I should be on my way – but I'll tell Susanna that she may call on you next week, shall I?'

'She will be very welcome.' I smiled as he got to his feet. 'It was good of you to call, Mr Walters. You have been helpful.'

'My pleasure, Miss – forgive me, Madame Heron.' His cheeks were slightly flushed as he corrected himself.

'I shall see you to the door, sir.'

'Thank you, but there is no need.'

'Marthe would never let a visitor see himself out.' I smiled as he raised his brows. 'Tante Marthe looked after me as a child. She was and is very dear to me.'

There was no need to explain the story of my life – that my mother had placed me in the care of a woman she hardly knew because it was too difficult to keep me with her in Paris. I had not suffered from the arrangement. Indeed, it seemed to me now, looking back, that Marthe's love for me had been more special than I had realised at the time. My life on the farm had been uncomplicated and wholesome, and because of Marthe I had lived a life of innocent happiness until I was forced to grow up.

At the door I shook hands with my lawyer, and he went off at a good pace down the busy London street.

Hesitating for a moment on the doorstep, I saw a smartly dressed woman enter the house next door but one. She had noticed me saying goodbye to my visitor but now gave no sign of having done so. I was frowning as I returned to the parlour.

Laurent's house had surprised me. I had not expected such grandeur nor that the area would be so exclusive. My mother's house in Paris – the house he had bought for her when she became his mistress – had been a much more modest establishment, and I had thought he would give me something similar. I would have preferred it: I did not think I should make many friends here.

'Well?' Marie said as she came in to the parlour to collect the tea trolley a few minutes later. 'What did he have to say?'

'It seems I own the house – so I could sell it if I wish.'

'Do you have a choice? You cannot afford to live here, can you?'

'I am to have an income of five thousand pounds a year.'

'Five thousand . . .' Marie looked thoughtful. 'It will probably cost you that to run the house. Did you know that your housekeeper buys the best of everything? I questioned the price of some new lamps for the kitchen and she told me the comte always wanted the best. If you stay here you will have to be more careful. I should sell if I were you.'

'Mr Walters suggested leasing. He thinks the property is too valuable to sell – an investment for the future.'

'Do you trust him?'

'I think so. Yes, I'm sure he is an honest man.'

'Then take his advice, Jenny. Besides, you won't want to be in town in a few months' time.' She wrinkled her forehead. 'I'm not sure about a village. People always want to know too much about a stranger in their midst. A small market town perhaps . . . or near the sea?'

'Mrs Walters is coming to visit me one day next week. I could ask her for her advice . . . where we should consider buying.'

'We can make inquiries ourselves,' Marie said, then pulled a wry face. 'Or *you* could – these stupid Londoners pretend not to understand me. Adele always said I spoke good English. Very good English.'

Usually Marie's English was more than adequate, but sometimes she became very French, waving her hands excitedly and speaking so fast that no one could understand her.

I smiled at the indignant note in her voice. 'You do, Marie – but your accent is very French. Remember, Mrs Benson finds it difficult enough to understand *me*.'

Mrs Benson was the housekeeper here. A thin, grey-haired woman, rather plain with unremarkable features, she had kept house for Laurent for years and was loyal to him, despite the fact that he had visited only once or twice a year in the past. She was polite, discreet but distant. She had not made me feel particularly welcome, and I thought she resented the fact that I had come to stay in the house – which might have been one of the reasons I felt a little uncomfortable living here.

Yet in my heart I knew it was not really the house or Mrs Benson that made me uneasy – or even my unfriendly neighbours. London itself seemed cold, noisy and strange. I was missing the sound of French voices and the sunshine. It had been cold and damp here ever since our arrival, although it would soon be June.

I recalled the glorious few days I had spent at the hunting lodge near Versailles with Gérard earlier in the year. Although it was only April then, the weather had been wonderful, as warm as summer – much warmer than it was here even now. It was there, hidden away in our love nest, that I had conceived our child. As yet, there was no outward sign to give my secret away, but soon my belly would begin to swell – and then I should not be able to hide my condition.

London seemed unfriendly, and I was experiencing a sharp

nostalgia for my home. I wondered if Marie felt the same. If she was homesick for Paris she had given no sign of it, and I knew she would never desert me while I needed her. As long as I was determined to stay in this country she would stay too – and I could never return to France.

My time at the chateau seemed part of a dream now, a fevered, vivid memory that kept me restless throughout the long nights when I hardly dared to close my eyes.

There were moments when I felt almost as angry with my mother as I did with Laurent. Why had she never told me she was the Comte de Arnay's mistress? Why had she never told me my father's name?

I had hoped to find something amongst her papers. Madame Leconte had told me there was a letter. She had packed it for me herself in Mama's trunk – the silk-lined trunk I had brought with me to London, which contained all her personal things. But when I looked there was no sign of the letter, even though I took everything out. What had happened to it? I believed the only person who could have taken it was my guardian – but why should he? It made no sense.

Only Mama had known for certain who my father was. Why had she not found a way of telling me?

Thoughts of this nature went round and round in my head, torturing me during those first, restless nights I spent at my new home in London. Sometimes I looked at two sketches, made by a street artist in Paris, of Mama and me when I was fifteen years old. A stranger had asked the artist to make them, taking the best two with him. I had never known who that stranger was – but I suspected it might have been Philip Allington.

I had met Mr Allington only briefly, when he called at the house in Paris to see Mama. He had been asking her if she would allow me to visit someone – a woman, I believed. Mama had refused, and afterwards she had cried bitterly, saying that the visit had brought back unhappy memories.

Mr Allington had tried to contact me after Mama's death,

but I had refused to see him. Perhaps I had been wrong. It might be that he could tell me some of the things I needed to know – and yet I was still reluctant to see him.

My mother had wanted to protect me from something she had thought might hurt me, something that had happened years ago in England. She could not have known that by keeping the truth from me, she would contribute to a terrible tragedy.

I needed to know the truth, and yet I was reluctant to probe too deeply into the past. And so the restless nights went on and on.

During the day I could keep busy, I could drive out the demons that came to haunt me, but at night they crowded into my mind. If I slept at all, it was to wake with tears on my cheeks.

Sometimes I thought of Laurent's comtesse, a prisoner in her own rooms at the chateau because of her poor health. I remembered the vivid tapestries of women in torment she had shown me. I had wondered what drove her to do such work, but I was naive then. Now I knew how she had suffered from her husband's jealousy. He had discovered her in the arms of a lover, and from then on they had lived apart, married only in name. It was then that Laurent and Mama had become lovers.

Now, after all that had happened to me, I could understand the torments of the mind . . . the darkness that could haunt the unwary . . . and I pitied Béatrix de Arnay. I pitied her, but I did not want to be like her.

I was determined that somehow I would live through this time of grief and pain, and I would find happiness again with my child.

Two

It was the first really warm day we'd had since our arrival and I was determined to make the most of it. I sat up and announced my intention when Marie came in to draw my curtains, letting the sunshine flood into the room.

'We are going out today, Marie.'

'You sound brighter this morning,' she said, giving me a thoughtful glance. 'You look better, too.'

'I am feeling better. There is no point in sitting in this house every day. My neighbours obviously have no intention of calling on me. So I shall go to the park – but first we shall go shopping.'

'You want me to come with you?'

'Yes. You are my companion, not my maid.' She pulled a face. 'Don't look like that, Marie. That is what we agreed. There are more than enough servants in this house. I want someone to talk to . . . and you are the only one who speaks French!'

Marie laughed. 'We are in England now, Jenny. You know the English expect everyone to speak as they do.'

'Well, I want to speak French today.' I laughed as I got out of bed. 'Why shouldn't we, if we feel like it? We can do anything we please. There is no one to stop us . . .'

And so Marie and I went on our first real excursion since we had come to London. The streets were busy and full of life and colour. I enjoyed watching the people passing by, the press of carriages and the traders' carts pulled by huge

17

horses with silvery manes and bright tackle that jingled as they passed, their hooves clopping noisily on the cobbles.

We spent an enjoyable morning shopping in Bond Street, looking at the large stores with their windows full of enticing goods, but bought only some chocolate from a shop selling Belgian confectionery, which made us feel at home. The assistant was English and stared at us in dismay as we chattered away in French while discussing our purchases.

'That was unkind,' Marie scolded when we left. 'The poor girl could not understand a word you said – and to pretend you did not understand English so that she had to point to everything and explain the price three times. Wicked. You were wicked, Jenny!'

'But it was funny,' I said. I took her arm, directing her towards a nearby café. 'Do not scold me, Marie. I wanted to laugh and I have not felt like laughing for a long time . . .'

I stopped laughing as I saw a man walking towards us, my heart jerking uncomfortably. He was very smartly dressed in a dark blue morning coat, silk hat and striped trousers, and had a flower in his top buttonhole.

He was clearly a gentleman of means, and there was something about him which seemed very familiar. I could not be certain, of course, because I had only seen him once at Mama's house in Paris, but I believed it was Philip Allington. If I did not do something immediately, he would see me – and if I had recognised him, he might also know me. I dived into the nearest shop, which happened to be a bookstore, leaving Marie walking along the street, still talking away to me until she suddenly discovered I wasn't there any more.

It took her a moment or two to realise where I'd gone, and then she followed me into the shop, looking annoyed.

'What did you do that for?' she said. 'You might have told me if you wanted to come in here instead of dashing off like that.'

'I'm sorry,' I said. 'I thought I saw someone . . . I came in here to avoid him.'

'Who?' she asked, looking at me oddly. 'Who do you know in London that you don't want to meet?'

'His name is Allington,' I said. 'He called at the house in Paris once. It was just before I went to school . . . and he upset Mama.'

Marie's eyes narrowed. 'I wish you had pointed him out to me. I've never forgotten . . . someone came to the house just before she died. I told you then, Jenny, if you remember? She told me she had had a visitor from England, though I did not see who came to the house, for I was out. I thought then it was a woman but it might have been him . . . I remember she was upset afterwards and that night I had to send for the doctor. That was the start of her last illness . . .'

'Yes, I remember you saying something at the time.' Marie had been upset after my mother's death. She had said a lot of silly things, even implying that Mama's death might not have been from natural causes. At the time she had thought it was a woman who had called and upset Mama, but now she was implying that it could have been Mr Allington. I did not think that she really knew anything, but had muddled it all up in her mind because she was so distressed by Mama's death.

'It might have been him, of course,' I said thoughtfully. 'He certainly upset her the day I met him, and he could have returned to see her again for some reason. Yes, it might very well have been Mr Allington, Marie. He did write to the comte after she died, asking if he might see me – but I refused. I didn't feel like talking to him then, and I'm not sure that I do now. I was very angry with him for upsetting my mother that day I saw him at the house – though she did not blame him. She said his visit had brought back distressing memories, and that it was not his fault.'

Marie was frowning. 'I wonder why he has been so persistent in trying to see you,' she said. 'What do you think he has to tell you that is so important?'

19

'I don't know.' A trickle of ice went down my spine. 'And I would rather not talk about it just now, Marie. Let's go and have coffee and cake somewhere . . .'

When we got in late that afternoon, I noticed a calling card lying on a silver tray on the hall table. I picked it up and clicked my tongue with annoyance.

'Mrs Walters called while we were out,' I said. 'What a nuisance! What ought I to do now, Marie? Do I return her call or wait for her to come again?'

'Who knows what the English consider correct?' Marie replied with an expressive shrug of her shoulders. She made a little puffing sound with her lips, which was very French. 'I do not understand them. They are crazy . . . this is a crazy country.'

'I think I shall write her a note and ask her to tea on Monday,' I said. 'That will give her three days to reply.'

Marie nodded but said nothing more. She walked upstairs as I laid my hat and gloves on the hall-stand and went through to the study. I preferred this smaller room, with its comfortable settee and chairs, to the more formal salons. It looked out on to the garden and there were French windows which could be opened on fine days such as this. I went out into the garden. Like many town gardens it was long and narrow with high walls at either side which were covered with creepers, clematis and roses. Some of them proved to have flower buds which were just beginning to burst – so perhaps it would be prettier than I had first thought. But I missed the space and freedom of the chateau garden with its pretty, secret walks and the rose arbours . . . but it would be madness to let myself remember.

I picked a few flowers and returned to the study as Mrs Benson brought in a tray of tea. She set it down on the table, then gave a little sniff which was intended to make me look at her.

'Will mademoiselle be joining you, madame?'

'Marie?' I sensed disapproval. 'I'm not sure. Perhaps it would be best if you brought another cup just in case.'

'Very well, madame. Shall I have these flowers put in water for you?'

'Yes, thank you. I should like to have them on my desk.'

She lingered a moment, obviously wishing to say more.

'Yes? You wished to say something?'

'I am not used to having my accounts questioned, madame.'

'Your accounts?'

'Mademoiselle Corbier has demanded to see them.'

'Has she? I see . . .' Marie was very suspicious of Laurent's servants, who she was sure had systematically cheated him for years. 'Well, I expect she is just trying to familiarise herself with the way things are done here. No one is questioning you, Mrs Benson. Marie takes care of things for me and we do need to know what expenses we shall need to meet each quarter.'

'Very well, madame.'

The look she gave me spoke volumes. She had been used to a more liberal regime under the comte.

I sighed as she went out. Marie had the frugal, practical nature of the French bourgeoisie and had been used to keeping a tight rein on my mother's accounts. I knew she had enjoyed noisy, fierce exchanges with the tradesmen in Paris, where such things were expected of her, and her feathers had been ruffled by Mrs Benson's refusal to understand her English. She in turn could not understand the reserved manners of the English woman. I could see trouble brewing between the two of them before long.

I carried a cup of tea over to the desk, which had a leather top and looked as if it had seen some service in the past. Opening the first drawer to take out a few sheets of writing paper, I frowned. They were all embossed with elegant engraving and bore my guardian's title. I dipped my pen in the ink and crossed Laurent's name through several times, then I began to write.

21

Dear Mrs Walters,

    I was sorry to have been out when you called. Please forgive me, but I was not sure when you would call and it was such a lovely day. I should be grateful if you could come to tea one day. Monday, if that would suit . . .

I sighed and chewed the end of my pen. Although I had written to Kate, I had not yet written more than a brief note to Henriette and Marthe. Although they had both played a small part in deceiving me – both must have known Mama's true situation – they did not deserve to be treated so shabbily, especially Marthe, who had loved me and cared for me during my childhood. It was time I told them I was settling in, and it might as well be done now.

I woke from a restless sleep with tears on my cheeks and knew I had dreamed of Gérard. I tried to recall my dream but could not. A sharp, stabbing pain struck at my heart as I realised I could no longer bring his face to mind at will. It was only a few weeks since we had parted and I could not remember.

    'Oh, Gérard . . .' I choked on my emotion. 'Forgive me . . . forgive me.'

    It was not that I had forgotten him or ceased to grieve, just that my memory would not always obey me. It had happened after my mother died, too – but I'd had photographs of her, the sketches that had been done by the street artist in Paris. I had none of Gérard.

    If I were living at the chateau, I could go every day to look at his portrait, which hung in the gallery there . . . I smothered a sob as a wave of longing and homesickness for France swept over me and I felt the weight of my grief pressing down heavily. Sometimes I wished I could just lay down and die.

    Suddenly the vomit rose in my throat and I made a dash

into my dressing room to be sick. I hung over the basin feeling dizzy and very unwell. Several minutes passed before I was able to sponge my face with cool water and return to the bedroom. Catching sight of my pale face in the dressing mirror, I smiled wryly. Gérard's son was reminding me of my reason for living.

I had to be strong for my child's sake. No matter how unhappy I might be, I had to go on.

On the following Monday the housekeeper came in to announce a visitor. 'Mrs Walters to see you, madame.'

I had been sitting in the back parlour reading a much-loved copy of Keats's poems my mother had once given me, because she wanted me to appreciate the English writers. It was a handsome volume, which Mama had had specially bound for me in thick leather. I laid it aside and looked up eagerly as Mrs Benson announced my visitor. I had been looking forward to this ever since I'd had her note accepting my invitation to tea.

Susanna Walters was a pretty, fair-haired woman in her late twenties. She had blue eyes, a soft mouth and a sweet smile – though, like her husband, she had a tendency to plumpness.

'Madame Heron,' she said. 'I hope I'm not too early? Your note said tea and we usually have it at half past three in our house. You may be accustomed to another time. Not that you drink much tea in France, do you? It's coffee and wine there, isn't it? Henry took me over for a week when we married, but we've never been back since. Pity really. I liked Paris.'

'My mother was English,' I said, amused. I liked the talkative Mrs Walters immediately. 'She often drank tea in the afternoons and I took the habit from her.'

'Ah yes, of course. You've lived in France all your life, but you're English really, aren't you?'

'I suppose I am. I've always thought of myself as a mixture of both.' I indicated a comfortable chair. 'Please, do sit down. Mrs Benson will bring tea soon – but I thought we might talk for a while first. Mr Walters was telling me you are a Suffragette. In France, I have a good friend who is a strong supporter of the Cause.'

'Henry talks a great deal of nonsense,' she said with a lift of her fine eyebrows. 'I did attend a few meetings before we married, but I have no time for such things since my son was born. I agree with their principles, of course, but that's about it, I'm afraid.'

'I have been reading about them in the papers since we came to London. It is interesting. The Movement seems very strong here.'

'Is it not the same everywhere? I think once these things start they soon spread – a friend of mine recently returned from America where he had seen several rallies in support of the Movement.'

'Kate says the women are more militant here.'

'Perhaps. Or mule-headed. Some of the things those ladies get up to!' She laughed merrily. 'Henry would have a fit if I joined them. I was invited to a meeting next month, but I doubt if I shall go . . .' She gave me a quizzing look. 'I could give you details if you were interested?'

'Would you? I'm not sure I shall go, but I might.'

'I'll give you the leaflet when you come to dinner this weekend – you will come, won't you? Henry was sure you would find it boring. We shall be a small company – just half a dozen friends and ourselves, but . . .'

'That will suit me very well,' I assured her. 'I shall look forward to it, Mrs Walters.'

'Oh, you must call me Susanna. I insist.'

'Thank you. My name is Jenny.'

'Yes . . .' She fixed me with her bright gaze. 'It suits you.'

We settled down to enjoy ourselves. It had been evident from the first moment that we should get on. I liked Susanna's straightforward manner. She was energetic and cheerful, reminding me a little of Kate.

We talked about France, of my life before my mother died – though not after. I did not want to speak of those things I still found so painful. She told me about her child and her parents, who lived in Cornwall.

'I had lived there all my life,' she said, smiling happily. 'I'm not a town person at all – but Henry's work was here and so . . .' She shrugged expressively. 'Here we are.'

'How did you meet?'

'He came down on holiday with some friends. It was love at first sight for me. Sometimes it happens that way.'

'Yes, it does.' My heart ached at the memory of my first meeting with Gérard. I had loved him from the first, though I had tried to deny it for a while. 'And he asked you to marry him straight away?'

'Oh no. Henry is not impulsive. Not at all.' She laughed at the idea. 'He asked me out a few times and he sent me postcards when he went home. He came down on holiday the next year and the next . . . I think it might have gone on that way forever if I hadn't received a proposal of marriage from someone else, a friend of my family I'd known for years. When I told Henry about it, it seemed to give him a jolt and he finally asked me. Henry is always careful. He's a lawyer, you see.'

Her merry peal of laughter made me laugh too. She was obviously well content with her marriage and her husband. For a moment I envied her safe, uncomplicated life.

We had been talking for well over an hour when Marie came in. She had refused to stay and have tea with my visitor and seemed surprised to discover that Susanna was still with me.

'Susanna – this is my companion, Marie Corbier. Marie, I want you to meet Mrs Susanna Walters.'

'Madame.' Marie's manner was stiff and distant. 'Forgive me. I should not have disturbed you if I had known you were here.'

Susanna glanced at the gilt mantel clock and gave a little

start of surprise. 'Good gracious,' she cried. 'Look at the time. I've been here ages, gossiping. I must go.' She looked at me. 'I shall expect you for dinner on Saturday, Jenny – at seven?'

'Yes, I shall be there. I'll see you to the door.'

When I returned to the parlour Marie was tidying the tea things. She clattered the delicate porcelain cups on to the wooden butler's tray, and I sensed that she was put out about something.

'You need not do that,' I said. 'Mrs Benson will see to it later.'

'It was always my job when Adele had visitors,' she said stiffly. 'I cannot be other than I am. You like to call me your companion, but I am not of your class. My grandmother worked in the fields and her people were always peasants. My mother married a shopkeeper and he took her to live in Paris – but I remember what I am and where I came from.'

She looked so proud and defiant that I could only apologise.

'Oh, Marie,' I said. 'Don't be cross with me. Tell me about your afternoon – did you enjoy yourself?'

She had been to an exhibition of French art. We had talked of going together, but when I'd received Susanna's acceptance of my invitation to tea, she had announced she was going alone.

'It was interesting.' Her frown eased. 'I met a pleasant French family. They are here for the summer. He has some meetings in London and then they are going to tour the country. She was telling me they are going to Oxford next week. Madeline says they were there two years ago, and that it is a nice place to live. Quieter than London but not too quiet.'

'Susanna was telling me about Cornwall,' I said. 'Her parents live in a place called Truro. I thought we might go there for a visit. We could stay and perhaps look for a house?'

'If that's what you want,' she said and turned away with one of her shrugs. 'I'll take the trolley back to the kitchen. I want to see how much meat the butcher delivered this morning. Last week we were charged for a side of pork we never received.'

'Oh, Marie,' I sighed as she went out. 'You are going to cause so much trouble if you're not careful.'

'I care nothing for this Mrs Benson.' She made a little hissing sound between her teeth. 'She may have cheated the comte but she will not cheat us.'

I felt a little nervous before I went to Susanna's dinner party on Saturday evening, spending a great deal of time over my appearance and trying to tame my hair – which had always been the bane of my life – into a neat knot at the nape of my neck. All my efforts were unable to prevent springy coils escaping into little curls about my face.

'You still look like a gypsy, Jenny Heron,' I told my reflection. My eyes were wide and serious pools of grey, but my hair was a wild flame of dark red colour against the cream of my skin. 'Even in mourning you don't look respectable.'

I fastened the little jade heart around my throat on a black ribbon. It was a modest piece of jewellery, not valuable like the things Laurent had given me when I was at the chateau – but I preferred it because it had been a present from Gérard.

'There – that's better. You look almost presentable now.'

I was talking to myself because I was afraid, of course: afraid that Susanna's friends wouldn't like me, because my accent would seem too French and I was a stranger – or because they would know immediately that I was only masquerading as a widow, that I was actually a shameless hussy who was carrying her lover's child.

I smoothed my hands over my stomach, which was still flat beneath my elegant gown and gave no sign that I was pregnant. How foolish I was. No one would know and by the time I did begin to show I would be out of London, away from anyone who might be interested.

Downstairs, Marie was waiting – of course I could not go out in company without my companion.

When we arrived at Susanna's home, which was a tall, attractive Georgian terraced house, she greeted me with a warm smile, drawing both me and Marie in and introducing us to two married couples. The Smiths and the Wilsons were of similar ages to their hosts and pleasant, ordinary people who seemed prepared to accept me as Susanna's friend, and were gracious if not friendly towards my companion.

'We have one more guest,' Susanna told me as her husband gave me a glass of rich golden sherry. 'Philip is a particular favourite of mine. He is seldom in London these days but when he is I always—' She broke off as a man came into the room. 'Philip, my dear, I was afraid you weren't coming.' She swooped on him, kissing his cheek and urging him towards me, an eager light in her eyes. 'You must meet Madame Heron. Jenny . . . this is my friend Philip.'

Something in her manner told me that she was matchmaking.

I froze as I saw the man she was introducing to me, and my heart jerked with fright. He was tall, dark-haired and harsh-featured – or perhaps his features seemed harsh because he looked angry. It was the same man I had seen walking towards me in Bond Street a few days earlier – and the man who had made my mother cry in Paris. Philip Allington! He had changed hardly at all since the day I'd first seen him, except that he looked a little older – and even angrier than the first time I'd seen him.

'Oh, silly me,' Susanna said, mistaking my hesitation. 'Philip Allington.' She looked at me oddly. 'Jenny?'

He was the one person I did not wish to meet that evening – the only one who knew that I could not possibly be *Madame* Heron. But there was nothing to do except brazen it out. I was breathless, my hand trembling slightly as I offered it in response to Susanna's introduction.

'Mr Allington.'

'Madame Heron.' He bowed over my hand. 'It is a pleasure to meet you.'

Could it be that he had not recognised me? Yet there was an odd gleam in his eyes that told me he had. Would he denounce me as a fraud? One word from him, and my chances of making friends this evening would be at an end.

I withdrew my hand from his. My manner towards him was reserved, stiff. His intent look made me uncomfortable. I knew he was wondering why I should call myself *madame* – and I saw him look at the gold band I was wearing on the third finger of my left hand. We stared at each other for a moment in silence, neither of us prepared to make conversation with the other.

I knew Marie was watching, her eyes narrowed, and I was afraid she might say something indiscreet. But she merely nodded when she was introduced to the late arrival, withdrawing immediately into the background, as she obviously believed was proper for a woman in her position.

Between Marie's dark looks and Mr Allington's palpable disapproval, I was most uncomfortable and felt relieved when Mr Walters came up to me.

'Are you feeling more settled in London now, Madame Heron?'

I turned to him with a smile, very conscious of Philip Allington's interest. He was listening to every word! 'I am beginning to, I think – though I have decided that the house is far too large for us. I shall definitely go away for the summer and I may ask you to find me a tenant. My companion has suggested we might find a house in Oxford, but I was thinking of somewhere in Cornwall.' Mr Allington's dark eyes narrowed at this and I averted my gaze, feeling distinctly uncomfortable. What must he be thinking?

'Madame Heron has recently come to live in Russell

Square,' Henry Walters addressed him directly. 'She finds London noisy and dirty, I'm afraid. You know Cornwall well, don't you, Philip?'

'Yes,' he replied. 'As you know, my home is there.'

'You might be able to suggest a suitable area for her to stay?'

'Perhaps – if *Madame* Heron would accept my advice.'

Mr Allington still seemed angry, and that anger was directed at me. I wondered what I could possibly have done to make him look at me that way.

At that moment Susanna started gathering her guests, directing them towards the dining table. I was afraid that I might have been placed next to Mr Allington at the table, but Susanna was too discreet, too thoughtful. She might hope that we would like each other – and we were the only two unattached persons at her dinner party – but she had seated us opposite rather than together. I was between Mr Smith and Mr Walters, for which I silently thanked my hostess.

Our eyes met a few times across the table, however. I was always the first to look away and I thought I detected suspicion in Mr Allington's face. I was embarrassed. It was unfortunate that we should meet in this way, especially after I had been so resolute in my refusal to see him at the chateau.

Apart from my guilty conscience, I found the evening enjoyable enough. Susanna's friends were the kind of people I had hoped to meet; I was well pleased to be invited to tea by Mrs Smith, and to a card afternoon by the Wilsons.

I wondered if Mr Allington might try to speak to me privately, but he made no attempt to make conversation with me at all – though I knew his dark gaze was often on me throughout the whole evening.

My coachman came to collect me as arranged at nine thirty. I kissed Susanna goodbye, thanked her for a pleasant evening and climbed gratefully into the carriage. I had managed to survive an embarrassing encounter and I could only hope that Mr Allington would not speak of his suspicions to the others after I had gone.

Susanna had told me he was hardly ever in London. With any luck I should not have to meet him again.

'So *that* is him!' Marie said as we drove home. 'Now I know who is to blame for her death.'

'Please do not be foolish,' I said, sighing. It seemed as if she must have someone to blame for my mother's illness, as if she could not let it rest until she had found a culprit. 'You do not know anything for certain, Marie. Even if Mr Allington did upset Mama that day – and neither of us can be sure he even visited – it may have had nothing to do with her death. I should not have told you about him if I had thought you would be so foolish.'

'How do you know what caused her to be ill?' she asked almost rudely. 'You were not there. You did not see her at the last – you did not see how distressed she was.'

She had touched a raw nerve, and because of it my reply was harsher than it might have been. 'You will not speak of this again. I do not particularly care for Mr Allington either, but I shall not tolerate such nonsense. You will oblige me by keeping your foolish ideas about Mama's death to yourself.'

She looked at me and I saw resentment in her eyes, but I did not relent. It had hurt me that I was not with my mother at the last – and I did not want to discuss it with Marie.

I dreamed of Gérard that night. He came to me as I stood in a beautiful, secluded garden and I knew that he was there to warn me.

'Take care, Jenny,' he whispered. 'Take care of yourself and the child. I fear for you, my love. You must be ever vigilant . . .'

And then he took me into his arms and kissed me. I awoke with tears streaming down my cheeks.

As I dressed that morning, I looked at myself in the mirror and saw heavy shadows beneath my eyes. Recently I had been feeling very tired, perhaps because I could not sleep – at night I was tormented by my thoughts and fears.

'Oh, Gérard . . . Gérard,' I whispered. 'Come back to me, my love . . . please come back to me.'

But he could not come back to me. He had gone from me forever and I must learn to accept that.

Three

Philip Allington called later that morning. I had been out shopping and saw his card lying on the silver tray in the hall when I got back. Mrs Benson was there, looking very prim and proper in her grey gown as she waited to take my hat and parcels. I looked at the card for a moment, then asked her about our visitor.

'Him!' she said with a disgusted sniff. 'He wouldn't believe me at first when I told him you were out. I thought he was going to force me to let him in so that he could search the house. Almost rude he was – accused me of not telling him the truth.'

The indignation in her face made me smile inwardly, but I was careful not to let her see it.

'That was unnecessary and not very polite of him,' I said. 'I do not think Mr Allington is someone I particularly want to see, Mrs Benson.'

'No, madame. I should think not indeed. I left his card here, because I doubted you would want to see him. I've taken your letters into the study, madame.'

'Thank you – that was thoughtful.'

I picked up the calling card and took it into the study. Perhaps it might be better if I asked Mr Allington to inform me of his business by way of a letter. It would save him another wasted journey.

But first I would read my letters. I was pleased as I saw there was one from Henriette. I broke the seal and began to read what she had written in her scrawling hand.

Dearest Jenny,

How I miss you! My poor Charles never stops asking for you. Though Kate is very good with him, she is not you. Will you not come back to us?

She went on in the same vein for some time, then:

Laurent is like a bear with a sore head these days. He spends most of his time in his own apartments and speaks to no one. I think he drinks too much.

I skipped over a lot more of this, then came to something that concerned me at the end of the letter:

A man called at the chateau asking for you. His name was Philip Allington and he was most insistent that I give him your address in London. Of course I did not. I hope that was right? Please think of us and come back if you can bear it.

I visited Gérard's grave and laid flowers from you today, and I said a prayer for you both. I think of you often, and wish that I had somehow been able to save you from this grief.

Love from your friend, Henriette

Tears stung my eyes as I read her reference to Gérard's grave. Had it not been for Henriette's letters I might perhaps in my grief have doubted that my lover was truly dead, for I had only Laurent's word and I had no reason to trust him. But I was sure that Henriette would not lie to me.

Blinking back my tears, I referred to the part about Philip Allington again. So he had been to the chateau once again to find me, and had been refused my address. It was not surprising, in the circumstances, that he had been angry when we met at Susanna's dinner party – and that he had been a little impolite to Mrs Benson this morning. He must imagine that I had been deliberately avoiding him.

I would write to the address on his card and ask him to inform me of his business by letter. There was really no need for us to meet. After all, if he had wanted to tell me something urgently, he could have done so at Susanna's house, instead of staring at me so rudely all evening.

I felt a shiver of apprehension, as though a dark cloud had passed over my world. The more I thought about it, the more I believed I would be wiser to have as little to do with the unpleasant Mr Allington as possible.

I entertained the Smiths, the Wilsons and the Walters to a small dinner party that weekend. Mrs Benson was an excellent cook; she produced several courses of really delicious food, and it all went off very well.

During dinner I was asked about the World Exhibition that had opened in Paris in April. It was by all accounts spectacular, covering five hundred and forty seven acres – the biggest of its kind ever held in Europe. But I was unable to tell them anything.

'Were you not still in Paris then?' Henry Walters asked. 'I understand the electrical illuminations in the Chateau d' Eau and the Hall of Illusions were particularly popular. There were huge crowds when the President opened it, I believe.'

'I . . . was not well at the time Monsieur Loubet opened the Exhibition.' I had been cast into the depths of despair by the news of Gérard's death and nothing else had made any impression on me.

'But surely—' Henry began and was immediately quelled by a look from his wife. He frowned, turned to Mr Wilson and began to discuss the Boxers uprising in China.

Susanna gave me a little smile. I knew she had seen my discomfort and tactfully stopped her husband from pressing me further.

'Are you happier here now?' she asked as she kissed me goodbye afterwards. 'Henry tells me you are looking for a summer place in Cornwall. I do hope you won't desert us altogether?'

'I haven't decided yet,' I said. 'But I can always come up to visit now and then. And I think we may buy a house nearer London. Perhaps Oxford . . . Marie likes the idea of Oxford. Don't you?'

I glanced at Marie but she was not listening. She had been quiet all evening, hardly saying a word except to answer when someone spoke to her. I suspected she was a little jealous of my friendship with Susanna.

'It is a pity you could not find a smaller house in town,' Susanna said, 'but I suppose you will make up your own mind when you are ready.' She glanced out of the window as she pulled on her gloves. 'It's raining again. We've had such awful weather this year. I wonder why you don't go back to France, my dear?'

'No,' I said. 'No, I shan't go back to France . . . even if it never stops raining here . . .'

A few days later the rain cleared up as if by magic. Summer had finally arrived and we had several consecutive warm, sunny days. I made the most of them, driving to Richmond in an open carriage, walking in the park or shopping. One morning I saw several younger members of the royal family as I was walking through Regent's Park. People were watching them, bowing respectfully, lifting their hats as their carriage went bowling past.

I was enjoying myself, watching some children playing with hoops. They were all dressed alike in little sailor suits, their hats made of straw with blue ribbons at the back. A nanny dressed in a grey uniform was sitting on the bench, watching them. She smiled at me, and I was tempted to go over to her – and then a voice spoke to me from behind.

'It's good to see the royal family out,' a woman said to me

as I turned. 'For years after her husband died, her poor dear Majesty hardly ever ventured out – almost a recluse, she was. It's such a shame Prince Albert died so young. They were a delightful family. She was such a good mother, always drawing pictures of her children when they were small – and quite a talented artist, I believe. A tireless worker – an example to the rest of us.'

'Yes, I am sure she was,' I replied.

'We shan't see her like again. The Prince is not the man his father was, no indeed. Albert was a fine man, a fine man. And the Queen is a good woman.' She looked at me curiously. 'You're in mourning yourself, dearie – not your husband, I hope?'

'Yes . . . Yes, as it happens.'

'And you in your condition . . .' She touched my hand in sympathy as I blushed. 'Yes, I thought I was right. I can always tell – it's my profession, you see. About two months, is it? Yes, I thought so. Well, you'll have something to comfort you, won't you? Children are a mixed blessing, of course – but when you've lost your husband . . .'

'Yes . . . Please excuse me. I have to meet someone.'

It was not true, but I felt flustered. My pleasure in the outing was spoiled. If a total stranger could just look at me and tell I was with child, perhaps it was time I thought of moving to the country.

Mrs Benson was waiting for me when I got in and I could see she was very annoyed about something.

'That man was here again,' she announced before I had even got my hat off. 'When I told him you weren't here he was angry. Accused me of lying, he did – said he would be back and next time he wouldn't take no for an answer.'

'What an unpleasant man he is,' I said. 'I wrote to him some days ago and asked him to inform me of his business by letter – and yet he still insists on seeing me.'

'Why don't you ask Mr Walters to go and see him?' she

suggested. 'It isn't right that he should keep coming here like that.'

'Yes, perhaps I will,' I agreed. 'And if he comes again without an appointment, tell him that I am not at home.'

'Yes, madame.' She set her mouth and I sighed as I realised there was more. 'It's about Mademoiselle Corbier . . .'

'Not now, Mrs Benson,' I begged. 'Please. I really do need a cup of tea. You can bring it to the study and tell me in a few minutes . . .'

I had known there was bound to be trouble if Marie insisted on checking the household accounts again and again. What was I going to do? I did not want to alienate Marie.

In the study I glanced at some details of a cottage in Cornwall which had arrived earlier that day. It wasn't what I wanted, but perhaps it would do for a while.

'Please try not to upset Mrs Benson, Marie,' I said that evening after dinner. We were sitting in the parlour, playing cards. 'Does it matter if she pockets a little of the house-keeping money herself? I'm sure it happens in most large households. Besides, she said it was just a mistake – she wrote the amount for the vegetables down twice, that's all. I am sure she did not mean to cheat me.'

'If you prefer to take her word . . .'

'You know I don't, Marie. Please do not be annoyed with me over this. I just don't want the bother of taking on new servants at the moment. We shall be leaving London soon anyway.'

'Very well. I shall apologise if you wish it, but I know she is cheating you, Jenny. It was not just a small error in her accounts – whatever she may have told you.'

'Let's forget it, shall we? Please? I just want everything to be peaceful.'

'Of course.' She looked a little ashamed. 'I did not want to make trouble for you, Jenny – but I must take care of you. You have no one else to look after you.'

I thanked her and told her I was grateful for her help. She was smiling as she went upstairs, but I was aware of a slight unease. Marie was so possessive of me. It was as if she wanted to keep me all to herself.

I did not sleep well that night. Once again I dreamed Gérard came to me in a garden. He was trying to warn me of danger.

'What danger?' I woke with the question on my lips and tears on my cheeks. 'Why are you so anxious for me, Gérard?'

I felt heavy-eyed and sluggish as I dressed that morning. My dreams were so vivid and emotional that they left me drained. Sometimes I felt almost ill. It was grief, of course. I had suffered a terrible shock when Laurent told me he was my father and then, within the space of a few days, Gérard had fallen from his horse and been killed.

Perhaps if I had been present at his funeral I might have been comforted. For me that had not been possible. I had not been there to say my farewells in church, and that might explain why I was haunted by these dreams.

'Oh, Gérard,' I whispered. 'I love you so . . . I love you so.'

I placed my hands on the slight swell of my belly. Had I ever considered the possibility of abortion? It could have been done had I wished it, though it was against the laws of God and man. But I did not wish it! As each day passed I became more protective of the life growing inside me.

The dreams would pass in time, perhaps after the child was born. I thought of holding my child, of the years when I would watch over him as he grew to manhood, and I was smiling as I went downstairs.

But what if that child were not normal?

It was a fear that never quite left me, despite my determination not to dwell on it. I fought my horror of such a possibility. I would love my child no matter what.

*   *   *

The next morning Mrs Benson brought the menus for the coming week to me in the study for my approval. It was a ritual she had started since Marie began to question her accounts.

I thanked her, approved the menus, then settled down to go through a pile of letters on my desk. One of them was from an agent who dealt in property and contained details and photographs of a pretty house in a Cornish village. Situated near to a beach, it was far nicer than anything else I had seen, and the rent seemed reasonable.

I thought I might take it for the summer and picked up my pen to reply straight away. I had just begun to write when I heard a commotion outside my door. I rose to my feet as it was thrust open unceremoniously and a very angry man burst in, followed by a red-faced, equally angry Mrs Benson.

'I knew you were here,' Philip Allington said, clearly in a temper. 'I shall not be put off yet again. I really must insist on speaking to you, Miss Heron.'

'I tried to stop him, madame,' Mrs Benson cried. 'He pushed me aside . . . I couldn't stop him.'

'There was no need for this, sir.' I glanced at my house-keeper. 'It's all right, Mrs Benson. Now that this . . . *gentleman* is here I shall see him. You may go.'

'Are you sure, madame?' She looked as if she could have cheerfully killed him. 'I could send for the constable, if you like? He had no right, pushing past me, forcing his way in here.'

'Quite sure, thank you. I don't believe Mr Allington has come here to murder me.' A little smile flickered about my lips as I saw her outrage. 'It's all right, Mrs Benson. I shall be perfectly safe, I assure you.'

'Thank you,' he said after she had gone. He looked slightly awkward now. 'I should apologise for bursting in on you . . .'

'Yes, you should.' I gave him a hard look. 'There was no

need for such behaviour – particularly as I wrote asking you to state your business in a letter before calling again.'

'Did you?' He seemed genuinely surprised. 'I have been out of town for some days. I tried to see you before I left, the morning after Mrs Walters's dinner – but you were out. Or so I was told. I returned to town yesterday morning and came immediately to see you; once again I was refused. I looked through my letters later, but did not see anything from you amongst the others waiting for me.'

'I assure you it was sent.'

'Then it must have gone astray.' He frowned. The intense anger had cooled somewhat but his expression was still harsh, still determined. 'I would have written to you and explained, but my letters have been ignored for months. I have been trying to see you for a very long time, since before your mother died, Miss Heron. I'm afraid my patience has worn thin.'

'So it would seem.' My tone was cold. I was not going to give way, despite his anger.

'I would not have persisted if it were not important.' Something flickered in his flinty eyes. 'I was surprised when we met at Mrs Walters's house. You may think my behaviour towards you that evening was rude, but what I had to say to you was private – and I thought it better to keep my distance. In the circumstances I ought to have waited . . . but what I have to say is nevertheless urgent.'

'Then you had better tell me, hadn't you? Would you like to sit down, Mr Allington? I should prefer to sit myself, and I don't care to have you towering over me like an avenging angel.' I raised my head, giving him a look that would have cowed a lesser man.

He hesitated and for a moment there was a glint of humour in that forbidding face, then his eyes fixed on me and the humour was gone. 'You look tired. Have you been unwell?'

I sat at my desk, which hid me from the waist down. He

perched on a fragile chair that I knew to be uncomfortable and which looked hardly capable of bearing his weight.

'I did not sleep well last night. Please do not concern yourself on my account, sir. I am perfectly well, I assure you.'

He was staring at the wedding ring on my hand, frowning. 'You are married? I had not thought it possible . . . the name . . . can it possibly be a coincidence?'

'I prefer to be known as Madame Heron. I have my reasons, but I am not prepared to discuss them with you, sir.'

He made no immediate answer, his dark eyes assessing me thoughtfully. His silence and the piercing intensity of his gaze unnerved me.

'Please go on, Mr Allington. I am expecting a visitor.' It was a lie, but it served its purpose, which was to bring him to the point of his visit.

'Very well, madame. I am here on behalf of Mrs Anne Ruston, widow of the late Mr Maxwell Ruston, who resides at Storm House, near Bude, Cornwall. Mrs Ruston has asked me to invite you to pay her a visit at her home in Cornwall.' His eyes narrowed intently as he saw the name meant nothing to me. 'Good grief! You don't even know who she is, do you?' He sounded angry, disbelieving.

'I am sorry, I have no idea – but no doubt you will tell me in your own good time, sir.'

I was cross with him and my tone was deliberately brusque, even sarcastic. This man was too sure of himself for my liking – too arrogant. How dare he force his way into my home merely to issue an invitation from a woman I had never heard of!

He in his turn was equally angry – this man was not to be lightly dismissed. His eyes were scornful as he went on. 'Mrs Ruston is your maternal grandmother. It was very wrong of your mother not to have at least told you of her existence.'

My heart gave an odd flip. 'My . . . Mama's mother?'

I was shocked and yet somehow it was not such a surprise. Laurent had once mentioned that I had relations in Cornwall

– a family with whom my mother had broken all ties years ago. Somehow I had assumed them to be distant cousins . . . not Mama's own mother!

'Mrs Ruston has long wanted to see you, Miss Heron, but all requests to have you visit her have been denied. She is almost seventy years of age and her health is not good.'

I stared at him in dismay, my mind reeling in confusion as I tried to sort out my feelings about this woman I had not even known existed until this moment. 'I did not know . . . I was not aware . . .'

'Your mother never spoke of her family?'

'Only once – after you came to Paris to see her that time. She was upset then. She cried after you left and begged me not to ask questions. I knew that she had been hurt by something that had happened to her years before but . . . she did not wish to speak of it.'

He frowned in disbelief. 'She has told you nothing more? Nothing of why she left her home – or the quarrel?'

'Did she quarrel with her mother? Yes, I suppose she must have done . . .' I met his gaze then; it was not unsympathetic, though I sensed frustration and anger beneath the surface. 'Why? It must have been serious.'

'Their argument was over something very personal and deeply upsetting to Mrs Ruston. An injustice was done by her to her daughter, which she has come to regret. I am sorry, Miss Heron. I am not at liberty to tell you more. Mrs Ruston naturally wants to explain about the breach herself. She wants to get to know you – to make amends. She did try to make up her quarrel with her daughter, but Adele was not prepared to listen.'

I was thinking now, remembering the first time I had seen him.

'Mrs Ruston sent you to Paris to ask if she could see me, didn't she? I heard you say something about it to my mother. I remember you were angry when she refused. Why did she ask you particularly?'

'Mrs Ruston is a family friend,' he said. 'That day in Paris . . . it was just after her husband died. I was concerned for her – even angry that your mother was not prepared to listen. Mrs Ruston had suffered a heart attack herself and had been very ill. My father was her lawyer for years, until he retired from ill health himself. She had no one else she could turn to . . . so she begged me to contact Adele for her. Mr Ruston had left his stepdaughter some money.'

I recalled that Mama had mentioned a small legacy . . . money she had told me was owed her. I'd asked her if it was a legacy from her family, but she had been vague, not wanting to talk about it.

I gazed inquiringly at Philip Allington. 'Are you also a lawyer?'

'No. I was left land by my grandfather. I am a farmer.'

'You don't look as if you work on the land, Mr Allington.'

'It is a fair-sized estate.' He looked angry again. 'I am not just one of the idle rich, if that's what you imagine, Miss Heron. I assure you I work for my living.'

I smiled inwardly. 'Oh, I am quite sure you do. I am sure a large estate must be a huge responsibility – especially if one is dedicated to the welfare of one's tenants.'

'Perhaps you may now understand my frustration in having all my efforts to contact you thwarted, Miss Heron? I am a busy man. I have made the journey to France several times . . .'

'Yes, I do see,' I said. I was angry. Marie might well be right. If he had visited at the time of my mother's fatal illness, he could have contributed to her death – though without the intention of harming her. 'Well, you have delivered your message, sir, and may rest easy. No more of your valuable time need be wasted on my affairs.'

He stared at me, a glint in his narrowed eyes. He had caught the inflection in my voice and thought I was mocking him. 'And your answer?' His voice was impatient, harsh, as if he sensed my refusal before I gave it. 'You will not turn

Mrs Ruston down? Not without a fair consideration of her request?'

I was on the verge of doing so. If my mother had been so steadfast in her determination not to make up the quarrel, she must have had good reason. I ought to refuse the invitation in justice to my mother's memory. And yet if I was ever to discover the secret of my birth, I had to start somewhere.

'I cannot promise anything,' I said, not wanting to give way to him. He was too arrogant, too demanding. If I wanted to see my grandmother, I could do so without his help or interference! 'But I *shall* think about what you have told me.'

'If you have any mercy in you, you will see her. She has not long to live, Miss Heron. She asked me to beg you in her name if need be. Anne Ruston is a God-fearing woman. She will die in torment and lie uneasy in her grave if you will not consent to see her.'

'Blackmail will not gain you your cause,' I told him coldly. 'I have the address of your London home. I shall write to you.'

'I am in town for another three days.' He took a card from his waistcoat pocket. 'After that you may reach me at this address.' He seemed to hesitate before standing up. 'I have taken up too much of your time, Miss Heron. Forgive me.'

'I am sorry you have been put to so much trouble because of me, Mr Allington.'

'It was for Mrs Ruston's sake – and for her sake I will risk your scorn once more. Please, I beg you, do not delay too long. I think you have a conscience, Miss Heron, and I doubt you would wish to condemn a good woman to eternal torment.'

I was shocked by the anger in him, watching in silence as he went from the room without another word.

After he had gone I began to recover, though I was still trembling, distressed. How dare he speak to me in such a manner? As if I were to blame for my grandmother's grief . . .

My grandmother . . . How strange that word sounded. What had she done to my mother that had caused a lifelong estrangement between them? I recalled the sad look I had seen in Mama's eyes sometimes and believed that this must have been one of the reasons for her secret sorrow.

Yet another of Mama's secrets had come to light. How many more must I discover before the web of lies was pulled aside and I could see the whole truth?

My mother's maiden name had been Heron – I knew that from her personal papers – so Mrs Ruston must have married again. Yes, I remembered now, the small legacy had been from her stepfather.

Thinking about it, I realised that I would have found it difficult to trace her without Mr Allington's intervention – but I was still not inclined to forgive him for his behaviour.

Laurent had taught me to distrust arrogant men who believed they could ride roughshod over other people's lives. It was this that had led to disaster. Had Gérard's father thought fit to tell us the truth sooner, perhaps my lover would still be alive.

And even now that I knew where to find my grandmother, I was afraid of what I might discover when the mystery was finally unravelled. Something dark and ugly lay at the heart of that web of lies; I knew it instinctively, sensed its evil like a shadow that had haunted my mother and had now thrust itself into my life.

'I caught a glimpse of someone leaving just now,' Marie said, coming into the study soon after my visitor had left. 'Whoever it was slammed the door and seemed very angry.'

'That was Mr Philip Allington,' I told her, sighing.

'That man! If I had seen him properly I should have gone after him and told him what I thought of him. What did he want?'

'He came to invite me to visit my maternal grandmother in Cornwall.'

'Your grandmother?' Marie looked startled. 'Did you know she was still alive?'

'Not until a few minutes ago,' I admitted. 'Mama never mentioned her. I'm not sure why exactly, but I was under the impression that she had died long ago. Apparently, she is the reason Mr Allington has been trying so hard to speak to me. She is unwell, and she would like to see me before she dies.'

'Why?'

'I have no idea.' Somehow I was reluctant to tell Marie everything. I was not sure why Mama had quarrelled with her mother, but suspected it might be something unpleasant. 'I suppose I am her only grandchild.'

'Adele never mentioned her to me . . .' Marie was clearly suspicious, uneasy. 'I do not think you should go there, Jenny. I did not like the look of that man. It might not be safe for you to visit these people.'

'What do you mean?' I looked at her in surprise. 'What can you be suggesting, Marie?'

She shrugged expressively, a strange, closed look in her eyes. I remembered the vague accusations she had made after my mother died, and sighed. Marie had such odd notions sometimes.

'I am sure neither my grandmother nor Mr Allington mean me any harm,' I said. 'I have not yet made up my mind whether or not I want to visit Mrs Ruston – but I shall decide when I have given it more thought.'

Marie shrugged again – I could see she was offended. She turned and walked from the room, her expression saying it all. This time I let her go without apology. She really could not be allowed to run my life for me. I knew she was concerned for me, and that she did genuinely care for my welfare – but I would make my own decisions from now on.

I was sitting by the window that afternoon, reading Kate's latest letter, when Susanna was announced. Kate had written that Henriette was worried about her son. It seemed that they did not get on as well as I had hoped they might, and Henriette still talked of me as if I might one day return to the chateau. I laid the letter aside and sighed as my friend came in.

'That was a big sigh,' Susanna said. 'Not bad news I hope?'

'No – just a letter from Kate. She is looking after Charles. You remember I told you about him? It seems his mother does not approve of Kate's methods of discipline. She is too strict with him. She makes him do his lessons, and will not play with him unless he remembers his manners.'

'She sounds like a very proper English nanny,' Susanna said. 'My friends say I should get one when I have my second child . . .' Her smile spread from inside her, bringing such a warm glow to her whole body that she seemed to light up the room. 'I wanted to tell you my news, Jenny. The doctor has just confirmed it . . . I am expecting again.'

'Susanna! I am so pleased for you.' I dropped my gaze, unable to meet her expectant eyes.

She hesitated, then gave me an understanding look.

'My baby should be born about four or so weeks after your own, I should imagine.' Susanna reached out to touch my arm, her eyes expressing anxiety for me but no condemnation. 'You haven't said anything, my dear, but I am right – aren't I?'

'Yes.' I could not lie to her. 'Yes, you are. I'm only just over two months gone. I thought I would be out of town before anyone noticed.' I ran a hand over my stomach self-consciously. 'I didn't think it showed yet.'

'It doesn't,' she said. 'It's a look in the eyes – just a feeling I had. When you've had a child yourself you know.'

'You know I'm not married, don't you?'

She nodded, her eyes sympathetic as they dwelt on my face. 'Yes, my dear. I guessed. Henry told me the comte's son was killed in a fall from his horse just before you came here. I thought perhaps . . . Was he the man you loved?'

I nodded, tears stinging my eyes. 'Gérard wanted us to be married as soon as possible. We were so much in love. I know we ought to have waited but . . .'

'It happens so often,' she said, and there was no censure in her eyes. 'You were unlucky, Jenny. You could have been married long before this and no one would have been the wiser.'

I turned away as the tears rushed to my eyes. If only that were true! I thought I could bear almost anything if only the burden of guilt could be lifted from my shoulders. It was because of our sin that Gérard was dead – because he had not been able to bear our parting and had ridden so carelessly that he had brought about his own death.

'Is the baby the reason you want to live somewhere else?'

'Not entirely.' I wiped my face with a handkerchief. 'How foolish of me to cry. Forgive me. It should be easier to bear by now – but it isn't.'

'How could it be?' She stroked my arm gently. 'Would you consider spending some of your time in London if Henry found you a smaller house at a reasonable rent? Something near us, perhaps?'

'Perhaps. I'm not sure.' I regarded her uncertainly. 'Would you continue to know me once the child is born – even if your friends guessed my secret?'

'If they were unkind to you, they would no longer be my friends,' she replied. 'But I won't put pressure on you, Jenny. You must do just as you wish. I simply want you to know that we care about you.'

'Thank you,' I said. She was so generous and kind, and I knew I had been lucky to meet her. In her place, others might have shunned me as though I had the plague. 'Thank you, my dearest Susanna.'

After she had gone, I thought about my situation. If Susanna had guessed my secret, others would not be far behind. I had not made up my mind about whether or not

49

to visit my grandmother, but it had occurred to me that it would be easy enough to pay a brief call on her when I was staying in Cornwall. However, if I decided to do so it would be wise not to leave it too long – unless I wished her to guess my secret, too.

Later that afternoon, I told Marie what Susanna had said about finding a smaller house in London. I knew she had begun to feel at home in the noisy, sprawling city and was doubtful about living in the country, but even so she could not quite conceal her feelings. She was cross and a little jealous, because the suggestion had come from Susanna and not from her.

'Do you want to take everything to Cornwall?' she asked. 'Or is Adele's trunk to be left here in storage?'

'I shall take Mama's rosewood box, but the trunk can stay here until I decide where to settle. I shan't take my thicker clothes either – I shall need new ones by the time the weather changes.'

'Are you going to see that woman?'

'Do you mean my grandmother?' She nodded, and I sensed her hostility. 'Why? Why does it bother you so much?'

'I cannot forget the letter your *maman* received just before she was ill – and then someone came to the house and upset her. I think now it was that man – the one who came here. Mr Allington. She was worried – frightened. I think . . .'

'Yes, go on. Tell me. What is worrying you, Marie?'

'I think Adele might have taken her own life – because of what was in that letter.'

I stared at her in horror. This was what she had been hinting at when my mother died! I had thought she meant something else, and so had Laurent.

'Mama – take her own life? No, that isn't possible,' I cried. 'You are imagining all this. Laurent told me her death was entirely natural – a recurring fever she had had before. It was not poison, nor was it suicide. The doctors would have known if that were the case.'

'Doctors don't always know.' Marie looked stubborn. 'There are things people can take that create strange symptoms. I know Adele was unhappy. She told me there was something troubling her – but she would not tell me what. She used to take a herbal medicine. It helped her with the pain – but too much can cause death.'

'And you think she deliberately took too much – why?'

Marie's expression told me that she was convinced she was right and nothing would change her mind. 'There was a letter that distressed her. I would know it if I saw it,' Marie said. 'If you don't want to go through her things, I could look for it. I wouldn't pry into any of her private papers.'

'I *have* looked, and there was nothing. Please stop this,' I cried. 'I don't want to talk about it, Marie. My mother was ill. You are being very silly. She would not take her own life because of something in a letter. That's ridiculous, and I do not want to hear it again.'

'If that's how you feel.' She gave me a look of deep reproach and walked out of the room.

I ought to have followed and made up the breach, but I was too upset. It was bad enough that my mother had died before I could see her. Of course Mama hadn't taken her own life – why should she?

'Come on, Marie,' I said the next morning. 'We are going shopping. It is time we both had some new clothes.'

'New clothes?' She looked at me uncertainly. 'If you want something new . . . but I don't need anything. I can make my own dresses.'

'Then I shall buy you a new hat,' I said, refusing to be put off. 'Or some summer shoes. I am determined to have fun, Marie – and I want to share my pleasure with you.'

She still looked dubious, but my mood was infectious. For

once I had slept well, and I wanted to make the most of our time in town.

'Do not deny me the pleasure of buying you a present,' I said. 'I want today to be fun – like it was the day we bought the Belgian chocolates.'

'If that is what you truly want . . .' She smiled at me. 'Then I should like a pair of shiny black boots.'

'You shall have them,' I promised. 'Only let's go now. It is such a lovely day, I do not want to waste a moment of it.'

I dreamed of Gérard again that night. As usual, I was alone in a garden and he sought me out. It was early morning and the mist was swirling all around us.

'Take care, Jenny,' he warned. 'Trust no one. There is darkness all around you. Take care.'

I woke with tears on my cheeks. It was impossible to throw off my grief when my dreams were so vivid. I felt that my lover was trying to reach me, to warn me . . . but of what?

Susanna called the day before I was due to leave for Cornwall. She embraced me and told me to take good care of myself.

'I shall miss you,' she said. 'I know things are not easy for you – but don't hide yourself away, Jenny. I am your friend. I shall always be here when you need me.'

'You are so generous,' I said. 'You are like Kate. I am very lucky to have two such good friends.'

At that moment Marie brought the tea tray in. She gave me a reproachful look and I wondered if she had been listening at the door – she did that sometimes. Was she offended because I had not included her amongst my friends? It was merely an oversight. Of course I thought of her as a friend. She had come with me to England when I was alone and desperate. I should always be grateful for that.

I smiled at her and asked her to stop and have tea with us, but she shook her head. 'I have packing to do,' she said. 'Talk to your friend, Jenny. I am busy.'

Susanna looked startled as the door closed behind her. 'Do you allow your companion to talk to you like that?' she asked. 'I think that's a little unwise, dearest. Women of the lower order . . . well, they do sometimes take advantage if they can.'

'You are wrong to think Marie would take advantage,' I said. 'She is a little possessive towards me, but she protects me like a dragon. Mrs Benson is at daggers drawn with her most of the time because of the accounts. Marie tends to niggle over small things – but it is her way.'

Susanna nodded, but I could see she was not convinced. 'You must do as you think best, of course,' she said. 'But I should seriously consider finding yourself a proper English companion – an older lady with good references. I could ask Henry to do that for you, if you wish.'

'No, please do not,' I said hastily. 'Marie is the companion I want. We speak French together and most of the time she is perfectly good-humoured. Besides, she was devoted to my mother. The comte did not treat her as kindly as he ought to have done after Mama died – and I feel I must make up for that. And I do like her – for all her faults.'

'Then there is no more to be said.' Susanna kissed my cheek as she left. 'Please write to me sometimes, Jenny. I do not want us to lose touch.'

'Nor do I,' I said and smiled at her. 'I do not know what I should have done had it not been for you and Mr Walters. I was nervous of making a new life here – but you have made it so much easier for me.'

'Then I shall wish you a safe journey,' she said. 'And I shall hope to see you on your return.'

Four

Two weeks had passed since we first came to Cornwall. The house was even better than I had expected, with five main bedrooms, two bathrooms, the housekeeper's wing, and three good reception rooms as well as a couple of small parlours. What I particularly liked was the comfortable furniture, the feeling of being in a home – so much nicer than the formal grandeur of Laurent's house in London . . . or the chateau.

Why could I not forget, even here? I had hoped I might sleep better when we moved from the noise of the city, but although the dreams had ceased for the moment, night after night I lay awake listening to the sound of the sea against the shore.

I sighed and walked over to my bedroom window. It was just possible to see the sea from here – beyond the houses and the treetops, there was a little patch of blue that seemed to shimmer and ripple in the sunlight.

I had walked alone in the cove that morning. Small and secluded, the beach was stony and the sea quite rough as it boiled around a spur of rock that jutted out for some distance. But from here the water looked dark blue and much calmer.

I thought I could be content in a house like this, once my grief had begun to subside – as it surely must in time.

'Madame Heron . . .' I swung round as a maid came into the room. 'There's a man downstairs. He says you wrote to him requesting an interview.'

'That must be Mr Allington?'

'Yes, I think that was the name he gave.'

'Very well, I shall come down. I had better not keep him waiting – he is rather an impatient man.'

'He is in the back parlour, madame.'

I thanked her and went downstairs. Philip Allington was standing at the window, his back towards me as he gazed out at the gardens. He turned as I entered, his eyes watchful, almost wary.

'Miss Heron,' he said with a little nod of his head. 'You are looking a little better. The Cornish air must agree with you.'

'Yes, it does. Thank you for coming so promptly, Mr Allington. I am sorry to have kept you waiting.'

'You wanted to see me about something in particular?'

'I have decided to pay Mrs Ruston a visit. I shall not stay long – just an hour or so.'

'She was hoping for a little longer. Could you not stay with her for a day or two?'

'You are asking a great deal, Mr Allington.'

'One night then – surely you can spare her that, Miss Heron? Is it so very much to ask?'

He was such an annoying man! Why did he always manage to make me feel guilty?

'Very well. I shall come on Saturday afternoon and stay until after lunch on Sunday. Will that be satisfactory, sir?'

'There is no train on a Sunday.'

'Then I shall come on Friday and return on Saturday.'

'There is no need. I can have you brought home in my carriage.'

'I would not want to trouble you, sir.'

'It is the least I can do – since you have been kind enough to accede to my request.' He was silent for a moment, then he added, 'However, I am sure you will find it is to your advantage to visit Mrs Ruston.'

It was a moment or two before I realised what he was implying. I felt the colour rush to my cheeks and was suddenly very angry. How dare he say such a thing to me!

'If you imagine I agreed to this visit because I think my grandmother may leave me some money you are mistaken.' I glared at him. 'I have sufficient for my needs. I do not want anything more.'

'Indeed?' His eyes were thoughtful as they dwelt on my face. 'Your mother was not a rich woman. Since she left you to the care of the Comte de Arnay – and since you were living in his house in London – I must suppose him to be your benefactor. I wonder why? I know that he was Adele's protector, but . . .' His mouth suddenly went hard and his eyes became colder than ice. 'I see. How stupid you must think me. You have replaced your mother in his affections.'

I gasped. Without thinking, I stepped forward and struck him hard across the face.

'How dare you!' I cried. 'How dare you insult me? Please leave this house immediately.'

There was a dark red mark on his cheek. His eyes had narrowed to slits of intense fury and his fists were clenched; I thought he wanted to strike me, but he made no attempt to retaliate. He seemed to hesitate and I saw a flicker of doubt in his face.

'Forgive me if I was mistaken, but . . .' He glanced at the ring on my left hand. 'You are using the same name as she used . . . living in his house . . .'

'What I choose to do with my life is my own business. I did not ask you to concern yourself with my affairs.'

'You invited me to call on you.'

'As a matter of courtesy. To tell you in person of my decision to accept the invitation you issued. I shall not make the same mistake again, I assure you.'

'Nor shall I, Miss Heron. I shall tell Mrs Ruston to expect you at the weekend – unless you have changed your mind?'

'Because you have insulted me, sir?' My head went up

and I gave him a look of such scorn that most men would have wilted under it. A little nerve jumped in his throat but he gave no other sign of having noticed my anger. 'I am not fickle. You may think ill of me if you choose, but I have given my word and I shall keep it.'

'Then I shall bid you goodbye, Miss Heron.' Was that a gleam of humour in his eyes – or simply controlled anger? 'I doubt we shall meet again.'

I turned my back as he left the room. I was seething with fury. What an arrogant, despicable man he was!

'Jenny!' Marie came hurrying into the room as the front door slammed behind him. I swung round and she saw I was close to tears. 'I couldn't help overhearing your quarrel with him,' she said, showing me a letter she was carrying. 'I was bringing you this . . . Now perhaps you will believe me when I tell you that man is dangerous!'

'Oh, Marie . . .' The tears came as she reached out and took me in her arms. 'How could he accuse me of being Laurent's mistress? As if I would sell myself for his money . . .'

Marie stroked my hair. 'Do not cry, Jenny. The man is a fool. I warned you not to trust him.'

'But he was not so very far from the truth,' I said in a choked whisper. 'I have accepted Laurent's blood money – that's why what he said upset me so much . . .'

'Money . . .' Marie shrugged. 'What is in this to make you cry? It is a business arrangement. The comte owed your mother a debt – and now he pays it. You are entitled to whatever he gives you.'

To Marie, with her practical French outlook on life, taking money from the Comte de Arnay might not seem anything more than a business arrangement – but to me it was something I had done only because I was carrying Gérard's child. Yet it was not the money that was upsetting me at this moment.

I was angry that the arrogant Mr Philip Allington could believe I would be any man's mistress. I *had* given myself without marriage, and many would condemn me for that, but I had done so out of love and to a man I had believed would marry me. To sell my body for a life of luxury – as Mr Allington had suggested – was something so abhorrent to me that I felt sick at the mere idea.

'Men . . .' Marie made a little puffing sound. 'They are none of them worth a single tear.'

'I'm being silly,' I said and wiped my face. I smiled through my tears. 'It's all right now, I'm not upset any more. Mr Allington is not worthy of notice. I only hope that I shall never have to see him again.'

'He won't be at your grandmother's house, will he?'

'No, I don't think so – why should he be?'

Marie frowned. 'I do not like him,' she said. 'You should be careful of him, Jenny.'

'Yes, of course,' I replied wearily, too tired to defend a man I did not much like. 'But I do not suppose I shall see him again . . .'

The letter Marie had brought me was from Henriette. I took it into the garden and sat under the shade of an old apple tree to read it.

> Dearest Jenny,
>
> I wish you would come back to us. You have no idea how our life has altered since you left. Laurent is like a brooding spectre. Sometimes I think he will go mad with despair. I never thought Laurent cared so much for Gérard – he was always so strict and disapproving – but since his death he has become a shadow of his former self . . .

I folded the letter and put it in my pocket, not wanting to read about my guardian's distress. If he was unhappy, it was his own fault. I blamed him for Gérard's death and I always would. My heart was made of stone as far as he was concerned. I hoped he was wracked with guilt, haunted by what he had done. He deserved to be!

Marie stopped me as I came downstairs that Friday morning. She looked at me accusingly. 'Why don't you want me to come to your grandmother's with you?'

'It isn't that I do not want you, Marie. I think I should go alone this first time, that's all. Mrs Ruston isn't expecting anyone else.'

'I do not like the idea of your going there alone. I do not trust these people.'

'I am meeting my grandmother for the first time,' I said. 'It may be awkward for both of us – it will be easier if I am alone. Please do not make a fuss about this, Marie. I really do not feel able to cope. I have been feeling so tired recently.'

A flush came to her cheeks. She looked slightly ashamed.

'Please, Marie. Try to understand.'

'All right. I'm sorry.' She smiled oddly. 'I'll look after things here while you're gone. You needn't worry about anything.'

'Thank you,' I said, and on impulse kissed her cheek. 'You know I couldn't manage without you, Marie.'

'I'm just trying to protect you – the way I did Adele. She wouldn't listen to me at the end – and she died. I should not want anything to happen to you, Jenny.'

'Nothing is going to happen to me.'

I went out of the house. The carriage was waiting to take me to the railway station. As I glanced back I saw Marie at the window, watching.

Where the storm came from that day was a mystery. It was mid-summer and the sun had been shining brightly when I left home. I was completely unprepared for the freak gale that met me as I left the train. The wind was so fierce that I could hardly stand against it and the rain was lashing down, hitting the ground so hard that it bounced up again, wetting the hem of my dress. I ran into the stationmaster's office to take shelter from its fury.

'Rare soaking you've got, miss,' he said. 'And you without an umbrella. It's a fair walk to the village. You'd best stay here until it eases.'

'Thank you . . . I shall, if you don't mind.'

'You'll be visiting friends, I dare say?'

He looked at me with dark, inquisitive eyes, obviously wondering who I was. It was a small station and I supposed he must know most of the people who used the infrequent service.

'I'm visiting Mrs Ruston of Storm House. Has the carriage arrived for me? I was told I would be met.'

He peered out into the yard behind his office. 'No one about, miss. Likely they're waiting for the storm to pass. You can bide here until they come for you.'

'Is there a hire carriage available?'

'There's Jed . . . from the village. He drives a pony and trap; folk use him if they want takin' anywhere local.' He lifted his cap and scratched his head. 'He might take you . . . but you'd have to walk a quarter of a mile to find him. Besides, I reckon he'll be at the market this mornin'. Folk usually let him know if they want fetchin' . . .'

'I was to have been met.' I felt a surge of annoyance. This was Philip Allington's fault! He had done it deliberately to punish me. 'Could I walk – is it far to Storm House?'

'Nigh on a mile or mebbe a bit more.' He peered out of the window again. 'You could walk it . . . if this rain stops.' He didn't sound optimistic.

'Do you think it will?' It was still beating hard against the window.

'Looks set for a bit. Never mind, you won't come to much harm in here. Fancy a cup of tea? I was just makin' one for myself.'

I sighed inwardly, wishing now that I had never agreed to

this visit. 'That is kind of you. Yes, thank you, I will have one, if it is no trouble.'

'I could send the lad . . . to see if Jed's home.' The stationmaster brought me a cup of hot, strong tea. 'When the rain stops a bit . . . if they haven't come for you from the house.'

'The lad?' I sipped the tea; it was horrible and I had to suppress a shudder of disgust.

'My son. He's in the house. He'll go for Jed if I ask him.'

'I should be grateful. It's very kind of you.'

His eyes were speculative as he looked at me. I felt an odd tingling sensation at the nape of my neck. Why was he staring at me in that way?

'Not often we get visitors, 'cepting on a Saturday. Jed waits in the yard on Saturdays, but it's market day today. He'll most likely be gone into town. Still, the lad won't mind going – when the rain stops.'

'Thank you.' I felt obliged to take another sip of the tea. It was so strong it almost made me sick. 'Perhaps when the rain stops your son would show me the way to Mrs Ruston's house?'

'Oh aye, he'd do that right enough. Walk with you most of the way . . . carry your bag.'

'I would be willing to pay him.'

'A shilling will do,' the stationmaster said agreeably. 'Robbie's a mite short in the head – but he'll know the way all right. He's a good lad as long as I tell him straight.' He peered out of his window again. 'Looks as if it might be blowin' over after all. I'll give the lad a shout for you.'

As he went into the back room I hastily poured my tea into the pot of a tired-looking fern. Then I went to stare out of the window. The rain had almost stopped and the sky was lighter. I could see the road. It seemed deserted as it wound away into the distance – no sign of any vehicles of any kind, not even a farm cart.

Obviously the carriage wasn't coming. Surely they couldn't have forgotten I was arriving this morning? I was certain that Philip Allington had done this deliberately to spite me. What a despicable creature he was!

I turned as I heard something behind me. The stationmaster had returned with a lanky, freckle-faced youth of about seventeen or so. Wearing a jacket far too large for him – which had obviously been his father's and hung on him like a sack – he looked awkward and unsure.

'Hello,' I said. 'Would you mind taking me to Storm House, please?'

He stared at me for a long moment, then suddenly grinned. I was relieved to see he was friendly, though his eyes were a little vacant, seeming to stare beyond me.

'I've brought you an umbrella, miss,' his father said. 'Robbie will carry your bag. He'll take you as far as the cliffs and you'll see the house from there.' He picked up my bag and gave it to the youth. 'Carry this for the lady, Robbie. She'll give you a shilling – and then you come straight back here. You hear me? No loitering about in the village. No drinking.' He gave the lad a fierce, angry look.

Robbie nodded. He took the bag and went out the door. I followed hastily, pausing for a moment to put up the umbrella. Robbie was striding ahead of me. I called to him to wait, but if he heard he did not look back, nor did he slacken his stride. I had to hurry to catch up with him. When I did he glanced at me and grinned, but said nothing.

'Could we walk a little slower please, Robbie?'

He looked at me again. For a moment he seemed puzzled, his eyes blank, then he nodded. 'You be town folk,' he said. 'Town folk ain't used to walking.'

'That's right . . . so can we go a little more slowly, please?'

He nodded, slowing his pace slightly. If I'd had the breath to spare I might have tried to talk to him, but Robbie had only one thing on his mind. He was to take me as far as the cliffs and then go straight home – and he obviously intended to do just that.

We came to the village after fifteen minutes or so; it consisted of a half-timbered pub, a small church and a cluster of cottages that looked as if they had been built for a fishing community and were quite old. There were two roads. One was just a sandy path that led towards the beach, passing a small wood and the village.

Robbie took the one to the left, which led away from the cottages and began to climb upwards. I could see other houses, larger and more modern, with gardens. Now I could see that the road led up beside a long, flat greensward that ran along the edge of steep, rocky cliffs, which seemed to stretch away into the distance as far as the eye could see. There, alone on a wide plateau looking out to the ocean, was a large grey stone house.

'There . . .' Robbie pointed towards it. 'That be it.'

He put my bag down and looked at me expectantly. I took a florin from my purse and gave it to him. He seemed puzzled, disappointed.

'Pa said a shillin' . . .'

'That's two shillings, Robbie.'

'Pa said a shillin' – that ain't a shillin'.'

His tone was stubborn. I took out a shilling and laid it beside the florin on his grubby palm. He grinned at me, took the umbrella I had closed and set off the way he had come at a cracking pace.

I smiled to myself, wondering whether Robbie was brighter than he let on. Not that I minded the extra two shillings. He had saved me the trouble of asking the way and the umbrella had kept me dry.

I wished I still had it as I saw the rain suddenly sweep in across the sea. I had thought the storm was over when I left the stationmaster's office, but now it had returned with a vengeance. Tucking my head down against the wind, I began to struggle up the steep incline towards the house.

*   *   *

Storm House was well named, I thought as I ran the last few yards towards the only door I could see and hammered frantically against its solidness. For a moment out there in the storm I had been frightened. I had felt as if the terrible weather was a sign that I should turn back. I was afraid of what I would find in this house – of the secret my mother had tried so hard to hide from me.

The door was opened suddenly by a thin, rather drab-looking woman, dressed in grey, who seemed surprised as she beckoned me inside to what I now realised was the kitchen.

'What a day,' she exclaimed. 'You're soaked through. It's no wonder, with rain like this.'

'I thought it had stopped when I left the station.'

The kitchen was warm and smelt of baking and herbs, reminding me a little of Marthe's kitchen at the farm where I had grown up.

'You've walked all this way on such a day?' The woman looked at me in dismay. 'From the station you say? Then you must be . . .' Turning her head, she addressed a stout, friendly-looking woman, who was busily kneading dough at the table. 'It's her, Mrs Morton. It's Miss Heron . . . she walked from the station.'

The cook looked up from her work. She was obviously just as surprised as the woman who had let me in. 'Well, I never,' she said. 'So you're Miss Jennifer – Miss Adele's girl . . .' She made a distressed, clucking sound. 'Whatever made you walk all that way in this weather?'

'It looked as if it had stopped raining. It was only when we got to the cliffs that the squall really hit me.'

'Aye . . .' She glanced towards the window. 'It's a strange day. Brilliant sunshine this morning and now as dark as night. A freak storm . . . come from nowhere.'

'The carriage wasn't waiting to meet the train as promised,' I said, shivering as I felt the chill of my damp clothes. 'The stationmaster seemed to think I might not be able to find anyone to bring me – and I did not realise there was another storm on the way. Nor that it would be so fierce.'

'Aye, our Cornish storms be fierce to those as are not born to them – and to some as are if they be seafaring folk. God rest their souls.' She made a small, discreet sign of the cross over her breast, reminding me in a way of Tante Marthe.

'It's an omen,' said the woman who had let me in. 'A warning of something bad . . .'

'Nonsense!' Cook shook her head and cast an authoritative eye towards two maids who were polishing some pans at the far end of the large kitchen. 'Rosie! Stop what you're doing and take Miss Jennifer up to the parlour.'

'Could I not stay here for a few minutes?' I asked, moving towards the warmth of the black iron cooking range. 'I should like to dry out a little before—'

My request was cut short as the door from the hallway opened and a man came in. When he saw me he looked startled. Our eyes met and my heart began to race wildly. How angry he looked! I was shocked to see him here and it set my nerves jangling. Marie was right. I should not have come here. It was a mistake.

'Miss Heron . . .' Philip Allington's deep voice sent a tingle down my spine. 'We were not expecting you until tomorrow.'

'No – today. Surely it was today.' I was angry, convinced that he had known exactly when I was due to arrive. 'You informed me that there were no trains on a Sunday and I said I would come on Friday instead of Saturday, as I had first suggested.'

'And I said I would put my carriage at your disposal on Sunday. I thought it was understood that you would come on Saturday.' His mouth thinned with disapproval. 'Could you not have sent a message from the station? You are soaked to the skin and you look exhausted. Surely there was no need to expose yourself to this weather?'

'I did not expect it to rain so hard.'

He was making me feel foolish. If anyone had the right to be angry, it was me. Yet here I was on the verge of apologising.

'Vera will show you to your room.' He turned towards the woman who had let me in and his expression softened. 'I am relying on you to look after this foolish girl, Vera. We don't want her to catch a chill, do we? Anne would be so upset.'

'No, Philip, of course she mustn't take harm from her soaking. I'll look after her.'

She was simpering, blushing like a schoolgirl. It was clear that she knew him well enough to be on first-name terms, but I thought her ridiculous to be taken in by his charm – which he could obviously turn on at will, since I had seen little of it.

Vera turned to me and smiled. 'Come along, Jennifer. Your room is ready for you, even though you are a day early. I'll show you up and you can take off those wet things. I can find you something to wear until they are dry, if you like.'

'I have a change of clothes in my bag, thank you.'

I followed her meekly from the room, mainly because I wanted to get away from the mockery in Philip Allington's hateful eyes, but also because I felt very wet and uncomfortable.

Vera led me along a dark hall and up the back stairs. The landing above was wider and lighter with a rich red carpet and pale oak panelling. There were several sentimental pictures hanging on the walls and some carved wooden chairs stood at intervals along the landing, rather like sentinels on permanent guard duty. The furniture was all rather heavy-looking and ugly. We passed several closed doors, walked up another flight of stairs and came to a small hall with a window at the far end. A potted plant stood on the window-sill, its huge, green leaves blocking out most of what light there was.

My guide stopped outside the first door and opened it. 'These are your rooms,' she said. 'I have been told they were your mother's when she was a girl. You have a bedroom, bathroom and sitting room of your own.'

I sensed disapproval and something more . . . resentment?

'Thank you. I am sorry . . . I am not sure what I should call you.'

'I am Miss Vera Lenton. Most people call me Vera – you may, if you wish.' She hesitated, adding, 'I am Mrs Ruston's companion. I've been with her for years. She relies on me completely.' There was an odd, defiant note in her voice.

'Were you here when . . . Did you know my mother?'

'No . . .' She walked into the first room, which was a little parlour with two comfortable chairs, a desk and a tall bookcase. 'I came to stay as a friend a year after Mrs Ruston's daughter left home, and continued as Anne's companion. I hope you will be comfortable here.'

I glanced round. It was a small room, a little dark and old-fashioned but pleasant enough, with a few pictures on the walls, a thick carpet, some pretty porcelain figurines and a white marble clock on the mantelpiece.

'Yes, I'm sure I shall. Thank you.'

I saw a sampler hanging above the mantel and went to look at it. It was beautifully done and signed by Adele Heron, aged nine.

It made me feel a little strange to see evidence of Mama's life in this house. I began at last to understand how it had been for her as a child. I thought of the house in Paris – of how light and pretty everything had been. How could I blame my mother for preferring her life as Laurent's mistress to the one she must have had here?

It was odd but in that moment of understanding, I felt the first easing of my grief – the first crack in the wall of ice I had deliberately built around my heart.

I heard Vera's voice behind me as from a distance. 'I was to have brought flowers in for you tomorrow,' she said. 'I always think flowers brighten a place up, don't you?'

I made an effort to control my emotions, and was calm

when I turned to face her. 'Yes, they do. Perhaps you could bring them later? I should like to change out of these wet things now . . . if you wouldn't mind?'

'I'll send Rosie up with some tea – unless you would prefer to have it in the parlour with Mrs Ruston?'

'That would be nice. Perhaps Rosie could show me the way? Shall we say in twenty minutes?'

'As you wish.'

She went out and closed the door with a snap. I had the distinct feeling that Miss Vera Lenton wasn't particularly pleased that I had come to visit my grandmother.

I was feeling a little sick and shaken. I had not realised how emotional I would feel at coming face to face with my mother's past. There was something about this house that unnerved me; I felt that there were secrets here. For a moment I experienced a rather unpleasant sensation. I seemed to hear a babble of voices in my head, all of them indistinct, none of them making the slightest sense, and I swayed slightly, catching at a chair to steady myself.

After the slight dizziness had passed, I went through to the bedroom and then to a tiny bathroom. The large white porcelain bath took up most of the available space, but there were plenty of fluffy towels and I was pleased to discover that the cast iron radiator was slightly warm. I laid my clean underclothes on it while I stripped off my wet things and rubbed myself dry.

Dressed in a fresh skirt and blouse I began to feel better. My hair was still damp so I left it hanging free about my face instead of trying to confine it in a ribbon – I would tidy it later.

I had unpacked my bag and was about to hang up a spare dress when someone knocked at my door. Guessing it was the maid Rosie, I called out that she might enter. She came in, carrying a huge bowl of fragrant pink roses.

'I picked these this morning so that the buds would be

open by tomorrow. They don't look much now, but they smell lovely. Shall I put them on the desk, miss?'

'Yes please. I love roses.' I picked up a fine wool shawl, wrapping it round my shoulders. These big old houses were never really warm, even in summer, and I was still feeling a little chilled after my soaking – or perhaps it was the atmosphere of these rooms? 'Shall we go down now?'

'I was wondering if you would like me to come back and unpack for you, miss? I could iron your dress, if you like.'

'It is a little creased,' I admitted. 'That would be kind of you, Rosie – if it's no trouble.'

'No trouble at all, miss. I'll be pleased to do it for you.'

'Thank you.' I smiled at her. She was a tall, pretty girl of about twenty or so. 'Have you worked here long, Rosie?'

'Five years. I came after Mr Ruston died. Mrs Ruston dismissed some of her maids then . . .' She faltered and blushed. 'You don't want to hear that, miss.'

'Was there any particular reason why the staff were dismissed?'

'I've heard rumours . . .' She glanced over her shoulder. 'They say the old man was a bit of a rogue where the maids were concerned. Madam didn't want anyone he had been messing around with to stay – at least that's what I've heard.'

'I see . . .' I smiled but took little notice. It was probably just servants' gossip. 'Thank you for telling me, Rosie.'

'You won't mention I said anything? Only, it's just old gossip. I don't really know for sure . . . and I wouldn't like to upset the mistress.'

'Oh no, I don't see why I should need to say anything – do you?'

She shook her head. 'You know what gossip is like, miss – especially in a small place like this. Cook was only saying to me this morning . . .' She glanced over her shoulder again. 'There's not been one of them attacks for months.'

'What attacks, Rosie?'

'Girls being frightened by a hooded man,' she said, crossing herself quickly. 'There were three or four of them last winter. No one was hurt or anything nasty . . . just grabbed and fumbled . . . you know.'

'That sounds very unpleasant,' I said. 'Did the girls know who had attacked them?'

'There was a lot of talk. Most of them were too scared to notice anything but my cousin Sally . . . she thought she knew him. She swears it was the stationmaster's son.'

'Do you mean Robbie?' I stared at her in surprise. 'He showed me the way here today. I wouldn't have thought he was capable of doing anything like that.'

'That's what Cook says. She reckons he's being maligned . . . because that's what gossip means in the end, doesn't it? People add things on and soon they'll be saying Robbie is dangerous and ought to be locked away – just because he's a bit simple.'

'Yes, I see what you mean,' I agreed. 'That kind of gossip can be very destructive.'

'I told Sally it wasn't likely to have been him, but she reckoned she recognised the jacket he was wearing. A sort of shabby, tweedy thing.' Rosie had been leading me downstairs and she stopped outside a door to the right of the main front hall. 'This is the parlour, miss. Go right in – Mrs Ruston is expecting you.'

I thanked her. She smiled and turned away. I stood for a moment without moving, almost too nervous to go in and meet the woman I had come to see.

My mother had called this an accursed house and sworn that neither she nor I would enter it. What was it that had made her feel such horror of her home? The house was perhaps a little dark and the furniture old-fashioned, and I had felt something in my mother's rooms, but it was nothing frightening or malicious – just the lingering echoes of some long-ago sorrow.

This was nonsense! Letting my imagination run wild would

do no one any good. I had come here to meet my grandmother – the woman who had quarrelled with my mother, who had made her run away to France and was in a way responsible for everything that had happened since.

But no, that was being unfair. She might have begun it all, but we each form our own destiny. I could not blame her. I must put an end to this dithering and go in.

I knocked. A soft, whispery voice bid me enter. I turned the fat china doorknob and went in, my heart thumping. A woman was sitting in a chair by the fireplace. She was alone, waiting for me. My immediate reaction was relief; I had half expected either Philip Allington or Miss Lenton to be there.

'Please come in, my dear,' she said, smiling at me as I hesitated.

Anne Ruston was not what I had expected, not the hard, demanding woman I had thought she must be. She was tiny, a delicate, bird-like creature with soft white hair swept up in an attractive roll about her head. She had a sweet face, and did not look as if she had ever quarrelled with anyone in her life.

'Come in, Jennifer,' she said again as I hovered just inside the door. 'I'm so pleased you've come to see me at last. Philip told me you were very pretty. You look a little like Adele when she was young . . .' She sighed and her hand fluttered slightly on the arm of her chair. 'But your hair is different.'

I put a defensive hand up to my wayward hair. 'I'm afraid it must look terrible. I got wet on the way here and it always goes wild after a soaking.'

'It looks pretty,' she said. 'I was told about the misunderstanding; that was unfortunate. I hope you will take no harm from your soaking. It was such a long way for you to walk on a day like this.'

'I'm sure I shan't. I was able to dry off quickly and change my clothes.' A sudden shiver caught me and she noticed. I pulled my shawl closer, but it was not the temperature of the room that had made me shiver. I had suddenly felt Mama close to me, smelt her perfume.

Imagination, of course, but disturbing.

'Are you cold?' My grandmother beckoned me forward. 'As you see, I have had the fire lit. I am seldom warm these days . . . the penalty for having lived too long, I suspect. Come and get warm, child. You need not be nervous. I shall not bite you.'

My common sense told me I was being foolish. Mrs Ruston was just a rather old and lonely woman. There was nothing to fear in getting to know her.

'No, of course you won't.' I saw a flash of humour in her eyes and relaxed as I took the seat at the opposite side of the inglenook fireplace. Now that I could see her face close up, I realised that she looked fragile . . . ill. 'I don't mean to be awkward with you. It's just that this seems so strange. I did not know of your existence until Mr Allington told me. Mama never spoke of her home.'

She nodded, looking sad but accepting. 'Philip was shocked that Adele had not told you, but I was not surprised. Why should she? She had every right to hate and despise me. In her place I might have done the same.'

'What did you do to make her feel that way?'

Anne Ruston's hand clenched the arm of her chair. She was wearing several valuable rings and the rubies flashed blood red in the firelight, but her skin looked papery thin, her veins dark blue and swollen. Something about those hands aroused pity inside me. She was old and tired, and vulnerable. Whatever she had done must have been regretted long ago.

'I accused her of being wicked,' she said in that soft, whispery voice. 'I shouted at her . . . struck her . . . told her that I would not tolerate her in my house . . .'

'And so she left.'

I tried to picture the scene . . . saw my mother crouching away from an angry woman . . . saw the blow . . . felt the pain.

'She ran away that very night.' A tear trickled down her lined cheek. 'I never saw her again. My poor, poor child . . . forced from her home by her mother's unkindness.'

'But you wanted to see her. You regretted what had happened – you sent Philip to ask her to see you, didn't you?'

'I had tried to reach her long before that – when I first began to realise how wrong I had been. I made inquiries, traced her to France, but she . . .' A deep sigh escaped her. 'But she would not listen. She could not forgive.'

I looked into Anne Ruston's eyes, eyes which had once been young and bright but were now so old . . . so haunted with sadness. 'You must have hurt her very much, don't you think? Mama was not cruel. Stubborn perhaps, sometimes careless . . . but not cruel. If she could not forgive you, you must have said something terrible to her.'

'I did. God forgive me, I did!' Her hand trembled. 'It was wicked . . . wicked. I have wished a thousand times that I could go back, unsay those words. Wipe out that night . . .'

She was clearly very upset. I waited for a moment to let her compose herself before asking questions.

'Can you tell me about your quarrel . . . what happened between you and my mother?' I said when she seemed to have recovered.

'It is very hard for me to speak of it, even now.'

'I understand. If you would rather not . . .'

'But I want you to forgive me. I want to make my peace with you before I die, Jennifer – and I must die soon.' She held up her hand as I would have protested. 'No, my dear. I am old and my time is almost done. I have lived long enough – but I shall die easier if I can make you see that I did not mean to be so cruel to your mother.'

I was silent for a moment, thoughtful.

'Mama always called me Jenny. She said I looked like a little Jenny Wren when I was born. All my friends use that name, though in France I was often called Jeanette.' I smiled at her. 'I was not sure I ought to come here. I was afraid –

of you and of being disloyal to my mother, but now I see it was right that I should come. I cannot hate you for what you did then.'

'I have suffered because of it.'

'Yes, I see that.'

'Do you, Jenny?' She sighed and shook her head. 'No, I do not think you could imagine – you are too innocent, untouched by the horror of what life can bring to the unwary.'

'I may not be as innocent as you imagine.'

If she knew the secrets I held in my heart, what would she think? Would she be as eager for my forgiveness then?

I glanced around the crowded room. There were several hard chairs with buttoned backs, their coverings a rather faded brocade which might once have been green but now looked a sludgy brown. A piano stood in one corner, its legs covered by more of the same brocade. On the chiffonier in the corner, I could see a clutter of silver vases, photograph frames and figurines of ladies and cherubs. On the wall were pictures of Queen Victoria and Prince Albert, and a huge aspidistra brooded in a corner like a malevolent spider. It seemed to me that it was a room in which time had stood still.

I brought my attention back to my grandmother as she spoke again.

'I pray that you will never suffer as I have – as your mother did here in this house.'

Her words sent a chill winging down my spine. I took a deep breath, knowing that the time for truth had come. It could not be delayed any longer.

'Will you not tell me what happened? I have sensed a dark secret. Something so awful that Mama could never bring herself to tell me.'

'Perhaps it is time . . . and yet I hesitate to burden you.' She closed her eyes for a moment. Her hand trembled. I could see she was deeply distressed. 'I want to tell you, Jenny. But it is so painful . . . so very painful.'

I reached across to touch her hand. 'If it upsets you too much do not tell me. I do not wish to cause you more grief.'

'It is right that you should know.' She took hold of my hand, clutching at it tightly. 'It began that summer. When your mother first met him . . .' Anne Ruston sighed and shook her head sadly. 'She was very young, younger than you are now. I had taken her to London for the season. She met him at her first dance. Even I could see how attractive he was . . . how much they liked each other. It was one of those things; it happened instantly, and neither of them was at fault – but he was married. I warned Adele that she must not fall in love with him, but it was already too late . . .'

I felt a tingle at the base of my spine as she paused, looking pensively into the fire. It seemed to me then that my worst fears were about to be confirmed, but I waited in silence for my grandmother to continue. And at last she did, her eyes looking beyond me, into the past.

'He must have followed her here when I brought her home, because they were seen in the village together. He was riding and had taken her up with him on his horse. People talk about that sort of thing in a village like this. She ought to have known that I would hear about it . . .

'I forbade her to meet him again, but she was defiant. She told me she was in love with him, that he had gone away – back to London on business – but would return to claim her in a few days. However, he was gone much longer than she had expected – several weeks I believe – and I knew that she was upset about something, almost frightened. I suspected that they had become lovers and I was afraid that she might be with child; there was something in her eyes . . .

'So when I found her weeping that night, I demanded to know what was wrong . . . and she told me she thought she might be carrying a child.'

'She suspected that she was with child but she was not sure?' I stared at her, the creeping chill beginning to spread through me as my fears grew. 'Who was the man she had fallen in love with? Please, tell me his name.'

My grandmother was not listening to me; her mind was wandering in the past, her eyes seeing that night as she remembered it. 'I demanded to know who the father was. She would not tell me. I accused her of being wanton, of having lain with her lover knowing he was married, that she could never be his wife. She begged me on her knees not to make her speak but I would not show mercy. I struck her. I was cruel and vengeful. I told her she was no longer welcome in my house . . . that I despised her.'

'And so she ran away that night?'

She nodded, her face grey with grief. 'I banished my own daughter. I would not listen to her . . .'

'You were shocked, because she had not heeded your warning?'

My grandmother had bent her head – she was weeping, the tears trickling silently down her withered cheeks. 'Adele hated me . . . blamed me for what happened . . .' She raised her head and looked at me. 'And now you will hate me.'

'No, I shall not hate you. It was not your fault.'

'I have not told you all yet . . .' I turned to face her, saw how grey she looked and was shocked. This was causing her such distress. 'She tried to tell me that night . . . but I would not listen.'

'I do not understand . . .' I felt the ice water trickle down my spine, its chill making me numb with fear. 'She ran away because she feared she was with child – what else is there to tell?'

'No, she ran away because I was cruel to her. She tried to tell me – but I would not listen.' Grandmother's eyes were bleak as she raised her head and looked into my eyes. 'She was raped, Jenny. My poor darling child was raped . . . I did not believe it at the time, but I have had time to reflect and I have come to believe that she was telling me the truth.'

A feeling of such horror overcame me that I jumped up

and began to pace the room in agitation. This was something I had not expected. Something that had never once entered my mind. My mother had been raped! Was I the child of that cruel act? Was that why she had tried to hide the truth of my birth from me all these years?

'And the name of the man she had been seeing? Was he the Comte de Arnay?'

My grandmother nodded but could not speak. She was too upset to continue. I felt sick with the horror of what she had just told me. Was Laurent my father – had he raped my mother?

It was so terrible that I could not bear to contemplate such a thing. Surely . . . surely it could not be true? Mama would not have been his mistress for so many years if he had raped her! Besides, even hating him as I did, I could not believe such a terrible thing of him.

'The Comte de Arnay raped my mother?'

'No . . . not him . . .' My grandmother raised her head, eyes mirroring her pain. 'She was in love with him, Jenny. It – it was someone else who violated her.'

'Someone else?' I stared at her. 'She was raped by another man? Who – who did that to her? Who could have done such a wicked, evil thing?'

'She would not tell me.' There was pain in Grandmother's eyes, and regret. 'I demanded to know, but she refused to answer – and because she would not name him, I would not believe her. I accused her of lying to cover for her lover . . . I called her terrible names, and I struck her again. It was only after she had gone – when I began to think more clearly – that I realised she had had no reason to lie . . . that she must have been telling me the truth.'

I stared at her in disbelief. How could she have been so cruel, so unfeeling? To call my mother terrible names when she ought to have been trying to comfort her – to help her to recover from a terrible ordeal!

For a moment I was so angry – almost demented in my fury

– that anyone could have hurt my beloved mother so terribly. I wanted to strike out, to hurt the man who had scarred her – scarred her so deeply that she had hidden this from me all these years. I no longer blamed her for keeping her secret, because I knew why she had done it. She had been trying to protect me from knowledge she believed would hurt me.

She had let Laurent believe he was my father because she could not bear to face the truth – that I might be the child of the man who had raped her. She had wanted me to be her lover's child, but she suspected that I was not. Because Laurent loved her, she had wanted to save him pain . . . just as she had wanted to protect me from this ugliness.

It was just as well that my grandmother did not know the name of the man who had hurt her, for I would not have been able to rest until he was brought to justice. Had I been a man, I should have thrashed him. Even killed him. I had never known such anger, such rage as filled me then: it was like a red mist that invaded my mind, blotting out every other feeling.

'Jenny . . . Can you forgive me for what I did to her?'

I ceased my frantic pacing as I heard the pitiful cry and turned to look at the frail old lady in her chair; my heart was wrenched with pity, and the terrible anger drained away as suddenly as it had come. My grandmother had set off a chain of events that had led to a terrible tragedy, but how she had suffered for it!

I went to her, kneeling at her feet to take her fragile hand in mine. I kissed it, then her cheeks and her forehead, tasting the salt of her tears. Then I gently wiped her face with my fingertips.

'There is nothing to forgive,' I said. 'You have suffered enough for what that evil man did – whoever he was. My mother could never have come back here after what happened, but I am sure she did not hate you. You were wrong – even cruel – but you tried to put it right.'

She reached out to touch my face with a kind of wonder. 'You are so special, Jenny. Where did your goodness come from? How have you become so wise so young? Adele was never like you – and nor to my everlasting shame was I.'

'Perhaps my wisdom, if I have it, came from Tante Marthe – the honest, kind woman who brought me up.'

'Or perhaps from Adele's father. He was a good man, a gentle man. My John was always too good for this world. Perhaps that's why he was taken so young.' She looked into my face and nodded. 'Yes, I can see a little of him in you – and his hair was much your colour. You do favour my John.'

'He was your first husband?'

'He was always a little fragile. They warned us he might not live long even before we married, but we loved each other. A day not spent together was a day wasted for us. We were happier than any two people had a right to be, I suppose . . . but it did not last. John took a chill. He died of a virulent fever when Adele was three years old. The doctors said it was an inherited weakness.'

'And so you married again . . . because you needed a father for your child?'

'Not for several years. Adele was seven when I met Max Ruston. He was wealthy, a gentleman – and he wanted me. I was flattered . . . but it was a mistake. We were not happy.'

She let go of my hand, her gaze drifting away as she lapsed into silence. I stood up. The story she had told of her first marriage made me think of my own tragic love affair. I had not been Gérard's wife, but in every other way it was the same: we had been the perfect lovers but our happiness had been cut short.

If Laurent had been sure whether or not I was his child, the accident might never have happened. Gérard would still be alive and I would be his wife. It was so unfair . . . so cruel.

My mind was whirling in confusion. I had been so angry on Mama's behalf that I had not immediately thought of the implications – the terrible events that took place after that fateful day at the hunting lodge might have been the result of my mother's refusal to tell Laurent what she believed to be the truth.

My thoughts went round and round, like a fairground ride, so fast that I could not make sense of them. I could not be sure that any of my suspicions were correct. Only Mama could have told me for certain who she believed to be my father, and she was dead. Oh, why had she never told me? Why had she never given me the least hint?

I was feeling odd . . . light-headed . . . my head was swimming. If Laurent was not my father I could have married Gérard. There had been no need to deny us. We were not related by blood, not forbidden to love by the laws of church and man. There was no good reason why we should have been parted . . . no need for my lover to die!

Round and round! The room was spinning faster and faster. I felt ill, sick, dizzy. My chest hurt and it was difficult to breathe.

The door opened. Vera Lenton came in carrying a tea tray.

'Have you had a nice little chat?' she asked innocently. 'I hope I haven't come too soon?' She stared at me. 'Are you all right, Jennifer? Jennifer . . .'

I was losing control. I gasped as the floor came zooming up to meet me and then everything went black.

Five

'It was my fault,' a woman's voice was crying in distress. 'I should never have told her. I had no idea . . . no idea that she . . .'

'You are not to blame,' a man's deep voice answered as I opened my eyes and began to focus on his face as he bent over me. He was fair-haired, a stranger, in his middle years. He smiled at me encouragingly. 'Ah, she is coming round. How do you feel, Miss Heron? You fainted, m'dear. Gave us all a fright.'

'Who are you?'

'I'm a doctor. Mrs Ruston's doctor. I had called to see her – just as well I did in the circumstances. You've been overdoing things. Ladies in your sensitive condition should rest more. You can't go gallivanting all over the country when you're—'

'I haven't,' I said, sitting up. 'I'm perfectly well. I was just upset about something.'

'That's as may be.' He took my wrist, checked my pulse and frowned. 'This can be a difficult time for some ladies. My advice to you is to go to bed for a week – unless you want to lose your child?'

I had been lying on a large, rather hard, velvet-covered sofa. Grandmother and her companion were standing behind the doctor, looking at me anxiously. I felt my cheeks grow warm. If I had wanted to keep my condition a secret from them it was too late now.

'It's all right, Jenny,' my grandmother said quickly. She

81

had seen the look in my eyes and interpreted it correctly as shame. 'I shall not condemn you – and Doctor Minter is very discreet, my dear. No word of this will leave this house. You have no need to tell me anything – unless you wish to?'

'I shall tell you in private,' I said. 'I am not ashamed. I was to have been married but . . . he died.'

Vera Lenton made a disapproving clicking noise with her tongue. My grandmother looked at her sharply and she stopped.

'You may show Doctor Minter out, Vera,' she said. 'Thank you for your help, sir. My granddaughter will take your advice – and you may call to see her tomorrow, if you will?'

'Certainly, Mrs Ruston.' He smiled at her. 'Now don't upset yourself any more. She needs to rest, but she is strong and, providing she does as she is told, will bear a healthy child.' He glanced at me. 'If you won't think of yourself, think of others. Your child's death would bring no good to anyone.'

'I want my child to live. Of course I do!'

'Good.' His disapproval vanished. 'Sensible girl. Do as I've told you and there's no need to worry. I'll call every day until you are well enough to get up.'

He left the room almost at once, and Vera followed him. My grandmother came to take my arm as I rose unsteadily to my feet. She looked at me kindly, anxiously.

'You will be sensible, won't you, Jenny?'

'Yes. If it is for my child's sake. I loved Gérard – I still love him. I want his baby more than anything else in the world.'

'Then you must take great care of yourself, my dear. I have sometimes wondered of late if Adele's illness was passed on to her by my husband, and if that was the reason for her early death. Besides, for some women there is no choice. Others can do as they please, but for some of us it is a difficult time.'

'Was it like that for you?' She nodded and I sighed. 'I must admit I have been feeling a little tired lately. I thought it was just grief, but now I see that this has been building up for a while.'

'And then I upset you. I am so very sorry. It was selfish of me to want to unburden myself to you in that way.' I shook my head and she put an arm about my waist. 'Could you walk upstairs if I help you? Or shall I call Rosie? She is very strong.' She looked at me anxiously. 'I should have thought . . . showed more consideration. You are not well . . . your mother . . . and grandfather . . . you may have inherited their weakness.'

'No, no, you must not think that,' I assured her quickly. 'I am seldom ill, I promise you. It was just the shock. If we could just sit quietly for a while, I think I could manage alone.'

'Of course, my dear. You will feel better in a moment.'

'My head feels strange.' I was relieved to sit down. The room still seemed to be moving and I was feeling sick. 'I rarely faint, though it did happen once before – in circumstances when I was deeply distressed. It is not a pleasant experience.'

'It was fortunate that Doctor Minter called. He comes most days – as a friend, to see how I am. I tell him not to bother, that I will call him if I need him, but he does it all the same.'

'You are fortunate in your friends.'

'Yes, I know,' She looked at me apprehensively. 'It was very wrong of me to lay my troubles on your shoulders, Jenny. I was thoughtless, selfish.'

'No, of course you were not – besides, as terrible as your story was, it was not only that which upset me.'

'Does it concern the man you loved?' she asked. I inclined my head, a little sob rising to my lips. 'Do you want to tell me?'

There was no one else I could talk to and I needed to release my feelings – especially now that I knew there was cause to doubt that Laurent really was my father.

'Gérard was the son of the Comte de Arnay. Laurent and Mama had had a long-standing relationship. I believe he loved her but, as you know, they could never have married because he was married before he met her – and his religion does not permit divorce.'

My grandmother was trying hard to conceal her dismay, but I could see the doubts and fears in her eyes. 'Philip has told me some of this – but he was not aware of your relationship with the comte's son. Did you know your mother was the Comte de Arnay's mistress when you fell in love with his son?'

'No. I believed they were friends, nothing more. Perhaps I should have guessed, but I didn't. When I was told the truth it was too late.' I blushed. 'We were so deeply in love. I know it was wrong to anticipate our marriage vows, but the strength of our passion was too much for us. We could not help ourselves.'

'I knew that kind of love once,' she said. 'If you had had your mother there to guide you, it might not have happened.' She touched my hand. 'And then Gérard died – was it an accident?'

'In a way, yes. He fell from his horse. Death was instantaneous. Laurent told me he would have felt no pain, and I am sure it was so, for Henriette wrote to me later to tell me that she believed he had not suffered. She laid flowers on his grave for me . . .' I choked back a sob – I had never seen my lover's grave and it hurt me, but I could never go back.

She looked at me sadly. 'You were the one who suffered. I am so sorry, my dear. You might have married him and been happy.'

'Laurent forbade the marriage.'

'Forbade his son to wed you?' She frowned. 'That was harsh. What was his reason?'

'I cannot be sure.' I closed my eyes as I recalled the night Laurent had come to the hunting lodge to tell us he believed he might be my father. 'He was angry . . . He said I had disappointed him.'

'But of course,' she said and I saw that she had guessed it all now. 'He wondered if he might be your father.'

I had stopped short of the truth, not wanting to hurt her. She was old and fragile and this would be an added burden for her.

'It was possible – is still possible,' I said. 'But, there is cause for doubt now. My mother had been raped before she went to France with Laurent . . .' – which meant that I could be the child of the brute who had raped her. It was difficult to choose which alternative was the least painful.

'This has been a terrible tragedy for you, my dear. If Laurent believed himself to be your father, he ought to have told you before you had time to become attached to his son. It was very wrong of him to leave you both in ignorance.' I closed my eyes and moaned as the grief swept over me. She gently touched my hand. 'Are you in pain?'

I opened my eyes and looked at her. 'It is the pain of grief,' I told her. 'Memories that will not let me rest . . . that haunt me constantly.'

'I know how you suffer, my dear.'

'Yes, of course. You have had more than your share of suffering.'

'Perhaps – but your grief is still raw. You must try to let it go, Jenny. For the sake of the child you bear. Remember that you have something to live for, my dear. Life will not be empty for you if you have Gérard's child.'

She could know nothing of the nightmares that had haunted me for weeks, nor could I tell her: that would have been too cruel. Yet it had helped to talk about my grief, and I was aware that somehow it had eased a little, as if discovering my mother's terrible secret had begun the healing process inside me. And perhaps meeting this gentle woman had helped, too.

'You are so understanding. I am glad I came to see you.'

'Even though what I told you was so terrible?'

'I have often felt that Mama was hiding something from me. It was perhaps time I faced the truth.'

'And yet I would not have told you if I had known you

were with child. I feel that I have burdened you with my sorrows.' Her hand trembled and she looked worn down with sadness.

'It is better that I know the truth.' I rose to my feet. 'And now, if you will excuse me, I shall go upstairs and lie down.'

'Your dinner will be brought to you,' she said. 'You will please oblige me by staying in bed for a few days.'

'Then someone must let my companion know I shall not be home tomorrow. I would not have Marie worry unnecessarily.'

'Philip will take care of that,' she said. 'Don't worry about anything, Jenny. All we want is for you to be well.'

I lay awake for some time before falling asleep that night. The wind had died away now, but I could still hear the sighing of the sea as it rushed against those forbidding cliffs. How strange it felt to be lying here in my mother's bed . . . knowing at last the terrible secret she had kept from me all those years.

She had tried to save me from the truth, inventing a kind, gentle man as my father. But what was the truth – was Laurent my father, or was it an unknown man who had cruelly raped her? It was horrible to think that I might be the child of a rapist.

How would that knowledge have affected me as a child? Would I have been scarred and wounded by it if I had known? Even now, when I was older, less naive, it was difficult to take in. It was almost easier to believe that Laurent was my father, despite what that meant.

Perhaps even more difficult to understand was Laurent's reason for denying happiness to both Gérard and me. Why had he done it? Nothing was certain. Only my mother could have told me the truth, and she was dead.

I could not understand why she had not found some way of telling me. Even if she did not want me to know as a child,

surely she must have realised I would want to know one day.
Perhaps she had meant to tell me in the letter I had not been
able to find . . . I would look for it again when I returned to
London. Although I had taken all her things out of the trunk,
it was just possible it had caught amongst the folds of a gown.
I had been in acute distress when I went through her things –
perhaps I had overlooked something?

In my distress, I had jumped to conclusions, blaming the
comte for taking Mama's letter. Perhaps I had been unfair?
Hating him for destroying my happiness, I had thought him
capable of anything. Now that I had begun to understand
Laurent a little better, I no longer believed he would have
taken such a letter and destroyed it. Indeed, he must have
wanted to know for certain himself whether or not I was his
daughter.

If he had denied us our happiness for no real reason . . . It
was a bitter thought and cost me some tears. By refusing us
the right to marry, Laurent had sent his son to a violent death.
If Laurent had doubts himself, then he too was suffering the
torments of hell. How must he feel, knowing that he had
ruined my life and caused his own son's death?

And yet I could not find it in my heart to forgive him. The
fact still remained that he had not told me of the possible
blood tie at the start, and by his carelessness he had allowed
Gérard and me to believe ourselves free to love – and in doing
so had brought us all so much grief.

I had ceased to hate him, but I could not bring myself to
forgive.

Rosie brought my breakfast tray in the next morning and laid
it carefully across my lap. She gave me a rather self-conscious
look, which meant the servants all knew what had happened
the previous day – and the reason for my fainting fit.

'Mrs Ruston says you're to stay in bed,' she said. 'If you
want anything, miss, you're to ring for it.'

'Thank you, Rosie, I shall.'

After she had gone, I started to read *Emma*, one of my favourite Jane Austen books. It never failed to amuse me and I was chuckling over something Emma's father had just said to her when someone knocked at my door.

'Come in,' I said, laying my book on the bed beside me.

'Are you decent?' Vera asked as she put her head round the door. 'I'm sorry to disturb you, Jennifer, but Philip brought these flowers for you a few minutes ago. May I bring them in?'

'Philip sent them for me? Philip Allington?' I was so surprised that I couldn't think of anything else to say.

'Yes, aren't they lovely?' She brought in a beautiful cut-glass bowl full of yellow, sweetly-scented roses and placed them on top of the dressing table, then glanced at me. 'Can you smell the perfume from there? Would you rather have them beside you?'

'They will do there, thank you.' I was suspicious, on my guard against this unexpected show of friendship.

'There is a note,' she said, bringing it to me. 'Philip called specially to see how you were. He is always so thoughtful.'

'Is he?' I noticed the wistful expression in her eyes and realised she had a girlish crush on him, which was a little ridiculous in a woman of her age. 'I have not always found him so.'

'How can you say that?' Her eyes strayed to the roses, then flashed angrily at me. 'After he went to so much trouble on your behalf . . . travelling at least twice to France at his own expense to see you.'

'I did not ask him to,' I said, sounding a little churlish even to myself. 'It was not for my benefit.'

Vera made no reply, merely giving me a reproachful look as she left the room, closing the door with a little snap after her.

I looked at the note she had given me, feeling irritated. What had the arrogant Mr Allington to say to me this time? I was tempted to tear the paper into shreds, and tell Rosie to take his roses away. Then I realised that would indeed be childish and laughed at my own petulance as I broke the seal of the envelope.

Dear Miss Heron,
  I hope you will accept these flowers as a peace offering. I am sincerely sorry for any offence my foolish tongue may have caused you. I cannot apologise enough for misjudging you, and hope that my unkindness did not add to the already considerable strain you have been enduring. Please forgive me, and accept my good wishes for your recovery. If there is ever any way in which I may be of service to you, I shall always be at your disposal.
                              Yours, Philip Allington

I read the letter three times before laying it aside. Obviously my grandmother had thought it right to confide in him. At least neither of them had condemned me, which they might well have done. My behaviour had flouted the rules of society, and there were many who would have no sympathy for my situation.

  It was thoughtful of Mr Allington to send me the roses, and I would be ungracious not to accept such an obviously genuine apology. I decided to write a note of thanks.

Dear Mr Allington,
  The flowers are lovely. You were hasty in your judgement, but perhaps by wearing a wedding ring to which I had no right, I laid myself open to misunderstandings and criticism. I am sorry for striking you as I did. Perhaps we could agree to forgive and forget?
                              Yours sincerely, Jenny Heron

When my lunch tray was brought up to me I gave the note to Rosie.

'Would you leave this in the hall for Mr Allington when he comes, please?'

'Yes, miss.' She smiled at me. 'He calls to see Mrs Ruston most days, if he can. A real gentleman, is Mr Allington. I don't know what Mrs Ruston would do without him. Before I go out, I'll make sure it's put where he'll see it if he comes.'

I smiled at her and lay back against the pillows, reading and dreaming as the lazy day wore on. With my eyes closed, and the sun warming the room, I could almost believe myself a child back at the farm with Marthe – and I realised I was feeling more relaxed than I had felt for a long time. Perhaps the shock of what Grandmother had told me had somehow released the well of pain and grief inside me, so that it had begun to drain away. It was still there in my heart, of course, but not so urgent – not so overwhelming.

My grandmother came up to sit with me in the afternoon. We had tea together in my room.

'How are you feeling, my dear?' she asked, bending to kiss my cheek. 'Any better today?'

She smelled of lavender and soap, and her hands were gentle as she touched me. Her kindness was easing the ache I had carried inside me for so long now.

'Much better, thank you. I really think I could come downstairs tomorrow. I'm sure I don't need to stay in bed all the time.'

'We'll speak to Doctor Minter in the morning. Perhaps if you rested for an hour or two in the afternoons . . .' She gave me an understanding smile. 'You must be patient for a little while, my dear. You were worn out with grief when you came here. It will do you good to rest for a few days. Besides, I am being selfish again. When you are better you will want to leave me, and I should like to keep you with me for longer.'

'Perhaps I could stay for another week or so,' I said, and the smile she gave me was reward enough for the small concession I had made. 'There is really no need for me to go anywhere in a hurry.'

It was another two days before the doctor would hear of my getting up, and only then on the condition that I had breakfast in bed and rested every day for two hours after lunch.

'You must not think of making the journey home for at least another week or two at the earliest,' he told me with a severe look. 'You were on the point of collapse when you came here, Miss Heron. Unless you follow my advice you may very possibly lose your child – even your own life.'

'Please do not scold me, sir. I am very willing to stay here – if my grandmother will have me?'

She smiled fondly at me from the end of the bed. 'You know that I should like nothing better than to have you stay here for as long as you wish, Jenny dear.'

'Then I shall stay here until the doctor says I may travel,' I promised.

I wrote a note to Marie, telling her not to worry.

> I was foolish to be nervous about coming here. My grandmother is far from being the ogre I imagined. I am being well cared for and will return as soon as Doctor Minter says there is no risk for my child.

I also wrote letters to Tante Marthe, Henriette and Kate. Kate was the only one I told about what had happened to Mama. To her alone, I was able to unburden my heart.

> So, you see, it is very possible that I am not Laurent's daughter after all – which means that I could have married Gérard. I do not hate Laurent as I did, Kate. I understand that he and Mama were in love, that they kept their secret for good reasons – but I still cannot find it in my heart to forgive him. He should have

warned me after her death – perhaps then we could have discovered the truth . . .

On the fifth day after my fainting spell I was allowed to come downstairs. I spent the morning in the front parlour – there was a magnificent view of the sea from the long windows. The windows led out to a tiny garden, where only a few hardy bushes and ground-covering plants were proof against the bitter winds that swept in from the sea during the winter. At the end of the mossy garden path was a wall and a gate, and beyond this I could just see steps leading down the steep cliff face to the stony beach below.

The weather had settled into a period of warm sunny days with blue skies clouded only by pink-edged, fluffy wisps that chased each other on the breeze like spring lambs. Tired of being indoors on such a lovely day, I walked as far as the gate and looked out: there was a narrow path and then, a little nearer the edge of the cliff, was the first wide step cut into the reddish-grey rocks. How I would love to clamber down those tortuous, twisting steps and walk at the edge of the sea!

I could see someone walking on the beach. I thought it was the stationmaster's son. He seemed to be hunting for something at the water's edge. I waved and called out to him. He looked up and waved back, beckoning as if encouraging me to go down. I was tempted and had my hand on the gate latch when I heard a sound behind me.

'Very unwise,' a deep voice said, startling me. 'Your doctor would never forgive you.'

I swung round to look into Philip Allington's eyes, and was surprised to discover that he seemed to be very amused about something.

'I was only wishing that I might go for a walk down there.'

'Do not tell me that you were not tempted?' His brows rose. 'I am not sure that I would believe you.'

'Am I so transparent?' I sighed as he inclined his head. His eyes were bright with laughter. 'You have no idea how tedious all this resting is. I have always been active. I long to walk by the sea . . . to be free of restrictions for a while.'

'And you will be soon,' he replied. 'I can imagine it must be very boring for you.'

'Yes, but I ought not to complain. They have let me get up for a few hours today. If I had been forced to stay in bed any longer, I think I should have gone mad!'

He was smiling at me in a way that made me think he really sympathised with my feelings. I understood then what Vera saw in him. He was an attractive man, even charming – when he wasn't scowling.

'I wanted to thank you for your note, Miss Heron. You were generous to forgive me. What I said to you the other day was very nearly unforgivable. I was misled by the wedding ring and . . . other things.'

My cheeks began to burn and I could not meet his eyes. 'I fear that my behaviour towards you that day was not very ladylike, sir. I should not have struck you. Please forgive me. It stung my pride that you could think I—'

'It was inexcusable of me,' he said at once. 'You have no need to beg my pardon – I should rather beg yours.'

'My grandmother has told you the truth concerning my situation, hasn't she?' I did not dare to look at him. 'I know that many would think my claim to any reputation false and that my behaviour has fallen shamefully short of what is considered respectable.'

'Foolish, perhaps,' he said gently. 'Reckless, certainly – but can there be shame in loving too well? You met a young man who captured your heart and you were lured into temptation. I understand that Gérard de Arnay was a very personable man, and you were thrown together by circumstances. It is perhaps natural that you fell in love.' He smiled oddly. 'My view would not find acceptance in the harsh codes of our society, Miss Heron – but it is an honest one.'

'Thank you.' I then managed to look at him, though still with a blush on my cheeks. 'You are being generous. I know what we did was wrong, Mr Allington – but love does not always act wisely.'

He was looking at my hand. 'I see you are still wearing your ring.'

'Mrs Ruston has accepted my situation – as you have, sir – but there are others who most certainly would not. Perhaps it is wrong of me to deceive them . . .' I twisted the ring uncertainly on my finger. 'I thought it best to be known as a widow. I do not think it would be fair to let my child grow up under the stigma of illegitimacy.'

'It does afford a measure of protection against censure by those who might otherwise shun you.' He frowned and looked thoughtful. 'Have you given much thought to the future . . . what you will do when your child is born?'

'I try not to think of anything other than the pleasure the baby will bring me. I know it will not be easy – it is never easy for a woman to raise her child alone. I shall be frowned on by some, I dare say.'

'And yet I sense you long for that child?'

'Yes.' I knew that my smile came from within, the secret, contented smile that lies in the eyes of women bearing a much-wanted child. 'Yes, Mr Allington, I do.'

'You are a brave woman,' he said and something in his eyes at that moment made me blush. 'I admire your determination.'

'Thank you.' I looked away, towards the house. 'Perhaps we should go in now? It must be almost time for lunch.'

'Yes, perhaps we should,' he replied. 'But I wondered if you would allow me to take you for a drive in my carriage? Not today, but when your doctor thinks it safe for the child.'

'You are very considerate. It would be pleasant to see something of the area while I am here.'

*　　*　　*

I walked to the end of the garden again the next morning. I was looking down at something I found vaguely disturbing happening on the beach when Grandmother called to me. I turned to her as she came up to me, still frowning.

'What is the matter?' she asked. 'Is something troubling you?'

'It was just that . . .' I shook my head. 'It was really nothing. I saw that boy just now . . . on the beach. The stationmaster's son. He was searching for something – pebbles, I think. And then his father came and . . . he hit him several times. Not just a cautionary smack on his ear, but brutal, heavy blows that sent Robbie flying. He ran off crying a moment or two before you called to me.'

I did not add that the sound of her voice calling to me had made the stationmaster look up – or that something about him at that moment had made me feel most uncomfortable.

My grandmother pulled a wry face. 'The boy is retarded. I think he has been a great deal of trouble to his father – not that I approve of such harsh treatment, of course.'

'No.' I smiled at her. 'It is not my business, but I do think it a shame that a young lad should be so unkindly treated by his own father.'

'I believe Robbie is usually no bother to anyone other than his father – unless he has been drinking. That's why his father never lets him have more than a few pence in his pocket.'

I remembered the three shillings I had given Robbie, and wondered if my generosity had been the cause of the beating. With the extra money, he could have bought several pints of beer in the village pub.

'Now, my dear,' Grandmother said. 'Philip has sent a message for you. He has consulted with Doctor Minter, and it is permitted for you to go for a gentle drive. Isn't that nice?'

'Yes, it is,' I agreed. 'Very nice.'

We went into the house together. Grandmother rang for tea, then she took something from the drawer of her bureau and handed it to me.

'I want you to have these, Jenny,' she said. 'They were given to me by my husband when we married – and I want you to have them now. I am sure John would have approved.'

I opened the box and gasped when I saw the choker of large, creamy pearls with an impressive square diamond clasp.

'You cannot give me these,' I said. 'They are far too valuable. Besides, they must mean a great deal to you.'

'They do,' she said, 'which is why I want you to have them, Jenny. It has meant a great deal to me to have you here, my dear.'

'I need no reward for that.'

She came to kiss my cheek, and I caught the sweetness of lavender water on her skin. 'I am asking you to accept them as a favour to me, Jenny. I want to know they are in safe hands – and if you have a daughter perhaps you will give them to her one day.'

Tears stung my eyes as I kissed her in return. 'You are so kind,' I said. 'I shall take them – and treasure them all my life.'

The next few days sped by and when it was finally time for me to leave, Philip insisted on taking me home in his own, very comfortable carriage. He had called every morning for the past ten days to see how I was, and I had come to look forward to those visits. Far from being the severe, cold man he had first appeared, he was gentle, amusing and good-humoured. I understood now why my grandmother counted him such a dependable friend.

She kissed me goodbye with tears in her eyes.

'You will never know just how much this visit has meant to me, Jenny. I am so grateful that you came. You will visit me again . . . when you are well enough?'

'Yes, of course. I shall come again before I return to London.' I looked at her face anxiously. She was so frail – and I had grown fond of her over the past two weeks. She was, after all, the only blood kin I had – and I refused to feel guilt for having come to like her. Mama had done her best to protect me from the past, but now I had faced it and I was the stronger for it. I believed my mother would forgive me and not think me disloyal for liking her own mother. 'Take care of yourself, Grandmother. And write to me, please.'

'Every day,' she promised and squeezed my hand. 'You have given me hope. I have something to live for now. I am determined to hold your child in my arms, Jenny.'

'Then you will,' I said and kissed her cheek. 'When my child is born I shall come and stay with you, I promise. And I shall see you again before that – providing I am well enough to travel.'

'You must think of yourself first, my dear. Try not to tire yourself too much. Promise me that you will rest each afternoon?'

I gave her my promise and we parted. Philip helped me into his carriage. I waved to my grandmother until I could no longer see her, then sat back against the squabs with a little sigh.

'Are you feeling unwell?'

Philip gazed at me anxiously from the opposite seat. I shook my head at him. 'Please don't fuss. I'm quite well. It was a sigh of content. This is a very comfortable carriage, sir.'

'I thought we had agreed that you would call me Philip? We are friends now – aren't we, Jenny?'

'Yes, yes, we are friends, Philip. You have been very kind these past few days . . . taking me for little rides in your carriage . . . bringing me flowers, and strawberries from your garden.'

'We have very large gardens and there is always plenty of fruit. Besides, it was the least I could do. I still fear that my bad temper contributed to your illness.'

He looked so anxious that I laughed. 'I am not so frail a flower, sir.'

'But I did upset you – I did cause you distress.'

'A very little, if at all,' I assured him. 'I have been grieving.'

Some of the shadows had been lifted from my life now that my grandmother had told me the probable truth of my birth. It was very possible that my love for Gérard had not been a sin . . . that my child was not the child of an incestuous relationship. I could still not be quite certain, of course – but it was surely the reason for Mama's deception. Why else would she have woven such an intricate web of lies about my father?

If I had been the Comte de Arnay's child, she need not have been ashamed to tell me – at least when I was old enough to understand. I would not have judged her. Such relationships were not uncommon. Indeed, now that I knew it had been a love match which had lasted until her death, I could see it was romantic. Laurent had not been able to marry her, but he had loved and cared for her while she lived – and afterwards, he had meant to care for me as his own daughter.

Little by little, the bitterness was melting away. Yet still I was not completely at ease; I felt as if a dark cloud hovered at my shoulder, waiting to drag me back into the pit of despair.

Philip was still studying me anxiously. 'There are shadows beneath your eyes. Do you not sleep well?'

'Not always . . .' I glanced down, twisting my gloves in my hands. 'Sometimes I dream of Gérard. He comes to me in a beautiful garden – a garden I have never seen in life. He comes to warn me of some danger, but I do not know what danger – it is never clear.'

'Dreams are often strange,' he said, looking thoughtful. 'You must have loved him very much?'

'Oh, yes, I did – I still do, very much.' I caught back a sob as I remembered our first meeting, the walks in the rose gardens. 'From the very beginning . . . when he laughed at me . . . I tried to resist him. But Gérard was . . . he charmed everyone. He was full of life and laughter and now he's . . .' Tears filled my eyes and I could not continue.

'You have his child.' Philip reached across to touch my hand. 'You must not let your grief make you ill. You are young, Jenny. You will be happy again one day. I promise you.'

'Shall I?' I blinked hard. 'Forgive me. It is so silly! I did not mean to cry.'

'Perhaps that's what you need.' He handed me his large, clean white handkerchief. 'There is no shame in tears when they are for a loved one. I cried when my mother died and for my father . . . just a year ago.'

It was unusual for a man to confess to tears. I was oddly comforted by his words.

'Thank you.' I wiped my cheeks with his handkerchief. I was about to give it back when I changed my mind. 'I shall have it washed and send it to you.'

'May I not call to collect it – as a friend? Anne will rest easier in her mind if I can give her first-hand reports of how you're getting on.'

I realised that I would miss his company if he did not visit me. 'Yes, of course. I should like that,' I said. 'I do not have so many friends that I can afford to lose someone as kind as you, Philip.'

Was that a flash of disappointment in his eyes? No, he was amused at something . . . some secret thought of his own.

'You would not have called me kind a few weeks ago.'

'Do not tease me, Philip,' I reproached him. 'I did not know you then – and you were not kind to me at the start.'

'No, I was not,' he said, his smile dying. 'You saw only the harsher side of me. You did not know me, nor I you. We both made hasty, unfair judgements – but all that is ended. How long ago it seems. I feel now that I have known you all my life.'

'Yes,' I agreed. 'I feel much that way. How pleasant it will be to have your friendship.'

'Yes, yes . . . very pleasant for us both.'

There was a look almost like regret in his eyes, but in another moment it had gone and his mouth relaxed into a smile again. He changed the subject, talking of Mr Gladstone, politics, and the weather.

Any tension I might have harboured drifted away as I listened to him. He was an interesting man, intelligent, educated, knowledgeable about the affairs of the world – the kind of man I thought a father should be. Philip was much too young to be my father, of course – he was no more than ten years my senior – but he might have been an older brother.

I was comforted by the thought. I should never love again, not in the way I had loved Gérard, but it was good to have Philip as my friend. A true friend. Someone I could rely on. How much easier that would make my life from now on.

I began to confide in him, to tell him of my hopes for the future.

'I considered buying a house in Oxford or a quiet market town – but Susanna hopes I shall return to London. I think I might like a smaller house there . . . and a cottage in Cornwall.'

'Are you not happy where you are?'

'Oh yes, indeed I am. I love the house I have now – but it might not always be available when I need it.'

'I'm sure it will be.' He looked a little nervous. 'Do not be angry, Jenny. The house is mine. When I discovered you were looking for something in Cornwall I had my agent send the details to you.'

'You did what?' I stared at him in disbelief.

'I heard you talking about your intention to take a house for the summer at Susanna's dinner party – do you not remember? And I'm afraid I took the liberty of sending you details of my own property.'

'That was devious of you, sir!'

'You *are* angry with me.'

I laughed at his crestfallen expression. 'I should be – but I love your house, Philip. I sensed it was someone's home the moment I walked into it. But don't you want it back?'

'I have Grandfather's estate now. I had almost decided to sell – then I thought I might let it to someone I liked.'

'But you did not know me then. I was not particularly pleasant to you at Susanna's – nor when you called at my house.'

'You forget,' he said with a wry smile. 'I had seen you twice before – in Paris. Once at your mother's house, and once out shopping with her. You were laughing that day, and your arms were full of flowers. I thought you looked . . . very pleasant.'

'So it *was* you who had the sketches drawn? I always thought it must have been! And so you sent me the details of your house – knowing that once I was living in Cornwall, I should most likely make the effort to see my grandmother.' I laughed out loud. It was amusing. 'Do you always get your own way, sir?'

'Not always.' His eyes gleamed. 'But if at all possible. Don't you?'

'I suppose I do. When I can.'

'Think of all the splendid arguments we shall have in the future.' His eyes were mocking me. 'I wonder who will win?'

'I shudder to think. Do not imagine I am always that easy to best, Philip!' I arched my brow at him. How good it felt to laugh. I had not felt this light-hearted in ages.

'Perhaps I shall let you win sometimes.'

'Shame on you! I promise you I shall not be so sentimental.'

He smiled and looked satisfied. He had chased away the shadows. They would no doubt return when I was alone, but for the moment they were banished.

Six

'It's good to have you back.' Marie was waiting at the door for us. 'Are you truly better now? I was concerned for you, Jenny.' Her dark eyes went over Philip, registering curiosity and, I thought, disapproval.

I took off my hat and gloves in the hall, walking ahead of both Marie and Philip into the large sunny parlour. How light and pretty this house was compared to Anne Ruston's – and how lucky I was that it belonged to Philip and would be my summer home whenever I chose to visit.

'Are there any letters for me?' I asked, ignoring Marie's pointed looks at Philip. 'I was hoping Kate might have written while I was away.'

'Your letters are in your room,' Marie said, seeming disgruntled. 'I do not know who they are from – I do not read your personal messages. If you will excuse me, I have work to do.'

Philip arched his brows at me as she went out. 'She does not seem as respectful towards you as you have a right to expect from a maid.'

'It is my fault.' I sighed. 'When I left France I needed a friend. Marie came here as my companion – but sometimes she seems to imagine she owns me.'

'Possessive,' he said, frowning. 'I've come across that type before. My mother had a personal maid very like yours once. She had to dismiss her in the end. She became obsessive. Before she left she smashed Mother's favourite porcelain figures and stole a diamond brooch.'

'How terrible! What did your mother do?'

'Nothing. She was sorry for the woman, and felt it was a small price to be rid of her. But my father wrote to his friends to cancel her references. He said he could not allow other people to be duped. Later, we heard that she had taken up work as a barmaid and in the end she married her employer.' His frown deepened. 'Some years after that, he fell down his cellar steps and broke his neck. It was rumoured – although never proved – that she might have pushed him, because he had lain with another woman.'

'You don't think that she murdered him . . .' I could see from his face that it was exactly what he thought.

'My father was certain of it. She was given to passionate rages – such women often are. You would do well to be careful, Jenny. Jealousy can be a destructive emotion.'

'Marie would never harm me.'

'Perhaps not . . .' His eyes were intent on my face. 'If you are ever worried about her – or anything else – please confide in me, Jenny. I would be happy to take care of any awkwardness for you.'

I understood what he was saying to me: if I found Marie too difficult he would take charge of the situation . . . dismiss her for me . . . save me from the unpleasantness it would create.

'I am glad to have you as my friend,' I said, 'but do not be too concerned for me. I shall talk to Marie. She is jealous and she sulks sometimes – but that does not mean she is dangerous.'

'You are too easy with her.'

'You do not know her. Your judgement cannot be other than flawed in this matter.'

'I may not know Marie, but I have seen the type before – and I am usually thought to be fair-minded.'

We glared at each other and then Philip laughed. 'I told you we should have glorious arguments.'

'Yes.' I smiled reluctantly. 'But you do see, don't you? It

would be easy to judge Marie too harshly. She is sometimes a little awkward in her manner, but she was good to me in Paris – and when I first came to this country.'

'I understand that you have a tender heart,' he said, his face softening. 'I can only pray that it does not lead you astray . . .'

Later, after Philip had left – promising to visit me within the week – I went upstairs to change my travelling gown and discovered a small pile of letters. There was one from Tante Marthe, one from Henriette and, at the bottom of the pile, the hoped-for letter from Kate. The seal looked rather odd, as though it might have been opened and resealed – but perhaps that was only my imagination.

> My dearest Jenny,
>
> How terrible for you to discover that Adele was raped in that manner. It must have been such a shock – but at least it should set your mind at rest over the other business. I did tell you not to worry. I have never thought it likely that Laurent was your father. Adele was still very much in love with him. I am sure she would have been only too delighted to tell you he was your father if that were the case. However, I can quite understand why she allowed Laurent to believe he was the father of her child – can't you? She must have wished it was the truth so many times . . .

Kate went on in the same manner for some time, putting into writing my own thoughts. It was very understandable that Mama should have let her lover believe he was my father – and perhaps in time she had almost convinced herself it was the truth.

And if he was not my father – then who was? The thought lingered in my mind unpleasantly.

I was replacing Kate's letter in its envelope when Marie

knocked at my door. I said that she might enter. She obviously had something on her mind and it would be better to let her tell me now rather than have her brooding. She stood looking at me, half wary, half sullen.

'What is it, Marie? Why are you worried?'

'That letter . . .' She looked at it lying on the bed beside me. 'I'm sure I've seen that writing before . . . on a letter to your mother. Just before her last illness.'

I sighed inwardly. Why could she not accept that Mama had died of a fever? Why must she always be trying to prove that some unknown person had done her harm?

'Very well,' I said. 'Bring me Mama's box, Marie. We shall settle this once and for all.'

She brought me the box and I unlocked it, taking out Mama's letters to Laurent and her personal papers.

'Look through her letters,' I invited. 'If you find the one you remember, we will read it together.'

She flushed a deep red colour and made a pretence of looking for it.

'It isn't there.'

'You knew it wasn't – because you had looked before, hadn't you?'

'Yes.' Her face was stamped with guilt. 'While you were at your grandmother's.'

'This is all nonsense, Marie. It doesn't make sense. Kate would probably have died if it were not for my mother – why should anything she had to say make Mama want to take her own life? Besides, my grandmother also wrote to Mama at about that time, and given that they had quarrelled so hurtfully, that was far more likely to upset her than anything Kate wrote – don't you think so?'

'I don't know.' Marie's eyes filled with tears. 'It's just that I can't get it out of my mind . . . She was so weak at the last, Jenny. I tried to make her well. Believe me, I did everything I could but she just got worse and worse . . . If it had been only a fever she ought to have got better. Why did she die?'

I had not realised Mama's death had been playing on Marie's mind this much. I had learned to accept my loss and had thought Marie must have come to terms with hers before now. Her obvious distress made me feel closer to her, banishing some of the annoyance I had felt recently. If she had cared so much for my mother, it made sense of her feelings towards me.

'Come, sit beside me on the bed,' I said softly, patting the coverlet. 'You must try not to grieve so much, Marie. Mama's death was entirely natural. She inherited a weakness from her father.' She stared at me incredulously. 'My grandmother told me about it – it runs in the family. It made her more vulnerable to fevers and chills than other people might be. But each time she was ill, she would have got weaker and weaker – and at the last, it killed her.'

'An inherited weakness?'

'Of the lungs. It means that she was prone to catching colds and fevers, and that she would suffer from reoccurring bouts that would eventually lead to death.'

Marie hesitated for a few moments, seeming thoughtful. 'She was not poisoned? She did not take her own life?'

'Laurent was certain it was a natural death at the time. Perhaps she had told him of her family history. Be easy in your mind, Marie. No one poisoned my mother. Nor did she take her own life because of a letter or anything anyone said to her. She might have been upset over a letter from someone – or a visit from Mr Allington. It is true that she did not want me to visit my grandmother – but that was for my sake, because she did not want me to know what had happened to her when she was a young girl. She was raped, Marie – and there was a child. She quarrelled with her mother because of it, and that is why she could never bear to be reminded of the past. So you see, there is nothing for you to worry about.'

I handed her a handkerchief. She dried her eyes, looking oddly ashamed and a little bewildered, as if she had been under a great strain.

'I have been foolish,' she said in a choked voice. 'I looked in Adele's box without your permission – and I opened your letters while you were away. It was because I was jealous of that friend of yours. I thought that if she came here you would not need me. But now you will be angry with me – you will send me away.'

She looked at me so pitifully that any annoyance I had felt over her behaviour melted away. Sometimes she *was* too possessive, and I knew she was jealous of my other friends, but I did not believe she would harm me. Her only fault was that she felt things too intensely.

'No, I don't want you to leave,' I said at last. 'But I have been told I must not worry, Marie. I must not be under too much strain. I have to rest . . . to relax . . . to be peaceful. I do not think I have inherited Mama's weakness, but the doctor is concerned for me. If you stay, there must be no more foolish jealousy. Do you understand me?'

'Yes.' She looked contrite, concerned. 'I should never forgive myself if anything happened to you, Jenny.'

'It won't,' I said. 'But I want us all to be happy. You, me – and my friends. And that includes Philip, Susanna . . . and Kate if she ever comes to stay with me.'

'I won't make trouble for you,' she promised, seeming upset at the idea that she might have contributed to my collapse. 'I'm sorry I've been so foolish.'

'Then we shall forget it,' I said. 'I've decided to lease a smaller house in London. We shall go back there in October – and come down to Cornwall each summer for a few months. Will you be content to live like that?'

'Yes.' She looked at me thoughtfully. 'You won't go back to France – ever?'

'Perhaps briefly to visit Marthe one day, but not to the chateau. No, I shall never go there again.'

I could not return, even though I no longer hated Laurent. There were too many memories . . . too many reminders of what might have been.

After Marie had gone I locked Mama's writing box and put it into a bottom drawer, covering it with my scarves and shawls. Most of my mother's secrets had now been revealed to me. I should not need to trouble myself further. There remained only one more mystery – the name of the man who had raped my mother and perhaps fathered me.

Sometimes, when I lay wakeful at night, I was haunted by the cruelty of fate. My life might have been so very different. Even now I might have been Gérard's wife.

But would the sharp, bright happiness we had known for such a short time have lasted? The thought came unbidden to my mind, lying there like a stinking maggot, twisting and turning as it taunted me. Gérard had always been restless – would he, could he, have settled down to being a husband and father? He had loved me truly and I him – but would that have been enough to content him?

But it was ridiculous to speculate! It was foolish to dwell on a past that was gone. Gérard was lost to me, but I had his child growing inside me.

I must look only to the future. I must think only of my child. I had friends to help me: my grandmother, Susanna and Philip – and, of course, Marie. I was not alone.

'The house is perfect for you,' Philip said, laying a coloured sketch on the table in front of me. 'The rent is half what you can get for your own house, and you will need only a handful of servants to run it. Far more sensible for a woman on her own.'

'You sound like Marie. She is always trying to encourage me to economise,' I murmured and pulled a face at him. 'But I think you are both right. I shall be happier in a smaller house.'

'So you will take it – for the time being?'

'I shall want a long lease,' I replied. 'Once I am settled there it will be my home – apart from the summer when I shall come here . . . if you will allow me?'

'You know the answer to that.' He looked serious. 'But a short lease is more flexible. Supposing you want to marry? You would have to find someone to take over the lease. Shall I suggest a year with the option of another five if you like it?'

'If you think it best – but I very much doubt that I shall marry.'

'You might. I know you feel you can never love again, Jenny, but time does heal, believe me.'

There was something in his voice then, a slight inflection that made me look at him.

'Have you been hurt, Philip?'

'There was someone I thought I cared for once – she married a much richer man. I was hurt for a while, but I have long forgotten the affair. I am perfectly happy as a bachelor.'

I turned my face aside as tears pricked. 'Your case was different, Philip. If Gérard had jilted me I should not feel as I do.'

'No, no, of course not. Forgive me. It is only that I cannot like the idea of your living alone for the rest of your life. It seems such a . . . waste.' He got up and walked over to the window, gazing out at the gardens. 'The weather is on the turn again. I think we shall have a few more fine days before you leave for town.'

'Philip . . . you will visit me in town sometimes, won't you?'

'Yes.' He turned to face me. I could see he was hesitant, unsure of himself. 'Jenny, I wondered . . .' He paused.

'Yes, Philip?'

'If I were to ask you something . . . you would not be angry?'

'Should I be? Speak plainly, if you please. What have I done to make you look at me like that? Have I upset you?'

'You have done nothing, nothing at all. It is merely that

I do not wish to lose your friendship. I would have spoken before this but . . .'

'Philip! You are worrying me.'

'Do not be anxious. It is just that I thought perhaps you might consider marriage with me.' He saw my frown and held up his hand just as I was about to speak. 'No, do not be angry. You would have security – and a father for your child.'

'Respectability,' I said. 'That's what you are offering me – isn't it?'

'Well . . . yes. At least, that would be a part of it.'

'But . . .' I was shocked by the suddenness of his offer. 'You cannot wish to marry me, Philip. You told me only a moment ago that you were happy as you are.'

'I meant only that I had recovered from my disappointment and was not holding a torch for anyone. I had not met a woman I wished to marry before . . .' He faltered uneasily.

'And now you have?' I gazed at him in distress. 'Please tell me this is just a foolish notion of chivalry, Philip! I value you dearly as a friend – you know I do – but I cannot marry you. It would be so unfair to us both. I loved Gérard. I believe that I shall carry that love with me to my grave.'

'I would accept that you could never feel such a passionate love for me,' he said in an odd voice. 'I should ask no more than you were prepared to give.'

'I can give you only friendship,' I said, my throat aching with emotion. 'I thought you understood that, Philip. I would not hurt you for the world.'

'Nor have you,' he said and laughed ruefully. 'What a mess I made of that! I meant only that I would consider it a privilege to be your husband – a father to your child. I have several houses and more money than is good for any one person. I should have been happy to share them with you.'

'But you are not madly in love with me? It won't break

your heart because I have refused you? Please, Philip, I beg you, I do tell me it was only kindness!' He shook his head, giving me a mocking smile and I was swamped with relief. 'Thank goodness! I could not bear to lose you entirely, Philip.'

'Nor I you,' he said. 'Forgive me for embarrassing you?'

'There is nothing to forgive.' I stood up and gave him my hand. 'Forgive me if I have slighted you in any way. I do care for you as much as I could for anyone.'

'Except Gérard.' It was a statement of fact, not a question. 'I was clumsy, Jenny. I shall never embarrass you in that way again, but if you should change your mind . . .'

I touched a finger to his lips and smiled. 'Tell me some more about my new house,' I said. 'It wouldn't be yours, by any chance?'

'Not this time. I have just one house in London – but if you would like to live there you would be welcome.'

'I think the house you have found me will suit me very well.'

'So I shall secure the lease for you – and you want me to tell Anne that you are going to see her soon, to stay with her for a few days before you go up to town?'

'Yes. Please do tell her not to worry. I have consulted my own doctor and he says the dangerous time has passed. I shall not miscarry simply because of taking a short train ride to visit Grandmother.'

'I promise you the carriage will be waiting this time.'

'And Marie will be with me. I shall be quite safe.'

Philip nodded. 'I may have been wrong about her. She seems calmer now, more respectful to you.'

I laughed and clapped my hands in delight at his confession. 'So you admit it at last?'

'No one could take better care of you than she does.'

'She would wrap me in cotton wadding if she could.' I smiled ruefully. 'It becomes a little tiresome at times.'

'I wonder why we all think you need looking after,' Philip said, a gleam of mockery in his eyes now. 'You are probably stronger than any of us.'

After he had gone I thought about his offer of marriage. It had shocked me so deeply that I had refused instinctively. Now I wondered if I had been too hasty.

Philip was a gentle, generous man and I was fond of him. I might have enjoyed being his wife. We got on well and shared many similar interests. We should have been good companions for each other.

Was that enough? I would never love him as I had loved Gérard, of course – but we might have found a certain happiness together.

But no! That was not fair to Philip. He deserved a wife who loved him deeply . . . passionately. As I had loved Gérard.

It was very hot the night I once again dreamed of being in a garden. I had lain without sleeping for several hours, and when I finally fell asleep there I was – alone, with the sound of birds singing sweetly all around me.

I could see it so clearly. It was a beautiful garden with a high wall around it, but it was neglected and overgrown. I felt a sense of peace and wished that I could stay there forever, that I could restore it to the glorious place it had once been . . . But then it was morning and I woke to see the sun streaming in through my window.

It was a beautiful day, my last day before I left to stay with my grandmother. I decided to go for a long walk on the beach. The dream of my garden had stayed with me, and as I walked by the edge of the sea, watching the wavelets break over the ridges of rock, I was planning the restoration of that wonderful, neglected place. I would have lots of roses, lilies and white lilacs. It would be a white garden . . .

How foolish of me! I laughed at myself. The garden

existed only in my imagination. And yet I had felt such a sense of rightness there ... such peace. I knew that if I could only find my way to that garden I would be happy.

Seven

'So you're back again.' The stationmaster's black eyes looked at me intently. I could see he was aware of my condition. It had not been so noticeable when I was here earlier in the summer, but this was the middle of September. I had less than four months to go until my child was born and there was no hiding the truth. 'Come to visit Mrs Ruston then, *Miss* Heron?'

There was something about the way he said my name, something disrespectful – a sly, knowing expression in his eyes as he glanced at Marie and then back at me. His manner towards me had been very different on my last visit, more courteous, without the underlying menace I felt now. I wondered what had changed him – or was I merely being sensitive because I was aware that my condition was more apparent?

Of course, Grandmother's servants would have gossiped in the village. They would all know that I was not married, despite the wedding ring I wore – which was for the moment covered by my white gloves. For a moment I felt vulnerable, exposed to this creature's ridicule and scorn. No doubt he thought me wanton, little better than the whores who plied their trade on the streets of London.

My head went up proudly. Let him and all such others think what they pleased. 'Yes. Yes, I have.'

'It's not raining today.'

'No, it isn't.' A shudder went through me. I was glad that I had not come alone this time.

'You'll not be walkin' today? You'll not want Robbie to carry your bag?' His eyes were on me, an odd, secretive look in them that disturbed me – but perhaps that was merely my imagination again?

'No, not today.' Thank goodness Marie was with me! I sighed with relief as I heard the clatter of hooves in the yard. 'That will be Mrs Ruston's carriage.'

'I remember your mother,' the stationmaster said suddenly. 'Oh yes, I remember her right enough . . . when she were a young girl like you.'

There was something about the way he said it that sent shivers down my spine. As if there was some secret about her that only he knew. Perhaps he had somehow known that she and Laurent were lovers – had seen them kissing . . . or even making love? The thought was abhorrent to me.

I hurried out into the yard. Rosie had come in the carriage and she got out to help me and take my bag. She noticed my expression and looked back over her shoulder at the stationmaster as he stood in the doorway, watching us.

'He gives me the creeps,' she said with a toss of her head. 'Now if it had been him they wanted to put away I wouldn't lift a finger to stop them.'

'What do you mean?'

'There's some as would like to see Robbie put away,' Rosie said. 'He likes playing tricks on the girls when he's had a drink or two – nothing bad, but it upsets some folk.'

'Yes, you did tell me that before, I believe – but surely it would be too drastic to put him away for something like that? I am sure there is no harm in the lad.'

'That's what I say. It's his father wants putting away – the way he treats that lad,' Rosie said. She nodded to Marie. 'You'll be Miss Heron's companion. Can you carry your own bag?'

'Certainly.' Marie's dark eyes flashed with pride. 'I would have carried Jenny's but she would not let me.'

'Miss Heron is independent,' Rosie said cheerfully. 'But

we'll look after her – she'll be all right now she's here with her folks.'

It was like a red rag to a bull! I sighed inwardly as I saw Marie's face. For the past two and a half months she had kept her promise and we had lived in peace, but she had taken an instant dislike to Rosie and I sensed that battle was about to commence.

As we drove away from the station I looked back at the upper windows of the house. A pale face stared out at us from behind the grimy glass and I knew Robbie had been watching us. Did he often stand there gazing out – trapped in his own home like a prisoner?

'How well you look, my dear.' Grandmother embraced me gently. I thought she seemed tired, more fragile than the last time. 'The journey hasn't upset you, has it?'

'No, of course not. You mustn't worry about me. I'm fine, really I am – much better than I was the last time I visited you.'

'Come and sit down, Jenny.' She turned her bright eyes on Marie. 'And this is Mademoiselle Corbier. Will you take tea with us, my dear?'

'I'll unpack Miss Heron's things first,' she said. 'I can have something in the kitchen later.'

'But you will dine with us,' Grandmother insisted. 'We have no formality here. Jenny's friends are always welcome.'

Marie thanked her and went off in the direction she had seen Rosie take earlier. I guessed she wanted to inspect the kitchens and the rest of the staff.

'That was kind of you,' I said to my grandmother after she had gone. 'Marie is never quite sure where she belongs – in the parlour with me or in the kitchens with the others. I suppose it wasn't fair of me to suggest that she become my companion in the first place. She would have known where she stood as my maid.'

116

'A companion's life is never an easy one,' Grandmother agreed. 'It must be much the same for Vera.' She paused, then said, 'I wanted to tell you, Jenny. My will—'

'Please don't,' I begged. 'I have all I need.'

'Perhaps.' She smiled in her gentle way. 'I know you wouldn't wish to live in this house, and it is Vera's home, so I intend to leave it to her for her lifetime and an income to support it. Everything else will come to you, as the house will in time.'

'Does Vera know?'

'I thought it best to tell her. She was a little jealous of you when you were here the last time. I think she felt threatened. Now that she knows she is secure, she will have no reason to resent you.'

'I'm glad that she has security for the future.'

'I thought you would approve.' Grandmother's gentle smile caressed me. 'Now tell me all your news, my dear. Philip visits you now and then, I believe?'

I saw curiosity in her eyes and smiled inwardly. 'We are good friends. Nothing more.'

'No, of course not . . . you could not think of . . . not yet.' Her eyes held a certain wistfulness. 'Perhaps one day?'

'No, I don't think so. It wouldn't be fair to Philip.'

'Well, we shan't talk about it. Besides, I think he may already have a young lady . . .'

'Oh?' I sounded surprised, which made her look at me intently.

'Yes. Vera saw them together at a tea shop in Truro the other day when she went in to do some shopping for me. She was quite upset. You may have guessed that she has a . . . feeling for him?' Grandmother paused, but as I made no comment, she went on. 'She was very beautiful, according to Vera. Dark hair and a wonderful complexion – but I dare say they are just good friends.'

Philip and a beautiful, dark-haired woman. I felt a twinge of jealousy but smothered it at once. It would be ridiculous to feel jealous. I was not in love with him. Besides, he had just asked me to marry him; it was hardly likely he was in love with someone else. And yet these things could happen in an instant. I of all people should know that – and it was more than a week since Philip had been to see me.

I had not thought it strange. Sometimes he visited several times in a week, sometimes he would not come for ten days or more. If he was busy he would write – but he had not written for a week either.

'And you will see Doctor Brownlee when you are in town?' Grandmother's words broke into my thoughts. 'He is the best in his profession. You should ask him to attend you at the birth, Jenny.'

'Yes . . . Yes, I will,' I promised. 'Philip gave me his address. I have already written to him, making an appointment. I move into my new house in two weeks' time. Philip has arranged everything.'

'Yes, he would, of course. He is always so thoughtful – the sort of man one can always rely on to take care of everything,' my grandmother said. 'I tell him it is high time he was married. He will make such a good husband for some fortunate young woman.'

'Yes, he will.' And when he married our friendship would change. He would be different, unable to give me so much of his time. His wife would resent it if he did, and rightly.

The door opened and Vera came in with the tea tray. She smiled at me. I could see the change in her – she no longer resented me. Indeed, she was prepared to like me now that I was not a threat to her.

'I haven't come too soon? I thought you two would enjoy a cosy little chat. How well you look, Jenny.' She set the tray down on the tea table, which had been opened up in readiness, and busied herself with the cups. 'You do take sugar, don't you, Jenny?'

'Yes, thank you.'

'I thought I had it right. It's Philip who doesn't.' She sighed as she handed me my cup, a wistful, regretful expression in her eyes. 'I saw them again this morning when I was out walking, Anne. He stopped and introduced her. Her name is Margaret. He is so fond of her. You can see it in his eyes. And she is madly in love with him. You can always tell.'

'We must invite her to dinner,' Grandmother said immediately. 'I shall write to Philip this evening. If he has found someone at last I want to meet her . . .'

I lay in bed listening to the rush of the waves breaking against the cliffs. The sea sounded very close and I knew there was a strong tide running; the wind had got up, reminding me of the day I had first come to this house.

I had been afraid of what I would learn then, and a terrible secret had been revealed to me. I had disliked Philip then, and now he was my friend – a friend I was afraid of losing.

How strange life was . . . how easily things changed.

Had I already lost him to the beautiful Margaret? He had laughed when I turned down his offer of marriage, but he was a proud man. Had he turned to someone else because I had wounded his pride?

It surprised me to discover that once again I was feeling jealous. It was an emotion that did not sit easily with me, an ugly, dark emotion that shamed me even while I was unable to conquer it. I was restless, angry. I had no right to feel like this. I was not in love with Philip . . . of course I wasn't. But I did value him; I did look forward to his visits.

It was not enough!

I wished I could go to sleep and dream of my garden. I had it so clearly in my mind now that I knew where each new plant, each new shrub, would go . . . but there was no garden, no haven of peace.

I got out of bed and carried my oil lamp to the window, holding the heavy brass base with both hands as I looked out. It was surprisingly light outside. I could see my grandmother's tiny, windswept garden and the sea beyond, moving restlessly, ever changing in the grip of wind and tides.

What was that? I put down the lamp and pressed my face against the window pane. There was someone down there in the garden! He was staring up at me and there was something about him . . . a stillness that I found unnerving. He was staring so intently . . . at me!

I suddenly realised that the light from my lamp must make it easy for him to see me. And I was wearing only a thin nightgown, which showed the dark circles of my nipples and the swollen mound of my belly.

I retreated hastily, turning down my lamp as I got into bed. My room faced seaward and I had never expected to see anyone out there. Who could it have been? My grandmother's house was a house of women; the gardener, coachman and bootboy all lived out, coming in daily to their work.

Who had been there in the dark – and why had he seemed to be watching my window?

For a few minutes it seemed quite sinister. I lay listening for sounds, as though I thought a face might appear at my window at any moment . . . that someone would come into my room and ravish me. I heard a faint cry somewhere out there in the blackness and I remembered the hooded man who jumped out at young girls and frightened them. I was certain it had not been Robbie watching from the garden – this man had been older, broader in the shoulder.

It must have been a tramp – or a poacher. Someone startled to see a light at the window. He had probably been more frightened than I, afraid to move out of the shadows in case he was recognised. He had been too far away for that, but there was something about him that made me feel I ought to remember . . . what?

No, no, I was imagining things again! It was just a tramp trespassing in a private garden – and the cry I'd heard had been that of a seabird as it perched on the rocky shore.

Smiling at my own foolishness, I turned over and went to sleep.

It was the first time I had walked as far as the village, but Philip had not visited since my arrival at Storm House and I had felt in need of some exercise.

'You will take great care?' Grandmother warned when I told her I was going for a walk. 'Why not let Marie or Vera go with you?'

'I shall be fine alone,' I assured her. 'Do not look so worried, Grandmama. The doctor told me it was good for me to walk.'

And so I took a gentle stroll down to the village. The sun was shining, though there was a gentle breeze which warned of a change in the weather. Autumn would soon be here, and I should be in London.

It was the girl's scream which made me turn suddenly. She came running from the direction of a small copse and she looked frightened. I called out to her, asking her what was wrong, but she just kept on running towards the row of houses, bolting inside one of them and slamming the door.

I looked towards the woods, catching sight of something between the trees. Was that a man . . . wearing a hood over his face? I could not be certain, and in another moment the shadowy figure had gone, disappearing into the trees.

There was a sandy path leading down to the beach. I moved towards it, feeling a little disturbed as I recalled Rosie's gossip. The village girl had certainly been upset about something – and I had thought for one moment I could see a man's bulky figure hovering in the copse.

I shivered as I recalled the face in my grandmother's garden the previous night. Had the man standing there been the same one who had been frightening village girls?

I walked for some minutes on the beach, venturing as far as the point where I could look up and see my grandmother's house. The steps leading up to it were steep, and there were some large boulders lying around where a part of the cliff had fallen at some time in the past, but it was perfectly possible for a man – or a youth – to climb up to the gardens of Storm House. And I had seen Robbie on this part of the beach at least twice. He had waved to me, beckoning me to come down to him, and it was here that I had seen his father strike him. Why had the stationmaster been so furious? Because the boy had been waving to me?

Had Robbie come to the house and stood in the gardens outside my window in the middle of the night? Was it he I had glimpsed in the woods a few minutes earlier? And yet I had thought the man in Grandmother's garden was bigger, heavier than Robbie . . .

I turned and retraced my steps along the beach to the sandy path that led to the village. As I reached it, I saw Robbie walking towards me. He had come from the direction of the copse, and as he came up to me, I noticed his face was flushed, his eyes very bright. He stopped when he saw me, then began to grin foolishly. His mouth was a little slack, as if he might have been drinking beer.

'You're her, ain't yer?' he said, and the slur in his voice told me I was right. He had been drinking. 'You're the one from up there . . .' He jerked his head in the direction of Storm House. 'The one Pa says is a wanton hussy just like her mother . . . Anybody's she was, the other one.'

I frowned, unsure the youth really understood what he was saying. From the way he spoke, I thought he was just repeating his father's words, rather in the manner of a trained parrot.

'When did your father tell you that, Robbie?'

'When he got mad and hit me,' Robbie said. His eyes glittered. 'He's always after me fer chasin' the lasses – but it's only a bit of fun like. I wouldn't hurt 'em, miss.' A puzzled expression came over his face. 'I wouldn't do 'em no harm. You don't think I'd harm 'em – do yer?'

'No, I'm sure you wouldn't, Robbie.'

'I could walk with you up to the 'ouse,' he offered hopefully. 'If you wus to give me a shillin' like you did the last time.'

'That's very kind of you,' I said. I was tempted to give him a coin, but decided against it. He would only spend it on strong drink, and if Rosie was right, he was already in enough trouble. 'But I think I can manage, thank you.'

He nodded, but I was aware of him watching me as I began my long, slow climb to the top of the hill.

'Philip cannot dine with us this week,' Grandmother announced at tea that afternoon. 'He is going up to town with Miss Lancaster. Her mother was a cousin of Philip's mother. He says she and her mother have been living in Italy with friends since Mr Lancaster died. They have recently come back to England and are looking for a house for a few months. Philip has offered to lend them his London house. He is going up to town with them to make sure everything is perfect for them.'

She smiled as she poured tea into a delicate porcelain cup, then handed it to me.

'How thoughtful he is – but you know Philip, my dear. You know he can never do enough for those he values.'

'Yes, I know. He is always generous.'

'You will be in London soon. You will meet Margaret and her mother. I'm sure Philip will arrange it.'

'If they care to know me,' I glanced at the ring on my left hand and blushed. Susanna and my grandmother had accepted me without censure, but not everyone would be as kind. 'Everyone in this village knows I am not married – they may have heard gossip.'

'Philip writes glowingly of Mrs Lancaster and her daughter,' Grandmother said. 'He would not like them so much if they were not kind people.'

I twisted my spotless white napkin in my lap. 'Has . . . Philip mentioned the possibility of marriage?'

'No. Of course, it is much too soon for him to be thinking of marriage. But I can sense something. If it does happen I shall be so pleased for him. Philip has seemed too busy to think of courting for years – but he needs a wife and children.'

'Well, perhaps you will have your wish.'

She looked at me, smiling serenely. 'Yes, perhaps I shall . . .'

I had the most terrifying dream of my life that night. I was in a wood, and running from a man with a hood over his head: the hood had slits for his eyes and a gaping hole for his mouth. I knew if he caught me he would do terrible things to me and I was breathing hard, my chest hurting as I felt the pain. If he caught me I was sure I should die.

But he was catching me. I could hear the rasp of his breath and his pounding feet. Then I stumbled and lay on the ground looking up at him. He stared down at me, his eyes glowing like hot coals.

'Who are you?' I cried, sure that he was the Devil and had come to drag me down to Hell. 'Who are you?'

'But you know who I am,' he said. 'I am your father.'

And then he snatched off his hood and I saw it was Laurent.

It was only a nightmare. I was almost sure now that Mama had believed I was the child of the man who had raped her. There was no proof, of course, and yet I thought it must be the reason for her silence all those years.

How I wished that she had told me the truth, however shocking, and then I would not be haunted by these shadowy fears . . .

The next day Grandmother, Marie and I went into Truro on the train. Grandmother's carriage took us to the station, and Marie bought our tickets from the stationmaster. I glanced at him once, but the expression in his eyes made me shudder and I turned away, feeling hot all over. Why did he stare at me like that – as if he knew something I did not? It disturbed me, making me feel a little uneasy.

Marie noticed it and looked at me oddly. 'Are you all right, Jenny?'

'Yes. Yes, of course. It was just a touch of indigestion. Please do not say anything to Grandmother. She is looking forward to this, and I do not want her feeling that she ought to take me home.'

We were going to buy some clothes for the baby. As yet, I had made no purchases, and Grandmother had been shocked at my neglect.

'You must be prepared, Jenny,' she had scolded me, but with a loving look. 'We shall go shopping together. I shall buy you a shawl and some clothes. I still have your mother's christening gown – would you like to have that?'

'Yes, I should, very much,' I said. 'But you are right – I suppose I ought to start buying some of the things I shall need.'

'And I shall so enjoy a little shopping trip,' Grandmother said. 'It is such a long time since I bothered to go into town.'

I saw the stationmaster grinning at me as we waited for our train. He had come out on to the platform, and I knew he was watching me . . . watching everything I did, as if it gave him some secret pleasure.

I turned my head and looked straight at him, pride and disdain in my face. I was not going to let him spoil my pleasure in the outing, nor would I let this awful fear in my mind gain a hold.

He saw my look and scowled, going inside his office when someone asked for a ticket. He was angry because I had shown my contempt of him. Perhaps that would teach him not to look at me so suggestively in future! I dismissed him from my mind, determined to enjoy the trip to Truro with my grandmother and Marie.

*　　*　　*

It was a very pleasant outing. We visited the draper's, which was a high-quality shop and had some pretty shawls – besides all the more mundane things I would need when the baby arrived.

Grandmother bought a very fine knit shawl in pure white wool, and I bought several gowns and bonnets, and a pretty lace-trimmed bassinet. We arranged for everything to be sent to Storm House, then we visited some other stores and finally had our lunch at a pleasant inn.

Seeing a flower seller near the station on our return, I was suddenly reminded of the flower sellers of Paris and I bought armfuls of them to take home with us.

'Goodness,' my grandmother said, indulgently. 'You must like flowers, Jenny.'

'Oh, yes, I do,' I said. 'One day I shall have a wonderful garden, and it will be full of roses. White roses . . .'

I was still smiling when we all got off the train. There was no sign of the stationmaster as we walked through to our carriage, which had come to fetch us and was waiting in the yard. Marie helped my grandmother inside, and then turned to assist me. I paused for a moment, then had a sudden urge to look over my shoulder.

The stationmaster had come round the corner and was looking at me. When he saw I had noticed him, he scowled and spat on the ground. A little shiver went through me as I saw the expression in his eyes . . . the gleam of malicious amusement had gone and he was staring at me as if he hated me.

'What is it, Jenny?' Marie turned and looked at the stationmaster. She made a little puffing sound with her lips. 'Do not let that one upset you,' she said. 'He is a pig. He has no brains in his head – they are all between his legs. He sees every woman as someone to use for his own pleasure . . . and would not care how he gained his pleasure.'

'Marie!' I was shocked at her vulgarity, but also at the

horrifying picture her words had created in my mind. It had been there hovering for some time, of course, but I had not wanted to admit it. Now I saw it clearly. Yet still I did not want to admit the possibility, though I knew it was a very real one. 'You shouldn't say such things. It isn't nice – not ladylike at all.'

'His kind are always the same,' she said. 'They think women are for one purpose only.'

I shook my head and got into the carriage before Grandmother started to wonder what was going on. Although I was shocked that Marie should say something so common, I knew what she meant – and I was sure she was right.

Which made it all the more horrifying that this awful man might just be my own father.

No, no, that could not be right! Where had such a terrible idea come from? It was foolishness. Just because he looked at me so oddly – as if he knew a secret . . .

Eight

After tea, Grandmother took me to her own bedroom. It was as dark and old-fashioned as the rest of the house, though on a different level to my own suite. There was another set of rooms next to hers, but the doors were shut tight, looking somehow unused – and when I mentioned them, she frowned.

'They were Max's,' she said. 'They are closed because I never go there. No one does anymore – not since he died.'

It seemed painful for her to speak of her second husband, so I did not press her. She had told me her marriage to Mr Ruston had not been happy at our first meeting, though I had been too upset by the discovery of what had happened to my mother to take much notice. Now, I realised that I had never seen a picture of Mr Ruston anywhere in the house, which seemed a little odd – or perhaps not if he had made her unhappy. She must have put them all away, out of sight, after he died.

'This is what I wanted to give you,' she said, and took a package wrapped in yellowed paper from the drawer of a large chest. 'I hope it will be luckier for you than it was for me, Jenny.'

I opened the paper to reveal a wonderful gown of white silk trimmed with delicate lace. A faint smell of lavender clung to the material, and some dried stalks fell out as I unfolded the gown to look at it more closely.

'Oh, it is so beautiful,' I cried and turned to kiss

128

Grandmother's cheek. 'It means so much to me to have this . . . to have something that Mama wore as a baby.'

'I am glad you have it,' my grandmother said. 'I am glad that we've had this time together.' She smiled, then took something else from the drawer. 'Philip brought me these . . .' She showed me the sketches the street artist had done of me and my mother in Paris. 'It was so clever of him to think of it . . . and it gave me something to hope for. I always prayed that one day Adele would relent and forgive me. I wrote to her a few weeks before she died, begging her to forgive me, but she did not reply.'

The mystery of Marie's letter was solved. Grandmother's request would have distressed Mama – because in her heart I was sure she *had* forgiven her own mother. She had probably longed to see her, but she was afraid to return to this house and the memories of her past.

I woke with a start. I was not sure if I had been dreaming or if it was something else that had woken me. Then I heard the noise and I was instantly alert. It sounded as if something was scratching against the wall outside; then there was a muttered oath and a bump. I threw back the bedcovers, and ran to the window to look out.

It was quite light outside, because there was a crescent moon in the sky. I could see someone running away towards the end of the garden, obviously intending to escape by way of the steps leading to the beach below. I thought whoever it was had been attempting to climb up the wall to my room. I could see a ladder lying on the ground; it was in several pieces and looked as though it had broken under the weight of whoever had attempted to use it.

My heart racing wildly, I opened the window and leaned out. 'Who is there?' I called. 'I know you are there. I can see the ladder. I'm going to raise the house and send for a constable . . .'

I doubted if the man – or youth, since his figure looked

slighter than a man's – had heard me. He had been running away even before I opened my window, and the noise of the sea would drown my voice. The wind was blowing hard and I could hear the sea crashing against the shore. Surely it was not safe to venture down to that beach now? But perhaps there was a path round the cliffs? I had not thought it wide enough when I had looked up from the beach, but for a man desperate to escape it might serve.

What had he hoped to gain by climbing to my window? He must have seen it was closed – and he would surely not have attempted to break in. No one in their right senses would do such a thing. So was it Robbie? I had thought it might be as I saw the shadowy figure running away. It was the sort of trick a slightly retarded boy might play, I supposed.

It made me a little uneasy to think of that ladder lying outside my room – thank goodness it had broken beneath the weight of whoever had tried to use it. The fall had clearly frightened the intruder, and common sense told me it was unlikely he would try again that night. Even so, I felt that I should not sleep for a while.

Slipping on my dressing gown, I went down to the kitchen. If I could make myself a warm drink it might help me to sleep. I was surprised to find Rosie already there; she had a saucepan on the stove and was warming some milk.

She turned to look at me in surprise. 'Is something the matter, miss?'

'Yes . . . Yes, there is, Rosie.' I explained to her what had woken me, and her eyes widened in astonishment.

'I can't hardly believe it, miss. I wouldn't have thought Robbie would do such a wicked thing.'

'I'm not sure it was him, Rosie. I only caught a glimpse of someone running away – and the ladder lying there on the ground. I just thought of Robbie, because it was such a foolish thing to do. He couldn't have hoped to get in without waking someone.'

'It's only you as sleeps on that side of the house, miss.' Rosie looked at me anxiously. 'Are you all right – has it upset you?'

'It did shake me a little,' I admitted. 'It isn't the first time I've seen a man in the gardens, only last time I thought . . .' I shook my head as Rosie raised her eyebrows. 'It definitely wasn't Robbie the last time – but it might have been his father.'

'The stationmaster?' Rosie frowned. 'Aye, it might have been Ned Watts. He's a bad man, Miss Heron. I told you before that he gives me the creeps, didn't I?' I nodded and she pulled a face. 'Treated his wife something awful, he did; they say that's why the boy is the way he is . . . that his brain was affected by the beatings Ned gave poor Mary when she was carrying.'

'Ned Watts – is that his name? I never knew. I always thought of him as the stationmaster.'

And as the man who might have raped Mama!

'Don't know why he would want to come scaring you in the middle of the night,' Rosie said. 'Do you, miss?'

'I'm not sure . . . I did notice him staring at me oddly when we were at the station, and I did give him what I suppose was a haughty look.'

'It might have been him,' Rosie said. 'Thought he would give you a fright to pay you back for looking down on him. Folk round here have looked down on him since the lad was born. I reckon he's got a chip on his shoulder.'

'Well, no harm has been done,' I said. 'Please, Rosie, say nothing of this to anyone. I do not want Grandmother to worry.'

'We ought to tell the constable,' Rosie said. 'It isn't right – going round like that in the middle of the night, upsetting people.'

'Well, leave it to me,' I said. 'I don't want Grandmother to hear it from anyone else.'

'I won't say a word,' she promised as she brought the

pan of hot milk to the table. 'Would you like some of this, Miss Heron? I am sure it would help you to sleep.'

'Yes, I'm sure it would,' I said. 'Thank you, Rosie, I will have some. We'll sit here and drink it together – shall we?'

'Oh yes, miss, that would be nice,' she said. 'We'll both settle better after that . . .'

I had tea with Grandmother that afternoon. I had not so far told her about my midnight adventure, because I still felt it would be too upsetting for her.

'I should think Philip will come down tomorrow,' she was saying. 'Perhaps then –' She looked up as Vera came in, carrying some letters she had collected in the village. It was obvious that she was very upset about something. 'Vera – what's wrong?'

'I heard something when I was at the shop. I'd been to fetch the letters as you asked, Anne – there are two for you, Jenny – and I heard them all talking. It gave me quite a turn.' She sat down on the sofa with a bump. 'Oh dear! I feel unwell. It is so unpleasant . . . right here in the village . . . and so close to us . . . To think it happened in the night while we were all asleep in our beds.'

A chill went down my spine when I saw the look in her eyes and I felt sick as I sensed what was coming. 'Has there been another of those attacks on girls?' I asked.

Vera put a handkerchief to her mouth. She nodded, her eyes avoiding contact with mine, as if she found it impossible to look at anyone. 'It was rather more serious, however. This time the girl was knocked to the ground and . . . she was . . .' Vera choked back a sob. 'I can't say it. I really can't!'

'Was she raped?'

'Please . . . Jenny . . .' She looked shocked that I should speak so bluntly, then nodded her head once, her cheeks bright red. 'I think that must be what they meant. It was so unpleasant. I couldn't bring myself to listen – and to think we all said that wretch shouldn't be put away!' Her voice rose shrilly in outrage. 'He is obviously mad and the sooner he's locked up the better!'

'How do you know it was Robbie?'

'Everyone says it was. The girl has accused him – so it must be.' She set her mouth primly. 'Why would she lie about it?'

I remembered the man who had stood looking up at my window. I was certain that was not Robbie. But I could not be certain it wasn't Robbie who had tried to climb up to my window.

'When did the attack happen? At what time last night?'

'Why, Jenny?' Grandmother was looking at me oddly. 'Why do you ask? Does it matter what time?'

'You mustn't be upset,' I said, 'but someone tried to climb up to my bedroom last night.'

Vera gave a little shriek and my grandmother's hand trembled on the arm of her chair. I reached over to squeeze it and reassure her.

'It was really quite funny, once I had recovered from the shock,' I said. I explained about the ladder breaking. 'It must have given him quite a fright – whoever it was.'

'Who would have done such a thing?' my grandmother asked, looking at me in distress.

'It could have been Robbie,' I said. 'It is the kind of prank that might appeal to him if he wanted to give me a little fright – but it wasn't him that I saw the first time.' I explained that I had seen a man standing in the garden looking up at me the first time I had stayed at Storm House. 'I am quite certain the man I saw that night was much older . . . heavier.'

'What time did you wake up?' Grandmother asked. 'Last night, I mean. Do you have any idea, Jenny?'

'It must have been almost twelve. I heard the clock strike midnight when I went back to bed, after having a drink of milk in the kitchen with Rosie.'

'It was half past eleven when the attack happened,' Vera

said in a hushed whisper, 'and not far from this house – between here and the village. Apparently the girl had been out late courting with her fiancé and had argued with him. He went off in a huff and she was walking home alone.'

'Perhaps it was her fiancé,' Grandmother said, frowning slightly. 'If they had quarrelled, he might have come back and . . . It happens sometimes like that.'

'She couldn't see his face because of the hood, but swears it was Robbie . . . said she recognised the coat he was wearing . . . that old tweed thing that hangs on him.'

'Oh dear,' Grandmother murmured, distressed. Her hand trembled as she poured hot water from a Sheffield plated spirit kettle into the pot. 'Perhaps he should have been locked up long ago.'

'She may have been mistaken – or she may be lying,' I said. I wasn't sure why I was defending the boy, but somehow I could not believe he was capable of rape. Of boyish pranks like jumping out at girls to frighten them, and climbing up to my room with a rotten ladder, yes – but not rape.

'Why should she lie?' Vera asked. 'If the girl says it was Robbie she must be right. They will have to do something this time. No woman will be safe until he has been safely shut away.'

'It isn't fair to condemn him without a trial or real proof of his guilt,' I said. 'Has it not occurred to anyone that someone else could have been wearing Robbie's coat?'

'He wouldn't let them,' Vera said. 'I asked if I could mend it for him once, meaning to clean it up for him – it's terribly filthy – and he started yelling at me as if he thought I wanted to steal it from him.'

'I still do not believe that makes him guilty,' I said stubbornly.

'But it might have been him.' Grandmother looked at me. 'Are you sure it wasn't him in the garden that night? The night you saw someone standing there? Could it have been him last night?'

'It wasn't him the first time – but it might have been last night. I did think at the time it might be Robbie. But don't you see, that makes it less likely that he attacked that girl. If he had been scared by his fall, surely he would not have gone on to rape someone? I shall report what I saw to the police. I think all the facts should be known.'

'Yes, you must do that. I'll send word down to the village and ask Constable Monks to call – but I doubt if it will help, Jenny. It doesn't prove anything either way. And if that poor girl is ready to swear it was Robbie, everyone will believe her.'

'Yes,' I said. 'I suppose they will. But I must speak out. I must say what I saw. You do agree, don't you?'

'Oh yes. You must do that – but I'm very much afraid it won't help.'

'Well, at least I shall have tried,' I said, taking my letters from the table where Vera had laid them. 'If you will excuse me for a while I think I shall go and lie down.'

I was uneasy in my mind as I rested on my bed, reading from the volume of Keats's poems that Mama had given me, and which was precious to me because of that. She had wanted me to appreciate the English writers, she had said, making quite a point of it.

Gérard had once told me that I had an original version of the second volume of the poet's works published in 1848 by Lord Houghton. 'It isn't the original cover,' he had said knowledgeably. 'Your mother must have had it recovered specially for you, Jenny.'

It was a very fine leather cover, very thick and smooth, and I liked touching it, handling it. It was a favourite thing of mine, and the poems often gave me comfort when I was bothered about something.

Surely Robbie's father could not be the man who had

raped Mama? He might have been a very respectable young man once, when Mama lived here in this house, but I refused to believe he could be my father. All my instincts were against it.

'Oh, Mama,' I said, stroking the cover of my book before I laid it on the table beside the bed. 'Why did you never tell me? Surely you could have found some way of ensuring that I would know the truth one day?'

I told my story to the constable that evening. He listened to me attentively, shook his head over what I had to say and made notes in his little book. Then he told us, 'Robbie has already been taken into custody, Miss Heron. That girl was hurt in the attack. She bled – and we found blood on his coat.'

He sounded as if he had discovered irrefutable proof and I was angry. Why were they all so determined to condemn him?

'It might not be her blood.'

'He tried to run when he saw us coming. He is not as simple as they say, miss. And he had been drinking earlier that evening. Sober he's a nice enough lad, I'll grant you that – but drunk is another matter. A lot of men turn nasty when they've had a few too many and I've a dozen witnesses who saw him down six glasses of cider in the pub.'

'But where would he get the money? His father never lets him have more than a shilling.'

The constable shrugged. 'That I can't say. All I know for certain is that the evidence against him was enough to justify our taking him into protective custody.'

'Oh dear. It seems so harsh. He cannot have had much of a life even before this, and now . . .'

'Don't worry, miss.' The constable gave me a patronising smile, which was perhaps meant kindly but made me angry. 'He won't go to prison, whatever he has done. They'll have to shut him in a secure hospital, though.'

'The asylum,' I said. 'From what I've read of such places, he would be better off in prison.'

'That's as may be.' He stood up, preparing to leave. 'I'm thankful it's not up to me to decide. I leave such decisions to them as know what they are talking about.'

It was meant as a rebuke to me, of course. I was a woman, a stranger, a foreigner even, as I had spent most of my life in France – what could I possibly know about a simple-minded lad I had met only twice?

Perhaps he was right and I was being foolishly senti-mental. Even Rosie had seemed less ready to take Robbie's part after this latest attack. Perhaps Robbie was guilty and would be best locked away for his own safety and that of others. It was probably only a matter of time before someone decided to take justice into their own hands and teach poor Robbie a lesson anyway. He might be safer away from the outraged inhabitants of his own village.

And yet I could not forget the pale face that had stared down at me from the window of the station house. I wanted to find some way of helping him. Perhaps Philip would know how. He had done so much for me, and I knew he was a compassionate man. I was sure he would know what to do.

I decided to write to him. He was still in London. Despite Grandmother's optimism, he had not returned to Cornwall since taking his friends up to town. But I would soon be there myself – surely he would find time to call on me then?

'You will take good care of yourself?' Grandmother said as I took leave of her a few days later. 'Are you sure you ought to travel by train all the way to London . . . in your condition? I could write to Philip, ask him to come down and escort you in his carriage. I am sure he would oblige us. It worries me to think of you . . . all alone on a train.'

I could tell she thought it a little shocking. In my grandmother's day ladies spent the last few months of their pregnancy in isolation, meeting only close friends or members of their families – a kind of social *purdah*. For me to travel by public transport at such an advanced stage of my pregnancy was something she felt not quite nice, but she was too sensitive of my feelings to make a fuss.

'I shall be perfectly all right,' I replied, kissing her soft cheek. She smelled of fine soap and lavender, her skin papery thin and soft to the touch. It made me aware of how vulnerable she was, and how grateful I was for this time we'd had together. 'We shall go first class, so it's likely we'll have the carriage to ourselves. Besides, Marie will look after me. There is nothing to worry about.'

'I'm such an old-fashioned thing,' she said and laughed at herself. 'You will come to see me when you can, won't you?'

'As soon as I'm allowed after the child is born,' I promised. 'Goodbye, dear Grandmother. I shall write to you often, I promise.'

I left her and went out to the carriage where Marie was waiting for me. When we got to the station there was no sign of Robbie's father. I asked the young man selling tickets where he was and he pulled a face.

'He has been given leave for his health, miss. Leastwise, that's what they said. But I reckon he won't be comin' back to work here no more. It isn't likely folk would want him – after what his son has done to them girls.'

'You mean he has been dismissed?'

'Put out to grass. They'll likely give him a few bob for his pension – if he's lucky.'

So Ned Watts had been another victim of the scandal. It was unfair, of course – and yet I was relieved not to have his eyes on me as I boarded the train.

Had it been Robbie's father who had stood in Grandmother's garden looking up at my window? I could not be sure, but something . . . some inner instinct told me it was. Why had he been there? One answer was that he had been out searching for his errant son . . . which made it more likely that Robbie was guilty after all.

Philip came to see me two days after I had moved into my new home. It was a four-storey Georgian terraced house in a square not far from Primrose Hill. It was large enough to accommodate the two maids and cook-housekeeper I had employed, as well as Marie, myself – and my child when he was born. Yet there was no ostentation, no excessive grandeur.

'Well . . .' Philip glanced round the parlour, which was at the front and looked out on to the quiet square with its neat green where children sometimes played. 'Are you comfortable here, Jenny? Is everything to your liking?'

'Yes. It will be better when we have more of our own things about us,' I replied. 'But it is just as you described it, Philip. Thank you. It was kind of you to settle all the details with Mr Walters.'

'I think your lawyer was a little put out that you did not ask for his advice, but I was able to smooth his feathers. In fact he has asked me to escort you to their house for dinner one night next week. It will be just them and us – so you need not make excuses about it not being proper for you to be seen in company at the moment.'

'I was not going to,' I replied, not meeting his eyes. I had been about to refuse, but only because I was cross with him for not writing to me for nearly three weeks.

'But you are cross with me – why?'

His intent look made me uncomfortable. I turned away, going to look out of the window at the back garden. It was pretty, but not the garden of my dreams.

'I am not cross – why should I be?' I said without looking at him. I knew I was being unfair, but could not help myself.

'I'm not sure. Perhaps you feel I have neglected you? I'm sorry I haven't visited for a while, Jenny, but I have been busy. It was not possible for me to call on you.'

I turned slowly to face him then, my hands folded demurely in front of me, giving no sign of my inner turmoil. I must not betray myself by showing the jealousy I felt. It was very wrong of me to be jealous of Philip's friends, to resent the time he had spent with them.

'I believe you have guests staying with you?'

'Yes. My mother's cousin and her daughter. You must meet them. I am sure you would get on well. I will bring Margaret and Mrs Lancaster here for tea, if you would prefer that to an invitation to dinner at my house?'

'I am too ugly and uncomfortable to be a good dinner guest, Philip.' I was very conscious of my shape, of the ungainly heaviness of my body.

He smiled gently. 'You could never be ugly – but I know you must be uncomfortable. This is an awkward time for ladies. So – shall I bring them here?'

'Yes, of course. Tomorrow, if you wish.'

'You won't find it too much trouble?'

'I have nothing to do but be waited on.'

'Is that why you are out of temper?' He gave me an understanding look. 'It will not be so much longer now.'

'Oh, Philip!' I laughed suddenly. 'What a crosspatch I am! I wonder that you can bear to visit me at all.'

'You know I would never desert you – only my duty has kept me from you this long. Please believe me, Jenny.'

The warmth in his eyes dispelled the foolish ache I had been carrying inside me since Grandmother had told me about the beautiful Margaret. Philip was still my friend. I was surprised how much that meant to me.

'You are forgiven – if I am?'

'There is nothing for me to forgive.' He frowned slightly. 'I received your letter, Jenny, but have not yet had time to do anything about Robbie Watts.'

'Do you think you might be able to help him?'

'I'm not sure. I agree with you that there is doubt . . . that he has been unfairly treated.'

'Do you?' I looked at him eagerly. 'Do you really?'

'Don't be too hopeful, Jenny.' His expression had become serious now. 'The most I might achieve – even if I could prove his innocence – is to have him moved to somewhere less harsh. A private hospital instead of the asylum. You see . . . his own father has signed for him to be committed. I could not have him removed from care – but I might be able to find him a better place.'

'You mean there is no hope of release for Robbie – ever?' I felt chilled. 'That is terrible . . . terrible.'

'Forever is a long time,' Philip said, sounding grave. 'Attitudes will change one day. It is not so long ago that it was fashionable to chain the mentally afflicted and let people in to poke sticks at them. Things are getting better, though the asylum is still a terrible place. But I do know of a hospital where they treat their patients with kindness and understanding. I might be able to arrange something . . . have him transferred there.'

'It would be so kind of you. Oh, Philip, you will try? You will try to help him – for my sake?'

I did not know why I was so concerned for Robbie – unless it was because I felt that fate had been kinder to me.

'I shall do what I can . . .' He gave me an odd look. 'But you must not be too upset if I fail. You must not be annoyed with me or blame me if I have raised your hopes for nothing.'

I moved towards him, smiling up at him. 'You have no need to fear my anger, Philip. I thought *you* might be angry with *me*. I thought I might have offended you.'

'You thought—' He looked puzzled, then laughed. 'Because you turned down my foolish offer of marriage? No, I am not offended. You were right to do so. We are friends, Jenny. Neither of us wants or needs more . . .'

*   *   *

I lay in my bed that night staring up at the intricate plaster rose on my ceiling. The moon was shining in through the open curtains. In a moment I would get up and close them.

Tears stung my eyes. Philip was so kind . . . so generous. I had refused his offer of marriage and he was relieved I had. When had he realised it was a mistake . . . was it when he first saw Margaret Lancaster? Had he fallen in love with her?

How foolish I was, how selfish! But I had begun to realise that I would miss Philip far more than I could ever have suspected only a few weeks earlier. If he were to marry someone else . . .

Foolish, foolish Jenny!

I brushed my selfish tears away and got up to pull the curtains. It was almost as bright as day outside, but there was no one standing in my tiny, walled garden . . . no one watching me.

Had it been Robbie's father that night? Why had he been staring at my window? And why had he signed to have his own son committed to the asylum?

So many unanswered questions. I forced them from my mind as I turned out the oil lamp beside my bed and lay down to sleep once more. Robbie's fate was a sad one, but it did not really concern me.

Did not concern me! Supposing he was blood kin? Supposing he was the brother I had often longed for but never had?

No, no, I would never believe that. Robbie's father was not mine. I felt it instinctively, despite the fears that came to me sometimes in the middle of the night. My concern for Robbie was that of anyone who hated injustice . . . because it was unjust that he should be locked away for playing a few pranks. And nothing would convince me that he was guilty of rape.

But there was nothing I could do personally, except rely

on Philip. He would do what he could to help the lad, I was sure of that.

I turned my thoughts to the following day. Philip was bringing his guests to tea. I would see the beautiful Margaret Lancaster for myself.

Nine

My worst fears were confirmed as soon as I saw her. Margaret Lancaster was indeed lovely: a cold, proud beauty with a creamy complexion and rich dark brown hair, which she wore in a smooth coronet about her head. Her clothes were fashionable, expensive, her manner regal as she swept into my best parlour, letting just the tips of her gloved fingers touch mine before removing them.

'*Madame* Heron . . . it is a pleasure to meet you.'

'The pleasure is all mine, Miss Lancaster.'

Her dark, chocolate brown eyes surveyed me with thinly veiled dislike. I sensed that she knew I was not entitled to the wedding ring I wore on my left hand. Whether Philip had told her, or whether she had discovered it for herself, I could not tell, but she knew. She was prepared to meet me because Philip had asked it of her, but she could not hide her feelings. She thought me beneath contempt – a woman who had fallen from grace.

Mrs Lancaster was kinder. A plump, pretty woman in her middle years, dressed in pale grey with more frills than suited a woman of her age, she did her best to bridge the all too frequent silences that fell between her daughter and me. She was obliged to step in often as the visit dragged on, seeming far longer than the prescribed half an hour or so that was thought polite for such occasions. She asked me a lot of questions about my grandmother and how I liked Cornwall, then fell silent as the subject was exhausted.

'And when do you expect to return to France, Madame Heron?'

The question startled me, coming from Miss Lancaster as it had after a longer than usual silence.

'I do not plan to return there, Miss Lancaster. I shall make my home here in London – and Cornwall. I enjoy Cornwall and was able to spend more than three months there this year. It was very pleasant, especially as the weather was good most of the time.'

'You stayed in Philip's house, I believe?' Margaret's dark eyes were hostile as they rested on my face. 'I should have thought you would find England too cold after the climate you were born to.'

Her tone made it clear to me that I was a foreigner and a stranger – and that she thought I would do better to return home.

'Jenny has not yet experienced one of our English winters,' Philip said, before I could think of a suitable answer. 'I can only hope she does not decide to leave us when she has. She has become one of us now and we should all miss her.'

His answer did not please Margaret, but she did her best to hide her annoyance, smiling up at him so sweetly that I could hardly believe the change in her.

'Of course, Philip. I merely wondered how Madame Heron's health would stand the winter – since she has not been used to our harsh climate.'

Surely he was not taken in by her expression of concern for me? It was false. He must see her for the spoiled, vain creature she was! I doubted she had ever cared for anyone but herself.

The thought was unworthy and I was ashamed of the jealousy that had prompted it. I made yet another attempt at polite conversation.

'And do you intend to return to Italy, Miss Lancaster? Or will you stay in England now?'

'We are not quite sure, are we, my dear?' Mrs Lancaster

spoke as her daughter gave me a haughty stare. *How dare I question her?* 'We had expected to stay here only a few months but now . . . Philip has been so kind, putting his houses at our disposal.'

'You are both welcome to stay for as long as you wish,' Philip said with a smile for her. 'I have space enough for us all. We shall not get in each other's way.'

There was silence for a moment. Margaret smoothed her gloves over her hands and I knew she was trying to think of a way to end the visit without offending Philip.

'Mother,' she began, 'I think we ought to be—'

She broke off as the door was opened abruptly.

'Jenny, my darling!' Susanna swept into the room unannounced. 'Forgive me. I did not mean to intrude when you have guests but I was unable to come before and I could not wait another moment. Marie was sure you would not mind so . . . here I am.'

I got up and went to her eagerly. We embraced a little clumsily, for she had almost as large a bump as me, despite being less forward in her pregnancy.

She laughed and pressed a hand to her swollen belly. 'Henry swears I am carrying twins this time.'

I was thankful for the easy, uncomplicated nature of my friend, who had saved me from an embarrassing situation.

'I'm so pleased to see you, Susanna. You must meet my guests. Of course you know Philip. And this is Mrs Helen Lancaster and her daughter Margaret. They are Philip's cousins. Mrs Lancaster, Miss Lancaster – may I present my friend Mrs Walters to you?'

'How rude you must think me for bursting in like this,' Susanna said, shaking hands with the older woman and then Philip. Margaret merely inclined her head regally, making no attempt to offer her own hand: she obviously did not think Susanna worthy of her notice. 'But it is ages since I saw Jenny and I have missed her so. Letters can never say enough, can they?'

'Oh, no, I do agree,' Mrs Lancaster said, giving her daughter a reproving frown. 'Do you live in town, Mrs Walters?'

'Mr Walters represents the interests of the Comte de Arnay in this country,' Philip said. 'I did mention that Jenny was the comte's ward, didn't I, Helen?'

'Yes. So you did. It was such a shame . . . a terrible tragedy,' Mrs Lancaster said on a sigh. 'We knew the comte's son so well. Such a charming young man and so handsome. He stayed with friends of ours at their villa when he was in Italy – and they all visited us most days, didn't they, Margaret?'

'Yes, Mama.'

There was a flush of embarrassment in her daughter's cheeks, as if she did not wish to be reminded of that time.

'I quite thought he meant to make Margaret an offer,' her mother went on. 'He was so attentive to her. It was very marked. He had promised to return the next winter and I think he would have . . . but it was not to be. We were both very shocked when we heard the news of his death.'

'Really, Mama,' Margaret said, looking annoyed. 'I gave Monsieur Arnay no encouragement. He was a little young and irresponsible for my taste – though charming, of course. It is just that I am more comfortable with people of intelligence and culture.'

She meant Philip, of course. I looked at her as she gave Philip a shy, confiding glance, and suddenly had a blinding flash of intuition. She would have taken Gérard if he had offered, but he was dead – so now she was looking elsewhere for a suitable husband.

I clasped my hands in my lap, finding their conversation both incredible and almost unbearable. My temples felt as if they were throbbing with pain. How dare they talk of Gérard in that way? Gérard could not have given either of them cause to hope. It was impossible. He had already given his promise to me. He had loved me! It was all I could do not to tell them the truth. The room seemed very warm all of a sudden and I was close to fainting.

'Are you unwell?' Philip asked, looking at me anxiously. 'Perhaps you should go upstairs and lie down for a while? Mrs Walters – would you go with her? I think it is time I took my cousins home. We have an engagement this evening and I am sure they would like to rest for a while themselves.'

'Forgive me,' I said, getting rather shakily to my feet. If I did not escape soon I would scream. I could hardly bear to look at Miss Lancaster. Gérard had never loved her, he could not! It was a lie, a cruel, hurtful lie.

'It was nice to meet you, Mrs Lancaster. If you will excuse me . . .'

I left the room immediately, going not upstairs but into a little parlour at the back of the house, where I threw open the French windows and let the cool air blow in on me for a few moments. When I closed them and turned to face Susanna, who had followed me from the drawing room, I saw that she was looking anxious.

'That stupid woman!' she exclaimed in outrage. 'If I were not a lady, I could slap her for upsetting you so.'

'Then perhaps it is just as well you are a lady. Do not worry, Susanna. I shall be calmer in a moment. It was just the shock,' I said and forced a smile. 'She could not have known the effect her words were having on me. I was upset, but it was not her fault. Sit down and talk to me, Susanna. We will go back to the drawing room when they have gone.'

She looked at me in concern. 'Would you not rather go and lie down for a while? I can come back another day.'

'I shall be better presently,' I promised her. The dizziness had passed and the pain was easing. 'Please stay, Susanna. I shall only brood if you go.'

'You don't believe what she said – do you?'

'No, not exactly.' I was silent for a moment as I considered. My thoughts were painful, but could not be denied. 'No, I do not think Gérard planned to offer marriage to Miss Lancaster

– but he *was* a flirt. He told me so when we first met. I know that he would have enjoyed spending time in her company. I do not believe he loved her, but he would not have been able to resist paying her compliments to see her reaction. He was very mischievous and she is very beautiful. If she did have cause for hope . . . then he was very wrong to mislead her.'

'She looks well enough, if you admire that type,' my friend said scornfully. 'I thought her cold and spoilt. A man would soon tire of a marble statue in his bed, however beautiful it was . . .'

'Susanna!' I cried and laughed. 'That is a shocking thing to say.'

'But true,' my friend said with a wicked look in her eyes. 'When it comes to marriage, most men prefer a flesh and blood woman to a remote goddess they can only set up on a pedestal and admire.'

'Perhaps . . . Anyway, let's forget Miss Lancaster. I want to know how you are – and whether you have thought of a name for your baby yet. I just cannot decide . . .'

Later, when I was alone in my room, I shed a few tears. It had hurt me unbearably to hear Gérard spoken of so intimately by strangers. And yet, they had as much right to claim acquaintance as I – for what had I really known of my lover?

I knew his smile made my knees turn to water and my heart race wildly . . . that his charm was felt by others . . . that his mood could change suddenly and without warning from laughter to a brooding silence . . . that he was a passionate lover . . . that he could be wild and restless . . . that he had loved me and I him.

But what did I know of the real Gérard? He had never spoken of his innermost desires, or his hopes for the future. We had been so immersed in our love for each other that we had not considered the reality of living – of the years ahead.

Despite Susanna's passionate denials, I believed it might

be true that Gérard had paid particular attentions to Miss Lancaster. He must have known that his parents would oppose his marriage to me – though he had not realised how terrible the outcome would be – and he might have toyed with the idea of wedding the beautiful Margaret for a while, even if in the end he *had* returned to me.

The thought caused me a kind of torment I had never felt before – a bitter, jealous anger that made me want to weep.

'How could you, Gérard?' I whispered as I gazed out of my window at the darkening sky. 'Why did you steal my heart if you never meant to keep it?'

But he *had* meant to marry me. He had loved me; he would have married me if Laurent had not prevented us . . . but would he have been faithful to me for the rest of our lives? I had always sensed the wildness in him, the restlessness of his nature. It was a question that could never be answered – a foolish, nagging torment that I would have done better to ignore.

Jealousy was an ugly emotion and I came close to hating Margaret Lancaster that day, but I was not sure why. Was it because of her past friendship with Gérard . . . or her present one with Philip?

In my distress, I looked for my book of Keats's poems, seeking the solace it always gave me – but it was not on the table beside my bed. Where was it? I always kept it near me . . . but now I remembered. It was still on the chest beside my bed at Storm House. I had meant to pick it up before I left that last day, but somehow it had been forgotten.

I missed it, but I knew it would be safe. I would find it there when I returned to Grandmother's house after my child was born.

When I fell asleep it was to dream of my garden. It had begun to take shape now – I saw the avenues of white roses, the beds of fragrant lilies. I touched their soft petals and smelt their perfume.

It was so peaceful in my garden. I knew I was happy. I could hear birds singing, the tinkle of a fountain as it played into a clear pool . . . and the sound of children laughing.

I saw the children clearly – there were two boys and a girl. In the dream they were my children. I loved them dearly. A man was walking towards me through the shrubbery, but I could only see him through a mist that hid his face from me . . .

I woke with tears on my cheeks. If I could only find my garden I should be at peace.

Two letters had been sent on to me from my grandmother's house in Cornwall. She had included them with a note of her own to say they had arrived some days after I left.

I glanced at the franking on the envelopes as I took them from the salver on the hall table after my walk the next morning. They had originally been sent more than three weeks ago. One I recognised as being from Henriette, the other was in a bold, fine hand I did not immediately know.

I opened this one first. It was from Laurent. When I saw the expensive engraving at the head of the notepaper I was shocked and almost threw it into the fire, then changed my mind. I must read what he had to say: if Laurent had decided to write to me, it must be for a good reason.

> Dear Jeanette,
>
> I beg you to read this. I have first to tell you that my wife Béatrix died two weeks ago. As you know, she had been an invalid for some time and I believe it was probably a relief to her at the end. She has suffered terribly these past few months and never recovered from the death of her son.
>
> It is because she is dead that I am now at liberty to tell you something I believe you may wish to know. I would be grateful if you would allow me to call on you when I come to London next month . . .

He did not know that Gérard had already told me the comtesse's story. No doubt Laurent hoped to make his peace with me by explaining why he had turned against his son, and why he and Mama had become lovers.

Gérard had told me that his mother had been betrayed by a lover and forced to marry Laurent, even though she did not love him. When her lover came back to her she had resisted for a long time, but out of loneliness had gone to him at the last. But Laurent had discovered her with her lover and his anger had known no bounds. He had suspected that Gérard was not his child, accusing her of foisting another man's bastard on him. Béatrix had sworn it was not true. She had wept and begged him to believe her, but he had remained contemptuous of her and cold towards his son.

Yet he must have known Gérard was his own. He surely believed it, for otherwise there was no excuse for what he had done that day at Versailles!

Angrily, I screwed the letter into a ball and threw it into the fire, but it fell on the tiled hearth and I left it there as I turned away, my eyes stinging with tears.

How dare he write me such a letter? How dare he! He had promised me he would not come near me again, and now he was breaking his promise.

Uneasy and distressed, I tore open Henriette's letter and read the contents. For a few moments I stared at what she had written without understanding, and when I did manage to focus on her words I could make no sense of them.

> I am sorry for the harsh things I said to you in my last letter. I was upset, Jenny. Please forgive me. I made false accusations against your friend and I should not have done. I have begged her pardon and asked her to stay on at the chateau, but she says we do not need her and intends to return to England . . .

Kate returning to England? I read the rest of Henriette's

letter hastily but there was nothing to enlighten me further. I had never received the letter she was apologising for and realised it must have got lost somewhere between Cornwall and London.

It was frustrating to say the least. Why should Henriette, who was usually the most tolerant of women, have made false accusations against Kate? What kind of accusations? And why had she now changed her mind?

I folded Henriette's letter and was just putting it into my letter case when I heard the tread of a man's feet in the hall, and turned to see Philip watching me from the doorway.

'Bad news?' he asked. 'You don't mind that I've called at this hour? I have appointments this afternoon and I wanted to see you . . . to apologise for what my cousin said yesterday. She had no idea that you . . . that Gérard is the father of your child.'

'You have not told her?'

'No, of course not,' he said, a little frown creasing his forehead. 'I would not dream of discussing your private affairs with my cousins – or anyone else. You should know that, Jenny.'

'Forgive me,' I said. 'I am a little upset. You asked me if I'd had bad news – and in a way I have. Laurent has written to me, asking if he may call on me when he is in London.'

'He *is* your guardian,' Philip said, his eyes a little wary as he watched me. He was remembering the morning we had quarrelled over the relationship he had suggested existed between Laurent and me. 'Is there a particular reason why you do not wish to see him?'

'Yes . . . no.' I smiled wryly at him. 'I suppose I ought to see him – but not alone. I don't want to be alone with him.'

Philip's eyes narrowed. 'May I ask why?'

How could I explain? I had no good reasons, but knowing my fears were irrational did not make them go away. 'No, you may not. It is for . . . personal reasons.'

Philip frowned, bewildered by my attitude. 'You are angry

because of what happened? Comte de Arnay refused his permission for you to marry, I believe. You blame him for Gérard's death – is that it?'

'That is a part of it . . .' I sighed. 'He says he has something to tell me. Something that he was not at liberty to tell me while his wife was alive.'

'The Comtesse de Arnay has died?' I nodded and Philip looked thoughtful. 'Perhaps it was not Laurent but his wife who was against the marriage.'

'I am sure she was,' I agreed, remembering the strange, angry words she had flung at me after she had sent her maid Flore to fetch me to her rooms. 'She told me once that she would never allow me to marry Gérard. He knew that there would be opposition, because of the differences in religion and class, but believed he could persuade his father . . . and his mother. Gérard always thought he could get his own way.'

'And yet he allowed his father to forbid the marriage?' Philip was very watchful now. 'You have never told me exactly what happened, Jenny. If you were so much in love, why did you not run away together?'

I turned away, trembling as I relived that terrible night.

'We did . . . We hid in a hunting lodge near Versailles. We had planned to be married in England and were waiting until Laurent had ceased to search for us. I could not tell you . . . anyone. I believed . . . until recently, I believed something so terrible that I could not speak of it. Even now I cannot be certain that it is not true . . .'

I drew a shaky breath. Since learning that my mother had been raped, I was finding it increasingly difficult to believe that Laurent was my father, but I still had no definite proof either way.

'Laurent found us . . . He led me to believe that I was his daughter. I truly thought it was so until Grandmother told me why they had quarrelled and what had happened to Mama. She was afraid it would upset me to learn that I was the child of a rapist – but she did not know that I had feared much worse . . .' I swallowed hard. 'That my love for Gérard was incestuous and evil. Now . . . I do not know what to think, but I want to believe that I am not Laurent's child.'

'My God!' Philip exploded with anger. 'How could the comte do that to you? He must have known there were doubts – he should have taken steps to find out more when your mother was alive. The man deserves to be thrashed. What you must have gone through . . . when you knew you were to have a child . . . the implications of such a relationship.' He paced about the room. 'No wonder you were on the verge of collapse when you went down to Storm House. This is beyond belief . . . disgraceful!'

'I do not believe that Laurent knows the truth himself,' I said as I saw the fury in Philip's face. His mouth was white-edged with temper and I believed he would have offered physical harm to Laurent had he been there at that moment. 'I have told no one else, except Kate and my grandmother, and neither of them would betray my confidence. Besides . . . I do not believe that either he or Henriette are aware that I am carrying Gérard's child. Kate knows, but I made her promise not to tell the others.'

'Does not know?' Philip stared at me, an odd expression in his eyes. 'Laurent will know it when he sees you.'

'Yes.' I bit my lip. 'Now you understand at least a part of my reason for not wanting to see him.'

'Yes, I do see . . .' He was thoughtful. 'I expect the comte will write to you again when he arrives, to make an appointment. I could be here when he comes, if you wish. Or I could ask him to come to my house and relay any messages he has for you through me. There is no reason why you should be forced to see him if you would rather not.'

'Perhaps – I'm not sure.' I listened to the hiss and crackle of blazing logs, feeling cold despite the warmth of the room. I could not explain my irrational fear that Laurent's coming would only bring more trouble on us. 'I think I would feel better if you were here, Philip – even if you were simply within call.'

He looked at my face. I was unable to hide my unease, the torment and fears that Laurent's request had brought back to me.

'Then I shall be here,' he promised. 'I am going down to Cornwall in the morning. I have some business there that needs my attention – and I shall make some inquiries about Robbie while I'm there – but I shall return to take you to dine with Mrs Walters next week.'

'Thank you. It was kind of you to call, Philip. I know you have so little time to spare at the moment.'

He hesitated, uncertain, awkward. 'Can you find it in your heart to forgive Margaret for her behaviour yesterday? She is not usually so . . . reserved. I think she was not sure what to say to you.'

Miss Lancaster had not been free to say what was on her mind. She had been forced to be polite to me when she would much rather not have had to meet me at all.

'Perhaps you ought not to have brought her here,' I suggested. 'She was embarrassed, Philip. You can hardly blame her. She has been properly brought up, taught that women such as I should not be noticed. And she does know I have never been married; I saw it in her eyes. You and Susanna have accepted me with all my failings, but you must not expect it of everyone.'

'Yes, she does know, but how, I cannot say. It was not from me.'

'I knew that as soon as you denied having told her that Gérard was the father of my child, Philip. Indeed, I was always sure of it in my heart . . . but I was too upset to think clearly the day she came here. However, I do not resent her for what she said.'

'Thank you.' He looked relieved. 'You are very understanding, Jenny. I was afraid you would think her rude. Once she gets to know you, I am sure she will be easier in your company.'

'Does she wish to know me better?'

'Oh, yes. She told me privately that she thought you were very brave – and asked if I thought you would allow her to call another day on her own. I told her I would ask you.'

'Your friends must always be welcome in my house, Philip.'

It was not true. I had not liked Miss Lancaster any more than she liked me, but I would not offend my friend by saying so openly.

'I must go,' Philip said, glancing at his gold pocket watch. 'I shall call on you when I return from Cornwall. Take care of yourself, Jenny – and don't worry too much about your guardian. He will answer to me if he upsets you.'

There was such warmth in his face, such fire in his eyes that I was touched by his concern for me.

'How good you are to me,' I said, hesitated, then moved closer to him. I gazed up at him for a moment, catching a faint breath of some woody scent about him, then stretched up to kiss his cheek. 'Your friendship means a great deal to me, Philip.'

'And yours to me.' His hand reached out to tuck a wisp of my wayward hair behind my ear. 'No one shall hurt you, Jenny. If I can do nothing more for you, I shall protect you from those who would harm you.'

After Philip had gone I rescued Laurent's letter from the grate where it had fallen, smoothing it out so that I could read what he had written once more.

I had calmed down after talking to Philip. My first reaction had been foolish and irrational. Now that I had begun to believe in my heart that Laurent was not my father, it was easier to face the idea of speaking to him again.

When I thought about it, he had always acted properly towards me. I had once imagined the passionate looks he

157

gave me to be those of a man who thought of me with lust; but now, looking back on the time I had spent at the chateau, I could see that he had been confused, disturbed in his mind. He had not known whether to think of me as his daughter or only as the beloved child of the woman he had loved for years.

Now that I knew Mama and Laurent's story, I realised it was a grand passion – a truly romantic love affair. They had fallen desperately in love at their first meeting, but he was married. They had tried to part, but then he had come after her, and perhaps they had become lovers. She had promised to go away with him . . . and then someone had cruelly raped her.

Had she gone to Laurent and wept of her pain? Had she told him what that evil man had done to her? Was that why he had never been certain whether or not I was his daughter? Mama had sworn to him that I was his . . . and because he loved her he had accepted it as the truth.

Yet when she died and he took me to his chateau the doubts had begun to torment him. Watching me, looking at me with the intentness I had mistaken for passion, he had begun to wonder – and so he had kept silent. Then he was informed that Gérard and I wanted to marry. At first he had tried simply to deny us, perhaps hoping for time to discover the truth – hoping that Mama would have left me something which would settle the matter one way or the other. But then, at the hunting lodge, he had realised we were already lovers, and he had been forced to tell us what he believed.

I had hated him for that . . . hated him so much that it felt as if my heart had been turned to stone. But the bitterness I had felt after Gérard's death had been easing little by little, until now, at last, I had finally come to an understanding.

How could I hate a man who had loved Mama so much? It was not his fault that I had flouted the rules that governed our society . . . that I had been reckless enough to lie with my lover before marriage. Yes, he *would* have been wiser to tell me of his suspicions at the start, but he had hardly known me. I believed now he had held back out of consideration for my feelings – had probably hoped I would discover the truth for myself through the letters he had sent to Mama. If I had gone through her things at the beginning, I might have done so. I was as much to blame for what had happened to me as Laurent.

Finally, I had come to accept what had happened. The black clouds were lifting, easing the ache I had carried inside me for so long.

I decided that I would see Laurent. I would talk to him, hear his side of the story. It might be that Mama had told him the name of the man who had attacked her. Laurent might have a clue that would untangle the last thread of the web of lies Mama had woven around her past.

Ten

S usanna insisted that I spend the morning with her at her house. She showed me her nursery, telling me where she had purchased various items, and talking about her last confinement.

'It wasn't easy,' she told me, pulling a wry face, 'but once it was over, I soon forgot all about it. I had my darling Charles, and that was all that mattered. I am sure it will be the same for you, Jenny.'

I was grateful for her advice. My nursery was as yet incomplete, and Susanna had saved me a great deal of trouble searching for the things I would need. I could simply send Marie to order what I wanted from the department store Susanna had recommended.

When I returned home after having lunch with my friend, I met Marie in the hall. She had an armful of books, and had obviously been to the library.

'I brought you *Tess of the D'Urbervilles* as you asked,' she said. 'And one of Mr Kipling's books that I hadn't seen before. Oh, and I managed to get a couple of books about rare plants – you said you would like some gardening books.'

'They sound very interesting. Thank you,' I said. 'I must ask Philip what he has on gardening in his library. He will call tomorrow or the next day.' I sighed. 'I shall be glad when the child is born and I can go out more. Reading and sewing are all very well – but I long for a really brisk walk.'

She pulled a face, as if a little annoyed that I should mention Philip's library when she had been to fetch books specially for me, and I knew she was still a little jealous of him, though she had tried very hard to hide it. She was being very considerate of me, treating me as if my health were still delicate, despite my telling her that I was very much better now.

'Why don't you go shopping tomorrow?' Marie asked. 'You still need more clothes for the baby . . . and the air would do you good. You've been sitting indoors brooding for far too long, by the looks of you. We don't want you ill again.'

'Will you come with me?'

'Of course I will,' she said, looking pleased. 'I saw some pretty material today that would make up into lovely baby gowns . . .'

As if to please me, the next day was fine and bright, even warm for the middle of October. Marie and I spent two pleasant hours buying baby clothes, materials and a pretty silver rattle with a coral teething ring.

We returned to the house feeling happy and laughing at our experiences. I thought it was almost like the first few days we had shared in London, before Marie had become so possessive towards me.

'There's someone waiting to see you, Madame Heron,' my parlour maid said as I entered. 'I told her you were out but she said she was a close friend and insisted on waiting for you to return.'

'Did she give her name?'

'Kate Blake.'

'Kate! Kate is here?' I cried, surprised and pleased. 'Where is she?'

'In your sitting room, miss. I took her in some tea an hour ago.'

'Perhaps you would bring some more to us now, Milly.' I glanced at Marie. She was frowning, an odd look in her eyes. 'Marie . . . ?'

161

'I'll take these things up to the nursery,' she said stiffly. 'You won't be needing me.'

The look in her eyes made my heart sink. Marie was still hostile towards my friends, still jealous. If Kate had come to stay in London, there would probably be friction between them.

I went into the little sitting room. Kate was standing by the window, her back towards me. The grey silk dress and coat she was wearing had a special elegance and could only have come from Paris, as must all the other expensive trifles she had with her: a fine fur muff, ivory-handled umbrella, kid gloves and beaded purse.

She turned as I entered and smiled, holding out her hands to me. 'Jenny dearest – how are you?'

We kissed. She smelled wonderful, bathed in a cloud of delicate perfume that seemed so right for her it could have been created just for her and was no doubt expensive.

'I'm very well, Kate. How did you know where to find me? I wrote to give you my new address, but I thought you might have left France before it reached you . . . after your disagreement with Henriette.'

'Henriette told you I had left the chateau then?' There was a flicker of something in her eyes.

I nodded. 'Yes . . . she did say she thought you might be coming back to England.'

'What else did she tell you?' Kate asked. I could see she was on edge, a little uncertain of my reaction.

I remembered Henriette's confusing letter and frowned. 'Only that there had been some kind of misunderstanding – and that she had quarrelled with you but afterwards begged your pardon and asked you to stay but you would not.'

'She was jealous of me,' Kate said. 'At first she seemed to like me – but when Charles became so attached to me she changed, and then Béatrix, too . . .' She stopped and blushed, looking uncomfortable. 'It was just a silly misunderstanding.'

'The comtesse liked you?' The surprise in my voice made Kate smile and I gave an apologetic shake of my head. 'I did not mean there was any reason why she should not, of course not . . . only that she was always so strange with me.'

'For some reason Béatrix took to me at once. I visited her most days. She liked me to read to her, said my voice soothed her . . . that it was like a soft breeze on a summer's day. She was always asking for me, wanting me to visit her.'

'Yes, I see. Henriette might not be pleased if her cousin seemed to prefer your company – she *has* devoted a lot of her time to Béatrix.' I looked at Kate curiously. 'And did you like her . . . the comtesse, I mean?'

'I felt sorry for her – she was almost a prisoner in her own rooms.' Kate sighed. 'I suppose you may as well know it all – she took her own life in the end. There was a medicine she used every day – it had an opium base, and was kept locked in a cupboard so that she should not use too much. One day the bottle was left by her bed and she drank it all . . . the whole bottle.'

'That is terrible! Do you think she meant to do it . . . to take her own life?' I recalled seeing the comtesse walking in the gardens once in the early morning. She had looked tired and ill, and I had thought then that she might have taken a drug of some kind. I wondered now if, at the last, she had accidentally taken too much.

'Yes, of course it was deliberate. She was tired of her life – and she hated her husband.' Kate twisted the fine diamond and sapphire ring on the third finger of her right hand. There was an odd expression in her eyes that puzzled me – somehow defensive, as if she felt guilty. 'On the morning of the day she died I overheard a conversation between her and Laurent. It was a terrible argument, Jenny.'

'But I don't understand. He always seemed to be considerate of her – at least in public – though I know there were times when he could be cruel, for Gérard told me so. But most of the time I think she had no reason to complain of his behaviour towards her.'

'He must have changed since you saw him last,' Kate said. 'Henriette told me Gérard's death affected him badly. I think he hated Béatrix . . . I think he may have left that bottle by her bed in the hope that she would drink it.'

'Kate! How can you say such a thing?'

'I'm not saying he gave it to her . . . I just think he might have left it where she could reach it if she chose.'

Would Laurent have done such a thing? I could scarcely believe it. Gérard had told me he had once saved his wife from taking her own life. Why should he help her to do so now?

'And did you say something of the kind to Henriette?'

'No . . . we argued over something quite different.' Kate looked awkward, slightly embarrassed. 'You see . . . Béatrix left me most of her personal money – the small amount she was at liberty to dispose of herself. Most of her dowry became Laurent's when they married, of course. I had no idea she was going to do it. I swear it, Jenny. I imagined she had left it to Henriette. I cannot think why she changed her will . . . just a week before she died.'

'How odd that she should do such a thing. What did Henriette say? She must have expected to be her cousin's heir.'

Kate hesitated, then said, 'She accused me of . . . of having told Béatrix that she and Laurent were lovers. Of course I did nothing of the kind. It isn't true. But Béatrix was convinced of it . . . and, at the last, she turned against Henriette because of it. I think her mind may have been affected, by the drug she had been taking for so long. She said a lot of terrible things to Henriette – and she was naturally upset. She blamed me, thought I had turned Béatrix against her, but I had done nothing of the kind. You must believe me, Jenny.'

'Of course I believe you. Why should you do such a thing? Henriette must have been jealous of you. Her letter to me complaining of your behaviour went astray, but in the next one she had obviously regretted making accusations against you and said she had apologised for it.'

'She did apologise, and begged me to stay on at the chateau – but I thought it best to leave, in the circumstances. And I am independent now that I have my own money.'

'This is all too much for me,' I said. 'Why did the comtesse leave you so much money?'

'It isn't really all that much,' Kate said. 'As I said, the money is mostly Laurent's – Béatrix wasn't particularly wealthy in her own right. And of course I shall not be able to touch a penny of it until everything is settled . . . So I wondered if you would let me stay with you for a while, Jenny?'

I hesitated for a moment, thinking of Marie's reaction if I invited her to stay. She had been barely keeping her jealousy in check, and was bound to feel put out if I asked Kate to live with us.

'You haven't said anything.' Kate looked at me oddly. 'Is something wrong? Don't you want me here?'

'Yes, yes, of course I do . . .'

'You don't think I had anything to do with Béatrix's death, do you? You don't think I persuaded her to change her will and then helped her to take her own life . . . do you?'

'No!' I cried. 'That's unthinkable! Of course you would never do something like that, Kate. Of course you wouldn't.'

I hadn't even considered the possibility. Kate wasn't capable of doing anything so evil. But I could see that my hesitation had upset her – I could not hurt Kate by refusing her request now. Besides, I would enjoy having her to stay. Marie would just have to accept it.

'You know you are always welcome in my home.'

'That's all right then,' she said and smiled. 'I've missed you – and the police must have forgotten all about that stupid incident with the helmet by now. I have brought Louise with me. She is being taken care of for the moment, but I thought you might like to see her. You seemed so fond of her in Paris.

And I shall be here when your child is born. I shall look after you, Jenny. Sit with you, wait on you . . .'

'You know you can bring your daughter here, Kate. I shall enjoy having you both to stay. I have been getting very bored recently and you always were able to make me laugh.'

She smiled and hugged me, laughing as she talked about how good it was all going to be. Yet I had the oddest feeling that there was something she wasn't telling me.

Kate had brought presents for all of us, including some expensive perfume for Marie, which I thought kind of her since she had only met my companion once or twice in Paris – but it was just like Kate to be extravagant with her money. I knew that she now had the allowance left in trust for her by her father, which had been denied to her after she ran away with her lover, until her brother managed to contact her and arrange for it to be paid into a bank in Paris for her. But I did not suppose it to be a fortune, and I wondered how she could have afforded to buy such lovely things.

I exclaimed over the gossamer shawl and bundles of exquisite lace she had brought for my baby – all of which was much finer than anything we had been able to find in London.

'Oh, Kate,' I said. 'Where did you find this lace?'

'I remembered one of the nuns made lace – so I went back to the convent and spoke to Sister Isobel. She asked after you – told me to remind you that you had promised to visit her one day.'

'Oh, dear. I suppose I ought to have gone, but I am surprised at your going back there. You couldn't wait to get away when we were at school.'

'I was a foolish girl then. Besides, I wanted the lace for you. You are pleased with it?'

'All these things are beautiful. But you've spent far too much money on me.'

'You are worth it,' she said and kissed me warmly. 'No

one ever had a truer friend than you, Jenny. Your mother helped me when I needed it most – and you welcomed me as a friend after I told you about the terrible things I had done. Now that I have money, I want to spoil you a little.'

'I did very little,' I said. 'We are friends, Kate.'

'I shall not stay too long,' she told me. 'Just two or three months, until you are over the birth and on your feet again – then I'm going back to France. I have written to my brother and told him I intend to buy a house near Paris. I shall have my daughter with me. I shall never be parted from my darling again . . . and I hope to make my peace with my brother. Thomas has been generous in making my allowance available to me. You were right, Jenny, when you said I should forgive him. When he refused to allow me to become engaged to Richard Havers, he was only trying to protect me. It was not his fault that it all went so wrong. If I had been a little less selfish . . . less headstrong . . . it might never have happened.'

I looked at her in surprise. Something was different – she was softer, the bitterness banished or at least put away to some secret corner of her mind. It seemed that she had come to terms with her unhappy past.

'You've changed,' I said. 'I don't know what it is . . . but something is different.'

'It is the clothes,' she said and her cheeks were a little pink. 'I am still the same otherwise.'

'No . . .' I shook my head. 'I'm not sure what it is – but you *are* different. If I didn't know that you had sworn never to trust another man, I should say you were in love.'

'Oh, Jenny, how like you to come right out and say it,' she said and gave me a mysterious look. 'Perhaps there is someone . . . but for the moment it is a secret.'

'Kate!' I cried, feeling pleased that the future looked brighter for her. 'Oh, Kate – is it true? Have you found someone? Is he an Englishman? Is that why you've come back?'

'Please don't ask,' she said. 'I promise I shall tell you when

I am certain . . . but nothing is settled yet. I am not sure how I feel about anything.'

'Then I shan't tease you about it,' I said, thinking I understood now. Knowing Kate as I did, I realised there must be good reason for her secrecy . . . it might be that her lover was already married. 'But I am glad for you, really I am.'

'I knew you would be,' she said. 'And I promise – as soon as I am able I will tell you everything . . .'

'How long is she going to stay here?' Marie asked, a sulky look on her face. 'I don't trust her, Jenny. She was in your room this morning and your jewellery box was on the dressing table . . . it was open.'

'I left it there. Kate wouldn't take my things. You must not be jealous of her, Marie. She is my friend, just as Susanna is – and Philip. But you are my friend, too.'

'I don't trust her. She was looking through your letters.'

'Kate brought the post up to me because I stayed in bed longer this morning. I asked her to fetch them, Marie, and we had hot chocolate together.'

I sighed and pressed a hand to my aching back. Kate had been with us for three weeks now, and Marie's jealousy seemed to get worse every day.

'Well, I do not think she is what she seems,' Marie said. 'And I do not like her.'

'I really do not want to hear this!' I snapped, suddenly angry. 'Kate is my friend, this is my house – and I want her here with me, at least until after my baby is born.'

Marie turned and left the room without another word. I knew my sharpness had upset her and I would have gone after her, but my body seemed so heavy and awkward, and I was desperately tired. It was less than two months now until my child was to be born; I had not had an easy pregnancy and I could not wait for it to be over.

Now that the birth was so near, I had begun to worry again

despite myself. Would my child be healthy and strong – and normal? I was almost sure that Laurent was not my father, but I could not be certain. And I needed to know, if I was to have peace of mind. Somehow I had to discover the truth for myself.

Mama's trunk! I had forgotten about it after my return from Cornwall, but all of a sudden I remembered that I had meant to search again for the mislaid letter. I rang for Milly, asking her where it had been stored.

'In the attic, I think,' she said. 'I remember it because it was full of things and heavy, but Marie said it would not be needed.'

'Will you have it brought down for me, please? I am so sorry to trouble everyone,' I said, apologising because I knew it was not easy to transfer trunks to and from the attic, and she would have to fetch a coachman to bring it down. 'But there is something I need to find.'

Milly gave me an old-fashioned look. No doubt she thought my odd request was because of my pregnancy. Just another folly, like ordering strange mixtures of food late at night – but I was suddenly impatient to examine the contents.

After all these months, it was foolish to feel this way, and I could only put my restlessness down to my physical state. When the trunk was brought in after a delay of half an hour or so, I unlocked it and then went down on my knees, beginning to take the contents out piece by piece.

There were several pretty dresses, silk underwear, fans, scarves – all the personal possessions of Mama's I had asked Madame Leconte to save for me. I unfolded everything, laying each article on the floor beside me until I had emptied the trunk. And still there was no sign of the missing letter. I was so frustrated that I could have cried, and I began to pull the clothes over again, sure that I must eventually find the elusive letter.

Kate came in to find me kneeling amongst a pile of

clothes, shoes and books. She looked at the mess and raised her brows.

'Well, I've heard of women cleaning the house from top to bottom in the last weeks of pregnancy,' she said and laughed. 'But this is something new. What were you looking for, Jenny?'

'A letter Mama wrote to me before she died.' There were tears in my eyes as I looked at Kate. 'Madame Leconte packed it in this trunk – but I've been through everything several times and it isn't there.'

'Can it have got caught up in something?' Kate knelt down in front of the trunk. She leaned over it, running her hands round inside, carefully examining every bit of the trunk, then stopped. 'What's this?'

There were just a few scarves and kerchiefs at the bottom. I had tossed them back in after emptying the trunk. Surely I could not have missed anything?

'I took everything out . . .'

'Not in the trunk,' Kate said. She was moving her fingers over the side of the leather trunk. 'I think there is something behind the silk, Jenny. Look – you can see where it has torn . . .' She gave a little cry of triumph as she extracted an envelope. 'It must have slipped behind the lining. Is this what you've been looking for?'

'Oh, Kate!' I cried, and took it from her eagerly. 'No wonder I couldn't find it. I thought Laurent must have taken it.'

'Why would he do that?' She looked puzzled.

'He wouldn't, of course,' I said, my cheeks warm. 'I blamed him when I couldn't find it, because he was the only one other than myself who had the key to Mama's trunk. It was stupid of me, but I was too distressed at the time to think clearly.'

'Well, now you have your letter,' Kate said. 'I shall leave you to read it, Jenny – and then I'll come back and pack this trunk for you, shall I? You really shouldn't be doing all this yourself.'

'Thank you for helping me,' I said. 'I should never have found Mama's letter without you.'

Kate smiled, got to her feet and went out, leaving me alone. I sat staring at my mother's letter for several minutes. I believed I was close to discovering the truth at last, and my hands trembled as I slit the seal and took out the single sheet of paper inside.

My darling child,

I have loved you so very much, and this letter is the hardest thing I have ever had to do. Believe me, Jenny, I never wanted to tell you any of this . . . but I have been ill and Laurent insists that you should be told.

My eyes misted with tears. Oh, Mama . . . Mama. I wiped the tears away and read on, my throat tight with emotion.

For many years I have been Laurent de Arnay's mistress. It is not the sordid arrangement you might think. I have always worked to support myself and you – though Laurent provided this house and he will never let me lack for anything. However, I have refused many of the expensive gifts he wished to give me, because to take them would have made me feel like a kept woman.

We have always loved each other, Jenny, but I knew from the beginning that he could not marry me. I want you to know that Laurent has made me very happy, and that he has always wanted to acknowledge you as his own child . . . though I believe in his own heart he suspects you are not his.

I fear I have not been entirely honest with Laurent, my dearest. I wish with all my heart that you had been his child, but it is not so.

I was not Laurent's child. My love for Gérard had not

been incestuous or evil. We might have been married if I had read this letter in Paris soon after Mama died – as she had obviously intended I should.

I could feel the tears rolling down my cheeks and for a moment I could not see to read the last few words Mama had written.

> You may wish to know the name of your true father one day. I have not written it here, because when you read this your grief will be too raw. I want you to think of Laurent as your true friend, and as the father he has always wanted to be to you. One day, in the future, when you are settled and happy, you will find the truth beneath the binding of the book of poems I gave you.
>
> For now all I shall tell you is that from the moment you were born I loved you. You were my own dearest child and my love for you never wavered. If one day you seek the truth I have tried to keep from you – and that must be your decision, dearest, for there are some things that may be best left to rest in obscurity – you must never believe that I resented having you. I loved you always, as I love you now. Remember me with kindness.
>
> Your loving mother, Adele

'Oh, Mama . . .' I sighed, the tears running silently down my cheeks. 'Why did I not read this when you intended I should?'

She had thought I would find it amongst her things. She had thought I would know all I needed to know for the time being – and she had made sure the truth was there for me to find if ever I needed to know it.

'Remember your heritage,' she had told me when she gave me the specially bound copy of Keats's poems. Gérard had noticed that the binding was unusually thick and must have been done specially for me – Mama had placed something between the original covers and that beautiful leather binding I loved to stroke.

It had been there all the time, waiting for me to discover it.

'At least you know that Laurent is not your father,' Kate said when I showed her the letter later that day. 'That should relieve your mind – if you were still worrying about it, Jenny. And I think you must have been, or you would not have had the trunk brought down.'

'Yes, I was,' I admitted. 'I was fairly certain Laurent could not be my father after Grandmother told me about the rape. My mother deceived him too, Kate. That was misguided of her – though I dare say it was because she wished so much that I was his child.'

'It is understandable,' Kate said. 'You must try to forgive her – and Laurent. I know you blame him for what happened.'

'No, not any more,' I said. 'I know it was my own fault, Kate. I should have gone into Mama's room after she died – or opened her trunk when it was first delivered to the chateau.'

'So you do not hate Laurent any more?'

I shook my head. 'No, I cannot hate him. He loved Mama so – and he made her happy. Besides, I am sure he has suffered enough for his part in Gérard's death.'

'Then you would see him if he were in London?'

'Yes, I shall see him when he comes,' I said. 'And I shall show him Mama's letter. It is only right that he should know the truth.'

'And the other letter . . . the one she concealed inside your book . . . the one that names your true father?'

'I don't know . . .' I felt an icy tingle at the nape of my neck. 'I left the book in Cornwall by mistake, Kate. I could ask my grandmother to send it . . . but I'm not sure I really want to know. For the moment it is enough

173

to be sure that my love for Gérard was not wrong – not incestuous.'

Kate frowned at me. She knew me better than anyone else, and she knew I was hiding something, but she did not pry.

She knew that when I was ready I would tear off that glorious leather binding and discover the final secret that had been hidden from me for so long.

Four weeks had passed since Philip had last called to see me – twice as long as he had expected to be away – but it seemed longer. It was now the end of November and I was feeling so tired. My back ached constantly, and I found it difficult to move. Sometimes I felt I could not bear to go on like this for another month.

I was sitting in the parlour that afternoon with a book on the table beside me, unable to concentrate. A deep sigh escaped me. Why had Philip not been to see me? He had promised he would come, but I'd heard nothing since his last letter, which had arrived ten days earlier. What could have delayed him?

'Why so gloomy? It may never happen . . .' a teasing voice said behind me.

I swung round with a cry of pleasure. He was here at last!

'Philip! It is so good to see you.'

He had noticed the signs of tiredness in my face. 'Why were you sighing just now?'

'No particular reason – I was just feeling bored.' I lifted my head, looking at him accusingly. 'It is a month since you last came to see me. I thought you had forgotten me.'

'I returned to town only this morning. My business took longer than expected,' he said. I saw the teasing smile had left his eyes. Something was wrong. An icy fear trickled down my spine. 'I came at once, Jenny. I am afraid my news is not good.'

'Is . . . is it my grandmother? Is she ill again?'

'Anne was well when I saw her yesterday. She sent you her

love.' He pulled a chair close to mine and sat down, reaching forward to take my hands in his. 'I'm so sorry, Jenny. I tried to help that lad . . . but I am afraid it is too late.'

'Too late? Robbie . . .' I saw the look in his eyes. He was upset, angry . . . guilty. He had no reason to feel guilt but would do so if he believed he had failed me. 'You mean something has happened to him, don't you?'

'He . . .' Philip held my hand more tightly. I sensed he was anxious for me. 'This must upset you, Jenny – but I would not have you hear it from anyone else.'

'Is he dead?' He did not need to answer; it was in his face. 'How did it happen?'

Philip took a deep breath. 'He hung himself. They say he had confessed to his crimes and knew they were about to move him to the asylum. It seems that he preferred to end his life rather than spend it shut away from the world.'

'Poor Robbie.' Tears stung my eyes. I was distressed but not really surprised. I had somehow been expecting bad news. It was the memory of that pale, unhappy face at the window of the station house that had made me urge Philip to help him. 'Poor, poor boy.'

'He did not deserve such a fate,' Philip said and I could see he was deeply affected by his failure to help Robbie. 'He must have been so confused . . . so afraid.'

I closed my eyes, feeling a deep sadness. I had not really known Robbie, but I did not believe him capable of doing the things of which he had been accused. He played silly tricks, and his manner was sometimes sly – but he had not been evil. I felt it instinctively.

'I do not believe he attacked that girl – not the one who was raped. He may have tried to frighten the others, but I do not believe he would have harmed anyone.'

I remembered the day I had met him near the village, and the puzzled look in his eyes when he had asked me if I thought he would harm anyone. Obviously he had known he was being blamed for something – something he hadn't done.

'We shall never know the truth, Jenny.'

'It is just that I hate injustice, Philip. It makes me angry that he was accused and condemned without being given a fair chance of proving his innocence. It was cruel . . . unfair. He was incapable of standing up for himself and even his father deserted him.' I swallowed the knot of emotion that rose in my throat and threatened to choke me. 'To lock him away without any hope of release. I am not surprised he chose death instead.' I took the handkerchief Philip offered and wiped my eyes. 'I shall never believe he was guilty.'

'The worst of it is not knowing,' Philip agreed. 'If he was guilty, they couldn't allow him to remain free, but if he was innocent . . .'

'Everyone is entitled to a chance in life, Philip. Even those who are not as able as we are.'

'Yes, I know.' He smiled at me. 'Your compassion puts the rest of us to shame, Jenny. I am sorry to bring you such news. Will you forgive me for failing you in this?'

'It is not your fault. There was nothing more you could have done, Philip. You cared – and that is more than most.'

'And this has not upset you too much? You will not fret over it . . . make yourself ill? I almost didn't tell you until after the child was born, but I thought you would prefer the truth – was I right?'

'I am glad you told me. It is because I know that I can trust you that I value your friendship so much, Philip.'

'Then I shall never lie to you.' He released my hands and sat back. 'Now, tell me all your own news. Have you heard from your guardian yet?'

'No . . . I thought he would have written before this.'

'Perhaps he has been delayed.'

'Yes, perhaps.'

'Would you like me to see him for you?'

'I have decided that I must see him myself, Philip – but I hope that he will not come until after the child is born. I do not think I could bear it.'

'Poor Jenny,' Philip said with a teasing smile. 'This is such a trying time for you. You must be patient for a little longer.'

'How patient you are with me,' I said and laughed at myself. I felt better for seeing him, despite his sad news. 'No husband could have endured my moans with better spirit.'

'We are friends,' Philip said, 'and friends should always help each other.'

I could not sleep that night. My mind kept going over and over the conversation I had had with Philip. Getting up, I walked over to the window and looked out. The sky was dark, lit only by a sprinkling of stars.

'Poor, poor Robbie,' I whispered. 'Such a cruel fate.'

The injustice of his treatment was what angered me. Surely it was the duty of those of us who were born sound of mind and body to show compassion to others less fortunate? He had been judged guilty by the gossips, condemned and sentenced without benefit of a trial.

At the back of my mind lingered the unpleasant thought that Robbie and I might have shared the same father. Was that why I felt so sorry for him – or was it merely the sympathy I would feel for anyone in his unhappy situation? Whatever, I was aware that somehow I had failed him and that distressed me.

Yet there was nothing more I could have done; Philip had tried to help but Robbie had taken his own way out, and perhaps in the end it was the best way for him. What kind of a life would he have had locked away in an institution? He would have been desperately unhappy, and who knew what happened to the poor inmates of those places? He might have been physically abused or subjected to unkindness. At least he was free now . . .

I must let it go. No good would come of brooding.

I felt the pain in my back intensify and groaned. Childbearing did not come easily to me. I wished desperately in that moment that Philip was with me . . . that I could rouse him from his sleep and beg him to talk to me . . . to make me smile at myself.

I should have married him when he had asked! Perhaps I would say something when he visited me next time. Perhaps it was not too late . . .

I gave a little scream as the pain suddenly ripped through me.

It could not be the child! It should not be due for at least another four weeks.

Oh, dear God! I had never felt such pain. I stumbled to the bed and lay down again, panting until the spasm had passed. Perhaps it was just a false alarm . . . perhaps I had eaten something for my supper that had upset me.

It was easing now . . . that was better. I lay staring at the ceiling, letting my body relax, breathing deeply. If Philip were here he would hold my hand . . . tell me to relax.

Oh, Philip, Philip. I need you so.

Several minutes passed before I felt the pain again; longer and stronger this time, it left me in no doubt that I was now in labour. Tears trickled down my cheeks. It hurt . . . it hurt so much. But at least the time of waiting was over and soon I would hold my child in my arms.

Eleven

'You have a beautiful little girl,' Kate said, smiling down at me. 'She looks just like you, Jenny.'

'I pray she will not have my hair,' I said, reaching out a languid hand to touch the rather red and wrinkled face of my baby as Kate held her for me to see. My labour had been long and hard and I was exhausted. 'She is beautiful, isn't she? Is everything all right with her?' I looked at Kate for confirmation.

'She has all her fingers and toes,' Kate replied, laughing at my anxious look. 'She's wonderful, Jenny. A perfect, healthy child – a little tiny perhaps, but the doctor thinks she was born a few weeks early, so it's understandable that she is small.'

'Yes,' I agreed. 'Doctor Brownlee said that I was lucky, because to have carried full term might have been very difficult for me. He had been expecting an early confinement, because of the trouble I had in the summer . . . but he told me there was nothing to worry about. Women like me do sometimes give birth a month or even six weeks sooner than normal, and it does not necessarily harm the child.'

'What will you call her?'

'Julia . . . yes, I shall call her Julia.' I looked at my baby and smiled. 'She is perfect, isn't she?'

'Julia suits her,' Kate said. 'Of course she is perfect. Why shouldn't she be?'

There was no reason, of course. I had lived in dread for months when I'd believed Gérard was my half-brother, but those fears should have been banished by Mama's letter.

And yet the shadow of fear for my baby had never quite left me. Even now that my child was born, there was a lingering unease at the back of my mind . . . something that would not let me be entirely at peace.

'You should let Jenny rest now,' Marie said and I heard the note of jealousy in her voice. Since Kate's arrival, she had retreated more and more into the background – and that was perhaps my fault. 'Give the baby to me.'

'Leave her here in the cot beside me,' I said, my eyelids flickering. 'I'm sorry. I must sleep now . . .'

'We should go and leave her to rest.'

'Of course. But she wanted to see the child . . . to be reassured before she could sleep.'

I heard their voices as from a long way off as I drifted into sleep. Why must they quarrel? I wanted us all to be happy, but I was too tired to think about it now.

As I slept, Gérard came to me in the garden. It was my own special garden, but no longer neglected. I was holding Julia in my arms. He smiled at me so tenderly that I cried out to him, calling his name.

'She is lovely,' he said. 'Take care of her, my love. And take care of yourself . . . take care of yourself.'

I woke to find Susanna sitting beside me. She had brought flowers for me, and presents for the baby.

'I came as soon as Philip gave me the news,' she said, bending down awkwardly to kiss my cheek. 'They told me you were sleeping, so I sat here quietly. You were dreaming, Jenny.' She reached out to smooth a tear from the corner of my eye, and I saw compassion in her face. 'Does it still hurt so much?'

'I was dreaming of Gérard.'

'I know. You spoke his name.'

'He came to see Julia.'

'Is that what you have decided to call her?'

'Yes – do you like it?'

'It is very pretty and she is going to be a little charmer.'

'Just like Gérard.' I reached out to take Susanna's hand as she sat beside me on the bed. 'You asked if it still hurt as much and the answer is no. I shall always think of him . . . always remember and love him . . . but the pain has become an ache. I wish that he could be here to see Julia, but I have accepted that it cannot be.'

'Dearest.' Susanna squeezed my hand gently. 'You were always so brave, Jenny. You deserve to be happy, my dear – and I pray that you will be.'

'I am happy,' I replied. 'I have good friends and I have my daughter. What more could I possibly want?'

I wanted the peace and happiness I had felt in my special garden – but it did not exist except in dreams.

'A husband and more children, perhaps?'

'Have you anyone in mind?' I asked with a teasing smile. My friend was a born matchmaker!

'I thought perhaps . . . It has seemed to me that you and Philip get on so well. It may not be a grand passion but—'

'He did ask me to marry him . . . so that my child could be born in wedlock. I refused his offer, which was made merely out of kindness.'

'Of course you would,' Susanna said, pulling a wry face. 'But I think you wronged him, Jenny. Philip cares for you – you can see it in his face, in the way he speaks of you. He has been so anxious for you. When he came to tell me of the successful birth there was such relief in his eyes . . . such excitement. No husband could have been prouder.'

'If I thought that I could make him truly happy . . .'

'I have no doubt of that, my dear.'

'Perhaps . . .' I sighed. 'Philip says he is content to be my friend but . . . when I went into labour I longed for him, Susanna. I wished he was there to hold my hand and comfort me.'

'Surely not while you were giving birth?' Susanna looked a little shocked. 'I would never dream of allowing Henry to be there – giving birth is so undignified and to see me in such pain would frighten the poor man to death.'

I laughed and yet I felt that if Philip were my husband he would not have left me while I needed him.

'I should go now,' Susanna said and sighed as she stood up. She put a hand to her back and I smiled in understanding. 'I envy you, Jenny. At least it is finished for you – and you have your darling Julia.'

'Yes.' I turned as I heard a whimpering sound from the cot beside me. 'Give her to me, Susanna, please.'

She lifted the baby gently, touching her face before laying her in my arms. As I looked at the fuzzy down covering her tiny head – hair which seemed to have more than a hint of red in it – I felt a wave of overwhelming love. I had suffered for her but it had all been worthwhile and I knew that I would love this child even more than I had loved her father. I would devote myself to her, protect and care for her always.

As Susanna went out, I put my baby to my breast and felt her begin to suck greedily. I stroked her head, smiling, contented.

'Julia . . . my precious daughter,' I whispered. 'I love you. I shall never let anyone harm you.'

I felt an icy trickle of fear. Why had that thought come into my mind? Why did I feel so protective towards her? Was it the natural feeling of any new mother? Or was it something more – a premonition, a sixth sense that she would need the special love I felt for her?

'Mademoiselle Lancaster has asked if she may come up,' Marie said. She watched as I rocked my baby in my arms. Julia had been grizzling non-stop for the past several hours. 'Shall I tell her you are not yet well enough to see her?'

It was six days since I had given birth and I was beginning to recover my strength, to feel less tired.

'I will see her,' I said, giving the child to Marie. 'I'm a little worried about Julia. Do you think she has a temperature?'

'Babies always cry,' Marie said with a careless shrug, which made her seem very French. Or was I becoming more English? 'Shall I take her away for a while . . . just until Mademoiselle Lancaster leaves?'

'Bring her back in twenty minutes . . . in case Miss Lancaster would like to see her.'

Marie nodded, her dark eyes going over me anxiously. 'You ought to be sleeping, Jenny. You have shadows beneath your eyes.'

'Don't worry. I am feeling much better.'

I lay back against the pillows as she took Julia from the room. I knew babies did cry a lot, but I could not help feeling concerned. It was this foolish fear that my child was somehow vulnerable . . . that she needed special care. Everyone told me not to worry, but how could I help it? To lose her would be more than I could bear.

'Miss Heron – may I come in?'

I had been lying with my eyes closed. I opened them to see Margaret Lancaster standing in the doorway. She was carrying a pretty basket of flowers and a gift wrapped in soft white tissue.

'Yes, of course,' I said. 'I was not asleep.'

'My mother thought it was a little early to come visiting,' Margaret said, smiling at me, 'but she is rather old-fashioned. I thought you would not mind?'

'It is nice to have company.'

I sighed inwardly. The one person I really wanted to see had not yet come to visit me. I supposed that Philip felt he ought to wait until I was up and able to receive him downstairs, but I longed for a smile and a few teasing words from him. Not that he had neglected me, of course. He had sent flowers every day and several gifts for Julia. I knew that he had seen my baby. Kate had taken her downstairs to him, but I had been sleeping at the time and no one had suggested that he come up to me.

It was not proper that I should receive a visit from a male

friend until I had been blessed and could greet him downstairs in my parlour. If we had been married it might have been so very different . . .

'I wanted to beg your pardon,' Margaret was saying, 'for the way I behaved towards you when Philip brought us here that first time.'

I brought my attention back to her. 'It was awkward for you. My situation makes things difficult . . . I understood your feelings.'

'No, no, I did not understand,' she said. 'Now that Mrs Walters has told me you were to have married the Comte de Arnay's son . . .' She stopped and looked dismayed. 'I cannot apologise enough for the dreadful things my mother said when we were here. She always imagines any man who is polite to me is preparing to offer me marriage . . . It was all nonsense, of course. There was nothing intimate in the relationship. We merely spent a few pleasant hours together, and always in the company of others.'

I could imagine Susanna telling Mrs Lancaster and I knew she had done it for my sake, but I wished she had not. I studied Margaret's face but she was expert at concealing her true feelings.

'Why are you telling me this?'

'Because I wanted you to know you had no cause to feel jealous of me, Miss Heron. Gérard did not make love to me in Italy. It was merely friendship.' She blushed and looked down, twisting her kid gloves in her hands. 'Besides, there is someone else I like very much. I know how I should feel if I had cause to suspect . . . Jealousy is such an unworthy emotion, isn't it?'

'Yes, it is.' I met her eyes. She was smiling and yet somehow I did not believe in this show of friendship. 'It was kind of you to tell me this.'

'I hoped we might become friends,' she said. 'Philip is so fond of you and I naturally want to be on good terms with all his friends.' She gave me a confiding smile. 'It

would be a little awkward otherwise. I'm sure you understand.'

'You mean . . .' I caught my breath. 'You and Philip . . .'

'Oh, nothing is settled yet,' she said quickly. 'Nothing
has been said openly . . . but a woman always knows these
things. Don't you agree, Miss Heron? I believe I may have
some happy news by next spring or even sooner.'

'Then I wish you happiness,' I said. 'And I hope we shall
be friends, because Philip's friendship is important to me.'

'Yes, of course. It must be so. You are in such awkward
circumstances.' Her voice was sympathetic. 'I told Philip I
thought you were very brave. Most women in your situation
would have gone away to have the child, and left it in the
care of a good woman.'

'I would never, never do that. It would begin a lie and I
hate lies. I am not ashamed of having loved Gérard.'

'No, indeed, why should you be?' She laid her gifts
on the bed. 'And now I should go. You look tired, Miss
Heron. Perhaps I may call again when you are over your
confinement?'

'Yes, please do,' I replied. 'Thank you for coming . . . and
for these.' I touched the flowers and the wrapped gift. 'It was
generous of you.'

'And you will forgive me for my bad manners on that first
occasion?'

'You were embarrassed,' I said. 'There is nothing to
forgive – and we must not quarrel . . . for Philip's sake.'

'How generous you are,' she said, smiled and went out.

I closed my eyes after she had gone, fighting against the
wave of anger and jealousy that assaulted me. How dare she
come to gloat over me?

The anger was swiftly replaced by grief and shame. I had
no right to be jealous. My anger should rather be directed at
myself than at her. Philip had offered me marriage and I had
turned him down without considering . . . Now I was paying
the price of my own stupidity.

'How selfish you are, Jenny Heron,' I chided myself softly. I should be glad that Philip had found someone who loved him. My own feelings for him were too muddled for me to be sure exactly what I was experiencing now. I had come to rely on him, to turn to him when I was worried, to look forward to his visits – but was this jealousy and pain only because I feared to lose his friendship?

When I had first felt the pain of labour I had longed for him to be near, to hold his hand and see him smiling at me – but was that love? Or was I simply being selfish – did I see Philip only as someone useful, there to solve my problems?

'Jenny . . .' Kate's voice broke into my thoughts. 'May I come in?'

'Yes, of course.' I looked up, relieved that she had come to banish my terrible thoughts. 'I've just had a visitor.'

'Yes, I know. I saw her leave – so I thought I would bring you this letter. I think it is the one you have been expecting.'

'From Laurent?' I took it from her. 'Yes, it is.' I tore open the seal. 'He asks if he can come to see me next week.'

'You will not see him yet? You are still not well enough, Jenny.'

'No . . .' I looked at her thoughtfully. 'He does not know I have had a child . . . You did not tell him or Henriette that I was with child?'

'You made me promise not to,' she said. 'So of course I didn't – though I was tempted. He was so wretched over his son's death. It might have comforted him to know that he would have a grandchild.'

'Do you think so? He refused to acknowledge Gérard for years. They quarrelled dreadfully, even before I was involved. I am not sure that Gérard would want him to know his daughter.'

'Is that not too cruel? Does he not have the right to know?'

'Perhaps . . . I am not sure.'

'I know that Laurent loves you – that he has suffered a great deal. Surely you would not want to deny him a little happiness, Jenny? It is not like you to bear a grudge.'

'I have forgiven him for what he did to me but . . .' I remembered the bitterness Gérard had felt because his father had rejected him, had threatened to disown him. I needed to think about this a little longer. 'Will you write to him for me, Kate? Please? Tell him I have had a nasty chill and that I cannot see him for another two weeks.'

'If that is what you want, of course . . . but I think –' She broke off as Marie came in carrying Julia.

'She is asleep now,' Marie said. 'She will not disturb you while you rest.'

I looked at my child's face. She was sleeping peacefully and looked so beautiful, so sweet and innocent that my heart was caught by the overwhelming love I felt for her.

'Lay her in the cot,' I said and smiled at Marie. 'You must have the magic touch. Nothing I could do would stop her crying.'

For a moment something odd flickered in her eyes, then it had gone and I was not sure it had ever been there.

'All babies cry,' she said. 'She will sleep now for a while.'

I lay back and closed my eyes as both Kate and Marie went out, leaving me alone with my child.

I did not sleep well the night before Laurent was due to call on me. I was restless, tossing uneasily in my bed. I felt hot and my head ached, and for a while I felt sick.

Was I worrying over what Laurent had to say to me? There was surely no reason – not now. Or was it just that I felt so unwell? I had been sweating, and my limbs felt heavy, as if I were sickening for something.

I got up and went over to my washstand, pouring cool water from the jug into a bowl and splashing my face. What was wrong with me? Why should I feel so nervous about meeting

Laurent? Was I afraid that he would renew his claims to be my father? No, no, that was foolish. Then . . . what?

The cool water had refreshed me. I returned to my bed, longing for sleep. Why did I feel so restless?

I remembered Kate's words to me when she first came back from France. She had half accused Laurent of helping his wife to take her own life . . . of leaving the medicine near Béatrix's bed so that she could commit a terrible sin – the comtesse had been a strict Catholic and her religion would condemn her severely for what she had done.

What else could it have been? Not murder surely! Who would want to take the comtesse's life? She'd had very little contact with the outside world . . . caused no trouble for anyone – except perhaps Henriette, who had been forced to neglect her own child to wait on her.

I had guessed soon after my arrival at the chateau that Henriette was in love with Laurent. She had stayed there as much to be close to him as for her cousin's sake. Would they marry now that his wife was dead?

Had Béatrix been in someone's way? Was that why the medicine was left by her bedside – so that she would make it easy for her rival?

What a wicked, terrible thought! I was ashamed of having had it. How could I think that Henriette – or Laurent – would be capable of such a thing? No, no, it was just my imagination . . . because I had been worrying too much over my child.

Julia did not seem to make as good progress as she had at first. She cried when she was awake and then slept for hours at a time . . . even past her feed. And when she did feed she seemed listless, as if my milk was not satisfying her.

I had spoken of my fears to the doctor.

'You have plenty of milk, Miss Heron,' he assured me. 'You must not worry. Julia is perfectly healthy. Some children cry more than others. And you must not expect her to put on weight too quickly. She was premature. It is natural that she should be a little tiny . . .'

It was natural, I supposed, but still I could not stop worrying. There was a shadow at the back of my mind . . . a loose thread from that tangled web of lies and deceit that had once seemed to ensnare me, waiting to drag me back into that pit of despair.

If Laurent was not my father – who was? It must be the man who had raped Mama – but who was he? Whose blood flowed in my veins and in my poor child's? I was not sure I wanted to know.

All this fretting was pulling me down. Marie was cross with me because I looked so tired and pale. She scolded me, taking Julia from me when she cried, and always, when she brought her back to me, Julia was sleeping.

'Marie is so good with her,' I had said to Kate only that morning. 'How do you think she gets her to sleep so easily?'

'I don't know.' Kate frowned. 'It seems a little odd that only Marie can stop her, doesn't it?'

'She has the right touch,' I said. 'I was going to employ a nursery maid, but I think I shall let Marie take charge of her.'

'I should think about that carefully if I were you.'

'Why? Marie is so good with her.'

'I don't know,' Kate confessed and looked half ashamed. 'There is no real reason, just instinct – perhaps because she doesn't like me.'

'You aren't jealous of her?'

'Good gracious no! Though the same cannot be said for her. She seems to imagine you are her own private property.'

'Yes, I know. It is so foolish of her – yet how can I complain of her taking too much care of me? Besides, she is sensible most of the time.' Marie had seemed much better recently, as if taking care of Julia had left her too little time to be jealous of my friends. 'I'm sure she doesn't dislike you, Kate. It's just that she cares too much for me.'

Kate had merely raised her eyebrows and said nothing. Perhaps she was right, perhaps I ought to have taken Marie aside and warned her that I would not tolerate her behaviour towards my friends – but Kate would be returning to France soon and then I should need Marie more than ever. Especially when Philip was married.

I glanced anxiously at the gilt clock on my mantelpiece; it was French and had belonged to Mama. It had been in her trunk and I had decided it was too pretty to remain there. I thought perhaps it might have been a gift from Laurent.

Where was he? I had been expecting him for ten minutes and his lateness was making me nervous. Had he changed his mind? Had he decided not to come?

I heard footsteps in the hall, then my maid entered and announced him. Laurent followed her in, looking at me with his sad, tired eyes, and my heart caught with pity. How he had changed! The lines of suffering had made him look older, banishing that youthful vitality I had seen in him when we first met in Paris.

'Forgive me for keeping you waiting.'

'Laurent . . .' I said, taking half a step towards him. 'You've changed. You look ill . . .'

'I told you I would suffer for what I had done – did you not believe me?' He smiled slightly. 'You look beautiful . . . different . . . older somehow . . . but lovely.'

'Thank you.'

Was this the man I had come close to hating? All my anger had somehow drained away. I could feel only pity for him now . . . and a sense of loss.

'I am grateful to you for allowing me to call on you, Jeanette.'

'You called me Jenny once. Will you not do so now?' I sat

down and intimated that he should do so too. 'I was sorry to hear that Béatrix had died.'

'It was a relief to her in the end,' he said, frowning. 'I dare say Kate has told you that she took her own life?'

'Then there was no doubt that she intended it?'

'None at all, I'm afraid. It was regrettable that she should do what she did . . . but I cannot condemn her. She took Gérard's death hard and never recovered from it. She said she had nothing left to live for – and we quarrelled bitterly. She hated me because of what happened to Gérard. Her life was meaningless. We should not grieve, neither should we condemn her.'

'No . . . I suppose not.'

'Forgive me for mentioning Gérard,' he said as I clasped my hands together in my lap, my eyes downcast. 'I did not mean to hurt you. And I see it does still cause you pain.'

'Did you think it would not?' I asked, looking up at him. 'Did you think my love so shallow, so careless, that I would forget him in a few months?'

'No, of course not – but you were so young. I hoped that you might find someone else in time . . . that you would learn to be happy again.'

'Perhaps I shall . . .'

'If you could forgive me for what I did to you both, I might begin to forgive myself.'

'I have forgiven you, Laurent – though I wish you had told me you thought I might be your daughter at the beginning, when you took me to the chateau.'

'I was not certain – but Adele always insisted that I was your father. I hoped you might find a letter amongst her things . . .'

'I have, though only recently. Perhaps you would like to read it?'

I removed the letter from my pocket and held it out to him; he took it, reading its contents slowly. I could see he was affected by what Mama had to say, and I felt sympathy for him as he got up and began to pace the room in agitation.

'You see how it was,' he said, turning to look at me at last. 'Adele wanted you to be mine and so for me you were. I loved her so much and I could never bear to deny her anything . . . because I could never give her what she truly wanted.'

'To be your wife?' I frowned as he nodded. 'Did you never think of divorce?'

'I never ceased to think of it,' Laurent cried passionately. In that moment his inner self was revealed to me and I saw how deeply he had loved my mother. 'At the beginning, I tried not to care for Adele. I tried to resist my feelings, but they were too strong for me – for us both. We met in London – at her first dance. Did you know that?'

'Yes – my grandmother told me when I met her this summer. You followed Mama home. She met you in secret, but you were seen together in the village . . . and her mother was angry with her.'

'I did not mean it to happen. I tried to do what was the right thing, the honourable thing,' Laurent said, his face working with emotion. 'I had told her that I was going back to France, that it was impossible for us to be together – but then I could not bear to be apart from her. I followed her to her home and we became lovers . . .'

'You *were* lovers then? Even before . . . But of course you must have been. Otherwise you could not have thought that you were my father, since Mama knew she was with child before you returned.' I had known it must be that way, but I wanted to hear everything from his lips, so that perhaps I might be able at last to understand and forgive what he had done to Gérard and me.

'Before she was raped? You know about that? Yes, I can see you do.' His eyes were bleak as he looked at me. 'Of course we were lovers. It happened for the first time after we had been riding together, Adele up before me on my horse. We were so much in love and our feelings overwhelmed us.

That was why I could never be certain whether or not you were my daughter.'

'Yes, I do see.'

'I told Adele that I was going up to London on business, but in fact I returned to France to beg Béatrix to release me,' he went on as if I had not spoken, his mind clearly dwelling in the past. 'I have wished a thousand times that I had taken her with me, kept her safe in my house in Paris – but she wanted to wait, to be certain that what we were doing was right.'

'You asked your wife to divorce you?' I was surprised. 'I had not expected this.'

'She refused.' Laurent hesitated, looking at me awkwardly. 'I should tell you her story . . .'

'Gérard told me,' I said. 'You were not kind to her, sir – or to him, I think?'

'You are right to condemn me.' A little nerve flickered in his cheek. 'She had hurt my pride. I *was* cruel to her. Abominably so. Adele made me see that, later, after we were together in Paris. Your mother was a wonderful woman. She told me that we had a right to our own happiness, but not to destroy Béatrix's. She made me promise that I would always behave courteously towards my wife, that I would visit her sometimes, and encourage her to mix in company. I have often wished to repair the damage I did when we were first married – but Béatrix could never forgive me.'

'So when you asked her to release you, she refused?'

'She said that I had forced her to live – and that if I tried to divorce her she would kill herself. She did not care that I had a mistress, only that she should not be disgraced by the shame of a divorce.'

'Oh . . . how terrible! For all of you.'

Béatrix's bitterness had trapped them all in a web of lies and sin that had in a way spoiled all their lives. Now it was all pouring out, as if a river had burst from its banks.

'Of course I could not divorce her after that. I was already ashamed of what I had done to her. Besides, it is very difficult for Catholics to divorce, and I realised I was being selfish. I returned to England, determined to see Adele again and tell her that I could not ask her to give up everything to become my mistress . . . and then she came to me and told me she was having my child.'

'Yes, I see.'

'It changed everything. She could not return to her home – and I wanted her so much.'

'Did she tell you about the rape then?'

'Not at first, not until after you were born, when we had settled in France. I had sensed there was something, but I was afraid to ask. She swore that you were mine, begged me with tears in her eyes to believe her. Of course I could not do anything else. She had given up so much for me – and I loved her.'

'But you were never sure it was your child?'

Laurent's eyes begged for understanding and forgiveness. 'It was impossible to know. You were born nine months after we first became lovers so . . .'

'You are sure of that?'

'Yes, quite sure. But I was told by the doctor who delivered you that you were born early, nearly three weeks too soon, because of a fall. Adele had tripped in the stairs and went into labour almost immediately. The birth was difficult and damaged Adele. We could never have another child . . .' His eyes carried the pain of remembered grief. 'If you were born too soon it was possible that you had been conceived while I was in France asking Béatrix for a divorce. There was no way to be sure – and it seemed not to matter. Any child of Adele's would have been welcome to me. And you were so beautiful, such a lovely baby.'

'I see . . .' I nodded, understanding how he had been deceived. 'If Mama had carried me full term I must have been yours . . . but if I was born a few weeks early then I could have been *his* – and only Mama could know for certain, if perhaps she had seen her womanly flow after you left her that first time.'

I had given birth to my own child a few weeks early, and I thought it more than possible that it should also have happened to Mama.

'But I *wanted* you to be mine,' Laurent said. 'For years I allowed myself to believe it, because I wanted you to be my child. I had seen you before that day in Paris when Adele introduced us. I used to come and watch you at the farm; I saw you playing with your friends, and attending church with your mother – though you were never aware of me.

'It was what Adele wanted. She told me she did not want you to misunderstand our relationship, to think it sordid or immoral . . . that one day she would tell you the truth. I believed her, because it was easier to let her have her way. It was only later, when I fetched you from school, that I began to question, to wonder . . .'

'It must have been difficult for you.'

It was so much easier to understand him now. His odd looks, his moods, his concern for me after Mama's death – and his gradual withdrawal after he found himself drawn to me.

'We were strangers, and yet I felt close to you. I did not know how to behave towards you. I felt affection for you. I wanted to spoil you, to give you things, but I was afraid you would mistake my feelings towards you – as I think you did for a while?'

I blushed and looked down. 'Forgive me for misjudging you. I have realised I was wrong.'

'Why did you give up the house I gave you, Jenny? Was it because you hated me too much to live there in my home?'

'No, I did not hate you. At first . . . yes. But not for some time now.'

'Why, then?' He looked at me intently. 'Did I not give you enough money to keep up the staff?'

'You were more than generous – you know that. I preferred

something smaller . . . and Marie did not get on with your housekeeper.'

'Why do you cling to that woman still?' He frowned. 'I never liked her. She was too possessive of Adele. Be careful of her, Jenny. Do not trust her too much.'

'Why?' I frowned at him. 'You were not kind to her after Mama died, turning her away with only a few months' wages. Why did you do that?'

'I had thought her a bad influence on Adele for a while.' He stood up again and walked towards the window, looking out. 'Your mother was in considerable pain towards the end, Jenny. She was taking something – some herbal medicine that Marie had got for her. It made her drowsy, changed her nature. I wondered . . .'

'Yes?' I asked as he hesitated. 'Please tell me.'

He turned to look at me. 'There is no more to say. Perhaps I am wrong – but I have never liked Marie. I loved Adele too much, Jenny. After I lost her, I did many things I regret. I know now that I was unfair to you and Gérard. I should have made the situation clear – but it was difficult for me. I could not speak of Adele, of how much she had meant to me – even to you.'

'We were both grieving for her. We should have comforted each other, drawn strength from one another.'

'Yes . . .' He looked so sad as he stood there. 'I was a fool – and now I have lost all claim to your affection. And I have lost my son. I was too strict with him, because I saw a wildness in him that I feared – and for a long time I was not sure he was mine. I was certain Béatrix had lied – that he was her lover's child. It was only in the last few months that I began to realise he was more like me than I had thought. I would give anything if I could change what happened, Jenny. I have been in torment these past months. God forgive me for what I did, for I cannot! I shall never cease to blame myself for his death. And I know I have forfeited all right to your respect.'

His face was grey with grief, his eyes haunted, revealing

the depth of his distress. Laurent had perhaps been selfish and careless, but he was not evil. And he had loved Mama desperately. I believed he loved me as the daughter he might have had.

I knew then what I had to do.

'We cannot change what has happened,' I said. 'But I think we might learn to be friends, Laurent.' I smiled as he turned to me eagerly, hope dawning in his face. 'And now I have a surprise for you. I am going to take you to meet a very special person . . . your granddaughter.'

'*My* . . .' He stared at me in disbelief. 'Gérard's child . . . you were carrying my son's child?'

'Her name is Julia,' I said. 'At first I did not want you to know – it was too painful – but now I think we understand each other better.'

'Jenny . . .' He looked at me humbly, pleading for forgiveness. 'What you must have gone through, carrying his child. I am so sorry. How can you forgive me after what I did to you and Gérard?'

'It has taken me a long time,' I said. 'But I have forgiven you, Laurent – and now I want to show you my darling Julia.'

He was silent as he followed me up to the nursery, but when I took his hand and led him to the cot, I saw the wonder and humility in his face.

'She is beautiful,' he said. 'Very like you as a baby.'

'Thank you. Would you like to hold her?'

'May I?'

I nodded, and he reached down into the cot, taking her carefully into his arms. As he gazed down at her, I saw that his eyes had filled with tears and I knew that I had made the right decision.

'She is your granddaughter,' I said softly. 'Gérard was your son, and Julia is his child – so you and I do have a blood tie we can both be certain of, Laurent . . . and one we can be proud of.'

He kissed Julia's forehead, laid her back in her cot and then turned to me as I gave a little cry of distress.

'What is wrong, Jenny?'

'I do not know. I feel faint . . .'

The room had suddenly started to spin. I made a little moaning sound as the floor seemed to rush up to meet me and fell forward into his arms.

Twelve

They told me afterwards that I was delirious for several days. I'd had a fever – an infection, the doctor called it, something that women who had recently given birth quite often suffered.

For a while everyone had thought that I might die. Perhaps at one time I might have let go, might not have fought against the sickness that had such a hold on my tortured body – but now I had my child and I was determined to live.

Susanna was unable to visit me, because she was very near her own time, but both Philip and Laurent came every day, bringing flowers and delicious fruit to tempt my appetite. At first they stayed only to make inquiries, but as I gradually became stronger, I asked that they should be allowed to come up to my room. I received them lying on a daybed I'd had brought in, wearing a silk robe over my nightgown and a lace cap to cover my hair.

Kate remained with me in the room during these visits for the sake of propriety. She often allowed Louise to join us for a few minutes, because she knew I loved her as much as if she had been my own. The child snuggled up to me, quiet and content within the circle of my arms, and as I began to feel better their visits developed into amusing tea parties. Philip and Laurent seemed to like each other, and I noticed that Kate's eyes sparkled when she teased Laurent – as she did unmercifully. He laughed quite often, and I began to see him as he must have been with my mother as a young man.

Laurent seemed to have shed much of the sorrow that had

weighed so heavily on him. He could not do enough for me, and seemed determined to spoil me. Presents began to arrive daily, but since they were all for Julia, I could not deny him. He was entitled to spend money on his own grandchild. He also brought a pretty fashion doll with a china head and a kaleidoscope for Louise, who was enchanted with her toy and forever showing me the different patterns it made.

The only black cloud hanging over me at this time was that Julia did not seem to be making progress as she ought to be. I worried about her, and of course it was to Kate that I confided my worries. Her daughter was so bright, so full of life. Why did my baby look so listless all the time?

'Do you think there is something wrong with her?' I asked anxiously. 'Has she inherited Mama's weakness through me?'

Kate tried to calm my fears. 'Stop worrying, Jenny, or you will make yourself ill again. Julia is as normal as any child can be.'

'How can you say that?' I asked, a sob in my throat. 'She cries all the time and then she sleeps like . . . It isn't natural, Kate.'

'No, I have thought her sleep rather too sound sometimes,' Kate admitted. 'Since you've been ill we've had a wet nurse to her – and she said she was worried about how little milk Julia takes.'

'There you are . . .' I said and tears started to my eyes. 'I was not affected by Mama's illness but it has come out in Julia. I'm so afraid for her, Kate. She is so weak . . . so vulnerable.' I was terrified that I had somehow passed on a congenital illness to my child.

'What nonsense,' Kate scoffed gently. 'You are still weak and overwrought yourself. It is not like you to be so tearful. You must make an effort and forget this nonsense.'

A sob rose to my lips. 'Oh, Kate. I think my baby is going to die and I do not know how I shall bear it . . .'

'She is a perfectly normal baby,' Kate said sternly. 'Stop

this at once, Jenny. Julia was premature; it may take her longer to become as strong as she ought to be – and you will do her no good by fretting. You must stop feeling sorry for yourself and get well again.'

'You sound like Philip,' I said, giving her a watery smile. 'Has he called today?'

'Do you not remember?' Kate said. 'He told you, he had to go down to Cornwall for a few days.'

'Yes, of course. I had forgotten. He has been such a good friend to me . . .' I stretched out my hand to her. 'I do not know what I should have done without him and you. You will not leave me, Kate . . . not until I am better?'

'You do not need to ask,' she said. 'I shall not leave you while you need me – but you must promise to stop fretting.'

'Yes, I shall. I promise. Will you bring Julia to me, please? I want to see her.'

'Of course.'

After Kate had gone I lay back and closed my eyes. I knew I was being foolish, but my illness had sapped my strength both mentally and physically. I felt as if my spirits were pressed down, as if a dark cloud was hanging over me – and I could not rid myself of the idea that there was something very wrong with Julia.

I told myself that I would stop this foolish fretting, but when Kate placed my child in my arms I found myself searching for signs of illness. Julia's eyes were bright and curious as she looked up at me, awake for once and aware of her surroundings. Kate was right, I thought. She was perfect.

I put her to my breast. She sucked but no milk came. My milk had dried up while I was ill. Julia began to wail pitifully. I looked at Kate, the panic starting to rise inside me once more.

'I can't feed her,' I cried. 'She doesn't know me – she cries every time I hold her . . . I can't bear it, Kate. I don't know how to comfort her. What can I do?'

'Give her to me,' Marie said in a scolding voice from the doorway. She came to take the child from me. 'I'll give her to the wet nurse, and then I'll settle her down. Stop worrying about her, Jenny. Leave her to me. I'll take care of her.'

I felt an ache begin inside me as Marie carried my child away to the nursery. What was wrong with me? I could not feed my baby and I was so terribly afraid that I was going to lose her.

Gérard had tried to warn me of danger in my dreams. I had wondered what those dreams meant, for they had seemed vague and strange, but now I knew that he was warning me to take care of our child.

Something was wrong with Julia, I felt it instinctively, but I did not know what to do and I was terrified.

My mind was in such turmoil over the next few weeks that I hardly knew what I did. The fever had gone and my strength was gradually returning – but I was haunted by the fear of losing my child. Once again, I began to have restless nights and dreams that made me start up in terror.

I slept very little, and in fits, often rising from my bed in the middle of the night to go and check that Julia was still breathing. She seemed to have put on a little weight at last. The milk she got from her nurse was richer than mine, and the doctor admitted that he might have been wrong – that perhaps my milk had not been enough for her.

'It is not unusual for new mothers to suffer a lowering of the spirits,' he told me. 'You will be yourself again before long, and in the meantime you must try not to worry. Your child is inclined to sleep more than is usual – but I am sure there is nothing to worry about.'

I should have been reassured by the increase in Julia's weight, but she seemed too quiet, too listless. She still cried for long periods, but more often she slept – a deep, unnatural sleep that frightened me. Sometimes I picked her up, giving her a little shake to waken her, terrified that she had stopped breathing.

'You will make yourself ill again if you go on this way,' Kate said to me. 'Stop fretting, Jenny. You are really being very foolish. I cannot understand you. You are normally so sensible.'

I was hurt by her attitude and could not be comforted. I was haunted by my fears for Julia . . . that she was going to die.

'Oh, please don't let me lose her, too,' I prayed as I stood by her cot night after night. 'Don't let her die . . . let her be strong and well.'

Philip came to visit me almost every day. He knew I had been ill, but he did not understand why I was so unlike myself.

'You are exhausted,' he said to me one morning when he found me alone in my small parlour staring into space. 'This isn't like you, Jenny. Won't you tell me what is wrong?'

'I am worried about Julia. She isn't well.'

'But Kate told me she is putting on weight at last. There is something more. Why won't you tell me? I thought you trusted me. I thought we were friends.'

'We are. Of course we are,' I said, 'but I cannot tell you, Philip. You have no right to ask it of me.'

'No right?'

He looked at me from puzzled, slightly angry eyes. I had shut him out, because I knew he was going to marry Margaret. I must not let myself rely on him too much. I wanted to confide in him, to tell him about the fears that haunted me, but I could not. I had to learn to live alone. Kate had begun to be impatient with me, and Philip would no longer come to visit me so often when he married. I had to find the strength to guard and protect my child myself.

'I am taking Margaret and her mother to my house in Cornwall for Christmas,' he said at last. 'I had thought of asking you and Kate to come but—'

'No,' I said hastily. 'I could not think of exposing Julia

to a change of air yet. She is not well enough to travel all that way.'

'Perhaps what she needs is to get out in the air more, Jenny. Perhaps she is being coddled too much.'

'How can you say such a thing?' I rounded on him like a tigress in defence of her cub. Angry, unreasonable, unjust. 'Please do not interfere, Philip. I know what is best for my child.'

'I did not mean to imply otherwise.' He looked at me sadly, as if he were hurt and could not understand my moods. 'You are overtired,' he said. 'Be careful, my dear. If you go on this way you will collapse.'

I turned away from him, tears stinging my eyes. 'Please – I would rather be alone . . .'

'Of course. You are weary. Forgive me, Jenny.'

It was so hard not to weep, so hard not to beg him to take me in his arms and cry out all my pain and fear on his shoulder . . . but I let him go without another word.

After he had gone I wept harsh, bitter tears that came from deep inside me. It was not like me to be so rude. Yet it was not just because I was tired and anxious for Julia. I felt so low. It was not like me. Even after Gérard's death, I had not felt so . . . I searched for the word . . . depressed. Yes, that described my feelings perfectly. I felt as if I were being squeezed tighter and tighter into a small space and that if I could not escape my head would burst.

The doctor had described it as a lowering of spirits, but it was much, much worse. I knew that I was foolish to give way to my fears, and I scolded myself – but I could not help it.

I had to pull myself free of this shadow that clouded my mind. I knew that I must learn to stand alone . . . not to rely on Philip. It would not be long before his engagement to Margaret Lancaster was announced and then I would lose him. Little by little, she would drive a wedge between us. No woman would tolerate her husband's friendship with another woman – not the kind of intimate, caring friendship that I had known with Philip.

I was already driving him away myself!

Foolish, foolish Jenny. I tried to tell myself that I could manage without Philip. I had Kate and Marie and Susanna . . . but I loved Philip. The realisation hit me quite suddenly, leaving me stunned, bewildered. When had it happened? When had friendship turned to love? It did not matter. It was too late. I had refused his generous offer of marriage and he would not ask again.

My heart was heavy as I went upstairs. Philip would have been such a comfort to me. If only I had been able to confide my fears in him . . . to tell him of my desperate love for Julia, a love that had only intensified since her birth.

If only . . .

A scream from the direction of the nursery brought me sharply from my reverie. As I ran down the landing towards Julia's room my heart was racing wildly. Had she stopped breathing? Was she dying? I could hear raised voices. It sounded as though there was a terrible argument going on.

When I burst into the nursery I saw that Kate and Marie were struggling together, embroiled in a desperate fight. It looked as if they were fighting over possession of a small bottle containing some dark liquid.

'What are you doing?' I demanded. 'What is going on here? Stop this! Stop it this instant!'

'She was trying to harm Julia,' Marie cried. 'I warned you not to trust her . . . over and over again. You would not listen – but I warned you.'

'She's lying,' Kate said. 'You cannot believe her, Jenny?'

I stared at them both as a terrible suspicion entered my mind. Had one of them given Julia something to make her ill? Was that why she seemed so lethargic all the time?

'What is in that bottle?'

Kate had it in her hand now. I remembered that Henriette had accused her of leaving the laudanum near Béatrix's bedside, and in my distress, I could not help what I said next.

'What have you done to my child?'

The colour left her face. She looked hurt, disbelieving. 'You cannot believe I would harm your child? Jenny . . .'

I was silent, remembering all Marie's warnings – and the fact that Béatrix de Arnay had changed her will in Kate's favour only a week before she died. The suspicions went round and round in my mind, driving me mad. Had Kate left that bottle within Béatrix's reach so that Laurent would be free to marry her? And had she used laudanum to quieten my child?

'It wasn't me, Jenny,' Kate said, as I did not answer her first plea. 'You said yourself that it was odd that only Marie could quiet her. She has been giving her this – some foul concoction of her own, no doubt.'

'Why . . . why would she do that?'

'To make you more dependent on her, perhaps?' Kate's eyes mirrored her hurt. 'Do you really believe that I would harm your child, Jenny? I caught her giving this stuff to Julia. I suspect it has opium in it. It smells much like the medicine Béatrix used to help her sleep.'

How could I know which of them was lying? I turned my gaze from Kate to Marie and saw the fear and guilt in her eyes and suddenly I knew. I knew without doubt. 'It *was* you, Marie. You have been poisoning my child. How could you! Why . . . why have you done this terrible thing?'

'It is not poison,' she said. 'You cannot believe I would harm her. It was just to stop her crying, to make her sleep . . . so that you would not worry. *Grand-mère* often used it, so did the other women when they needed to keep their children quiet while they worked. It is not harmful in small doses. I did it for you, Jenny, because you had been through so much . . . for you. Only for you . . .'

'You have been drugging my child for my sake? How dare you! Don't you realise that I have been out of my mind with worry over her? Thinking that she was backward in some way . . .' A wave of anger swept over me. I wanted to strike out at her, to hurt her. 'You disgust me. I can hardly believe that you would be so wicked. So stupid!'

She seemed to crumble and wilt before my eyes.

'It was for you,' she whimpered. 'I only wanted to help you – just as I tried to help your *maman*. You said Adele wasn't poisoned . . . that she died of an inherited weakness. I only wanted to ease her . . . to make her rest better. I didn't want her to die . . . I didn't want her to die.'

For a moment I was too distraught, too concerned for my child to realise what she was saying. Then I suddenly understood. She had always insisted that Mama's death was not natural . . . *because she believed that she herself had poisoned her*. When Marie insisted that Mama had taken her own life, and that she had done so because of a letter that had upset her, it was because she wanted so desperately to find proof of someone else's guilt – because she could not bear her own.

Now I understood Marie's fixation with the letters, her belief that Mama had killed herself . . . It was all to cover her own guilt, to convince herself that she had not really contributed to the death of a woman she had truly loved. For she *had* loved Mama. And she must have suffered the torments of Hell since her death.

This was what Gérard had tried to warn me of in my dreams!

Julia was awake and crying. Kate hesitated, then, seeing I was too stunned to move, picked her up to comfort her.

'You gave Mama something,' I said, looking at Marie. 'Didn't you? You poisoned her with your foul mixtures – just as you were poisoning my baby.'

'It was supposed to help her . . . for the pain,' Marie whimpered, tears starting to her eyes. '*Grand-mère* gave it to me. It is not harmful unless you take too much. I would never have harmed Adele. I loved her. I wasn't hurting Julia . . .

only helping her. You must believe me, Jenny. I would never harm her.'

'You should send for the police,' Kate said. 'She could have killed Julia. Goodness knows what damage she has already done.'

'She did not intend to kill,' I said, 'but she must go. I cannot bear to have her near me or Julia again.'

'Jenny . . .' Marie gave a cry of despair. She fell to her knees in front of me, wringing her hands, tears running down her cheeks. 'Forgive me. I beg you. Do not send me away. I will do nothing you do not wish. I beg you to pardon me.'

She looked so desperate, so pitiful, but my heart had turned to stone. I was angry, cold, unfeeling. She might have killed my child and deserved no pity from me.

'You will leave this house now – as soon as you have packed your things.' I turned to Kate and took Julia in my arms. 'See that she has money – her fare to France and six months' wages. You will find sufficient in my dressing case. Please take her away now. I never want to see or speak to her again.'

I turned my back on Marie, rocking Julia in my arms as she cried, a long, thin wail that tore at my heart. To think that Marie had been giving her opium to stop her crying . . . It was evil, wicked! No wonder her sleep had seemed so unnatural.

'Come on,' I heard Kate say behind me. 'Stop that snivelling, you wretch. If I had my way they would lock you in a cell and throw away the key. Think yourself lucky Jenny has such a soft heart.'

Marie had lapsed into French – perhaps because she thought Kate would not understand her – and she cursed and pleaded with me in turn as Kate dragged her forcibly from the nursery. I would not look at her. What a fool I had been to keep her in my household. All my friends had warned me of her obsessive nature. I had known her jealousy was beyond all reason, but I could never have suspected that she would drug my child simply to make me think I could not manage without her.

What kind of a person would do something like that? I believed that her motives in giving my mother the drug had been purely selfless – she had tried to help her. But perhaps Mama had come to rely too much on the drug . . . perhaps like Béatrix she had taken an overdose without meaning to. I would never know the truth. I was sure that Marie's fear of having contributed to Mama's death had played on her mind ever since. To such an extent that she had become slightly deranged? Surely no one in their right mind would give such a dangerous medicine to a newly born child! It was a miracle that Julia had not died.

She had finally quietened but I was afraid to put her back in her cot . . . afraid to let go of her for a moment in case something happened to her. My poor darling little girl. My heart ached as I thought of her suffering, of what she must still suffer. How could Marie have done such a wicked, wicked thing to her?

I was still sitting in a nursing chair by the window when Kate came back to me more than an hour later.

'How is she?'

'She seems to be resting.'

'She may be addicted to that disgusting stuff,' Kate said, looking angry. 'I've heard of unscrupulous women using it before. Once, when I was going to leave Louise with a woman who ran a baby farm, I discovered that she used it to keep other babies in her charge quiet and I took Louise elsewhere. It is a terrible thing to do, but I can only think that Marie did not realise the harm she could cause. You must have seen she was not really intelligent. By making her your companion, you tried to make her into something she wasn't – and she was afraid you would dismiss her because she could not be like your other friends.'

'Yes, I see that I have been partly to blame,' I admitted. 'But I cannot believe she would harm my baby.'

'She may not have intended to harm Julia. We shall probably have some weeks of restless nights with her, Jenny, but perhaps no lasting harm has been done. It might be a good idea to speak to your doctor.'

'Yes, I shall ask him to call tomorrow,' I said. I glanced up at her. 'Forgive me for questioning you at first, Kate. I was so shocked, so confused. The bottle was in your hand and I could not think clearly. Tell me, did you suspect Marie . . . before you caught her?'

'I suspected something. Julia's sleep wasn't natural – and I knew the effects of opium.' Kate's eyes were dark with remembered grief. 'I have never told you this, Jenny, but my mother became dependent on laudanum when she was very ill. In those last few months before her death she changed . . . becoming confused, difficult . . . even violent at times. Sometimes she would fly at me in rage and accuse me of deliberately keeping her in pain. She demanded more and more of the drug but I had been warned not to let her have it – but she was dying anyway and when the end came I was almost glad. Glad that she would not suffer any more, and that I should not have to watch her.'

'Oh, Kate,' I said. 'No wonder you were so restless and unhappy when you first came to the convent.'

'I meant it when I said I did not know what I should have done without you, Jenny. You were always my one true friend and I loved you – that's why I came here to this house. Laurent had always distrusted Marie. He believed Adele had become too dependent on her towards the last – that is why he dismissed her.'

'He asked you to come here, to keep a watch over me?'

'Yes, after I told him Marie was with you. He became alarmed for your safety. I thought he was being over-protective. Like you, I could not imagine that Marie would actually harm you. Then, when Julia seemed drugged, I wondered . . . but at first could not believe that Marie would do such an irresponsible thing. I decided to watch her. I saw her put something into her pocket as she left her own room earlier this morning and I followed her to the nursery. She put a few drops of the stuff on a spoon and was about to put it in Julia's mouth when I grabbed it from her.'

'Thank God you discovered what she was doing before it was too late.' I looked at her anxiously. 'Do you think she *has* harmed Julia?'

'I doubt that there is lasting harm – but we must be prepared for her to cry a lot. Opium-based medicines *are* addictive, Jenny. My mother was not the only one to suffer from the effects: Béatrix had been using one for years. She needed more and more to help her sleep and she had terrible nightmares if she was forced to go without.'

If the drug had such powerful effects on adults, it must be even worse for a tiny child. I was horrified.

'How could Marie have given such a drug to a baby? How could anyone do such a thing?'

'I do not know, Jenny. I think she is a little mad – she must be.'

'Has she gone?' I shuddered. My anger had abated a little but I was still shocked and distressed that she could have done such a terrible, wicked thing.

'Yes – and the staff have instructions never to let her near you or Julia again. I have told them that they are to send for the police if she tries to enter this house.'

'Oh, Kate . . .' I choked back a sob as Julia awoke and began to cry pitifully. 'I should have sent her away long ago. If anything happens to my child . . .'

'Julia is strong,' Kate said. 'Give her to me for a while, Jenny. We shall take it in turns to nurse her through this. She will be well again – I promise you. She is not going to let this defeat her, are you, my precious? She's a brave little mite . . . just like her mother.'

I watched as she put Julia to her shoulder, patting her back as she began to walk about the nursery, shushing her cries, which were becoming ever more frantic.

'I pray you are right,' I said. 'Oh, Kate . . . you must be right!'

Thirteen

During those tortured days and nights that Kate and I spent watching over Julia we became closer than we had ever been before, even during our schooldays. She told me more about her mother's illness and of the terrible time when she had been left alone and friendless in Portsmouth . . . when she had been forced to earn her money as a prostitute until she could buy her passage on a ship to France. And she told me something I had suspected but not dared to believe.

'I shall go back to France when Julia is better. And I think I may marry Laurent.' She looked at me uncertainly. 'I believe he truly cares for me – and he needs me. He has been so lonely since he lost your mother. I know I can never replace her in his heart, but we can be companions, lovers. He asked me to marry him before I left the chateau, but I wasn't ready to decide. I wanted to tell you before, Jenny, but I wasn't sure how you would feel. I do not want to upset you – or make you feel I had betrayed you. If you had not been able to forgive him, I should not have married him.'

'I am glad you have found someone you can care for,' I said. 'I have forgiven Laurent, and I hope you will both be happy.'

'I had nothing to do with Béatrix's death,' Kate said. 'At first I wondered if Laurent had left that bottle there deliberately, but he swears he did not – and now I think she must have had a key to the cabinet herself. Perhaps she persuaded her maid Flore to get it for her. I do not know why she should have taken her own life – I can only think that she must simply have tired of living.'

Flore had been devoted to her mistress. She had guarded the comtesse like a dragon, and I believed the mystery was solved. Flore would have done whatever Béatrix wanted – even if what she planned to do was a sin.

'I am sure that was Béatrix's reason. Had I not been carrying Julia, I might have taken my own life after Gérard died. Besides, Laurent would never have helped her to kill herself. Had he wanted her dead, he would have divorced her years ago and married my mother,' I said and explained what he had told me about his wife's threats. I embraced Kate. 'You must forget about it now and be happy.'

I thought for a moment of Henriette, who had loved Laurent, and I was sad for her. But perhaps now that Béatrix was dead, she would leave the chateau and begin a new life for herself and her son.

Julia had begun to cry again. I picked her up, held her to my breast and kissed the top of her head and the soft down of her hair, which was growing redder every day.

I was happy for Kate and Laurent, but my child was ill. I felt that she was vulnerable. My mother had inherited a weakness from her father – what might Julia have inherited through mine? A tiny fear nagged at the back of my mind, a fear I did not even wish to name because it was too horrible to face.

For how many days and nights did Kate and I share our vigil over my poor, tormented baby? I could not tell one day from another and hardly knew when Christmas came and went, despite all the cards and visits from people who came to share my anxiety and my grief.

'What a wicked girl she was to do this to your child,' Susanna wrote to me – she was herself confined to bed after the birth of her own twin daughters. 'I never liked her, Jenny, and now I wish I had spoken out . . .'

*   *   *

Philip called to see me when he returned from Cornwall. Kate had written to him, telling him what had happened, and he was full of concern for me and my child.

'Have you had the doctor to see her?' he asked. 'What did he say?'

'That she will suffer from having the drug withdrawn for a while but should not be permanently damaged.' I smiled at him. 'She is getting better, Philip . . . but it takes time. She was such a little thing to be given such a terrible drug, though the doctor believes Marie could only have given her tiny doses.'

'It is a wonder she did not die!' he said, looking angry. 'I warned you to be careful of that woman. You should have listened to me – and you should have had her arrested. While she remains free she could be a danger to someone else.'

'Please do not be cross with me,' I pleaded. 'You do not know how I have regretted our last quarrel.'

'I was not aware that we had quarrelled.' He looked at me oddly. 'Have I offended you in some way?'

'No, of course not. I was harsh to you when you were last here . . . but I was so worried about Julia.'

'And with good cause, it seems.'

'Julia was not improving as she ought,' I said, 'but that was not all. Philip, there is something I must tell you – something you may find shocking . . .'

'I knew you were fretting over something,' he said, his eyes intent on my face. 'Please tell me, Jenny.'

He listened in silence as I told him what had been playing on my mind since I had read Mama's letter telling me I was not Laurent's child.

'So you see, there is a possibility that Robbie and I might share the same father,' I said. 'It was foolish of me, I know – but when Julia was so strange, I wondered . . .'

'If she might be mentally retarded, like Robbie?'

I looked for horror or disgust in his eyes and saw nothing but sympathy and understanding.

'No wonder you were half out of your mind with grief,' he said. 'You should have told me at once. We could have talked . . . eased your mind. I would have fetched the book from Anne's if you had asked. You must have known that, Jenny?'

'I have been afraid of what I might find.'

'What nonsense is this? It is not like you to shrink from the truth, Jenny. You must know it is better to face up to it – whatever it is.' He gave me a searching look. 'It cannot change you or what you are. And there is no reason why Julia should be retarded. I mean this, Jenny! There are many reasons why Robbie might have been the way he was, and most of them are not hereditary. You have been ill, and for a long time you were suffering from grief – and you have allowed your fears to prey on your mind. Now you must put all this out of your mind and look forward. Promise me?'

He cupped my chin in his hand, making me look up at him. I felt his strength flow into me and my doubts seemed to fall from my shoulders like a heavy cloak I had cast away.

'How do you always manage to make me feel better?' I asked, smiling through the tears that stung my eyes. 'Oh, Philip, I have missed you these past weeks – I shall miss you so much when you leave me . . .' I stopped and could not go on as the emotion rose in my throat to choke me.

'I shall be in London for several weeks now,' he said. 'And now that Margaret and her mother have returned to Italy, I shall be able to spend more time with you. I was duty-bound to look after them while they were here, and I cannot pretend it was always a pleasure.'

'Margaret has returned to Italy?' I stared at him in surprise. 'But I thought . . . I mean, she said . . .' I flushed as he stared at me.

'What did you think, Jenny?' He saw the flush in my cheeks

and frowned. 'Good Lord! You did not imagine . . . What did Margaret say to you when she visited you?'

'It does not matter.' I turned away in confusion, my heart racing wildly. 'I was mistaken . . .'

Philip was not in love with her! He was not going to marry her! A black cloud had suddenly lifted, halving the load I had been carrying, and I realised how much I had dreaded his marriage.

Philip caught my arm, swinging me back to face him. He was very alert, his eyes bright and searching as he looked into my face long and hard.

'Did she tell you I was going to ask her to be my wife?'

I knew that I must tell him.

'She . . . she said that she might have good news in the spring or perhaps sooner . . . that she wanted to be on good terms with all your friends, because it might otherwise be awkward for her.'

'And you believed her?'

'Why should you not marry?' I asked, hardly daring to look at him. 'I would have tried to be happy for you, Philip . . .'

'Would it have hurt you to see me wed to another?' he asked, his voice suddenly hoarse. His hold tightened on my arm until it became almost painful. I held back my cry. He gave me an impatient look, shaking me so that I met his demanding gaze. 'Would you have minded, Jenny? Tell me truthfully.'

'I should have been . . . I should have missed you,' I whispered. 'I have often wished . . .'

'What have you wished, Jenny?'

'You know . . . you must know.'

'How should I, if you will not tell me?' He was determined to make me speak plainly. 'Is it that you have changed your mind . . . that you would consent to be my wife if I were to ask again?'

I nodded, my throat too tight to speak.

'Say it, Jenny. I want to hear you say it.'

217

'When I was in labour I wished that you were with me to hold my hand and laugh at me . . . to make me laugh at myself,' I said in a voice that was little more than a whisper. 'I have longed for you so many times, Philip. When I could not tell you about Julia and we quarrelled, it was the worst moment of my life. I wanted you to hold me . . . to make me safe in your arms . . . to make us both safe.'

'Why, Jenny? You must have known that I would always be your friend . . . that I am always ready to come if you need me.' His eyes seemed to burn into me, demanding, compelling me to open my heart to him.

'That is not enough for me,' I confessed, my cheeks burning. 'I want to be with you – I want to be your wife, Philip . . . if you will have me, because . . . because I care for you. I need you.'

'My sweet, lovely Jenny,' he said and put a finger to my lips. 'Foolish, foolish girl. I never once considered marriage to Margaret. Did you imagine that I would settle for a cold beauty when I had seen you? Did you not understand? Did you not know it was you I wanted as my wife? I was prepared to wait, my dearest – until you were ready to be happy again.'

The dark clouds were parting, lifting the heavy burden of grief that had almost overwhelmed me these past weeks. For the first time since Julia's birth, I felt truly well again. And it was Philip who had given me the strength to face whatever was hidden between the covers of the book Mama had given me.

'I think I could be happy with you,' I said softly. 'I know that it is a lot to ask of you . . . Julia . . .'

He silenced me with a gentle, loving kiss that made me melt into his arms. I loved the familiar smell of him, the comfort of being close to him. Philip was so strong, so steadfast and dependable – a rock to cling to in times of trouble. I looked up at him when he released me and reached out to stroke the line of my cheek.

'Julia is *our* child,' he said. 'She will be my daughter as much as yours and we shall have other children so that she is never lonely – she will be loved and cherished always. Even if she was not as perfect as we could wish, she would be protected and cared for – but I know that your fears are groundless, my love. She is beautiful, and quite perfect.'

'How wise you are, Philip.' I sighed and smiled, knowing that whatever might happen in the future I would be strong enough to face it with him. 'How soon can we be married?'

'Just as soon as it can be arranged,' he promised. 'But first I think I should take you down to Cornwall. You can stay with Anne. She is anxious to see her great-grandchild – and you will be safer there.'

'Safer? What do you mean?'

He frowned. 'Only that I think Marie may try to see you. I would prefer that you and Julia were out of her reach.'

'You do not think that she would try to harm either of us? Oh, Philip! She is not so evil. I am sure she meant to help – she was misguided, but not wicked.'

'I think she had become slightly deranged,' he said, his mouth drawing into a hard line. 'If I had been here, I should have made sure she could be of no further danger to you.'

I could see that he had set himself against her. I knew that what he said made sense, but in my heart I felt that I had been a little unfair to Marie. She had not meant to harm either my mother or my child. I had sent her away in anger and I would never want her to live in my house again, but I should have liked to see her once more . . . to tell her that I had found it possible to forgive her.

'Listen to me, my darling,' Philip said, tipping my chin once more so that I looked up at him. 'Marie is dangerous. You must promise me that you will not see her if she tries to contact you.'

'Very well,' I said. 'You know best, Philip. Kate says that I am too soft-hearted, too forgiving – and perhaps she is right. You are both right. Besides, I am sure that Marie has gone back to France. Why should she stay here?

She never really liked this country. She only stayed for my sake.'

I could see that Philip was not convinced. He believed that Marie was a mad, bad woman and nothing would change him.

'I shall go and tell Kate that we are to be married,' I said when at last he was ready to leave me. 'I think she wants to go back to Paris . . . to Laurent. She loves him despite his faults, and I think she might be his salvation. She was reluctant to leave me, but now that Julia is getting better . . . now that I have you, she will feel able to go on with her own life.'

'We shall invite my old nanny to come and help you with Julia,' Philip said. 'She will guard her like a dragon – but she is kind and clever and our little girl could not be in safer hands.'

'Thank you,' I said and smiled up at him as he kissed me once more. 'I shall rest easier for knowing Julia is being cared for by someone you trust, Philip.'

'You will like Nanny,' he promised, looking down at me lovingly. He stroked my cheek with the tips of his fingers. 'And now, my dearest, I must go. We shall leave the day after tomorrow for Cornwall . . . and then we shall be married and I shall take you to my home.'

I kissed him once more before he left, and then I went upstairs to tell my friend the news.

Kate was preparing to leave. Her trunks had been sent ahead to Dover and Laurent had arranged all the details of her journey. He had been to see me the previous day, to say goodbye and wish me happiness for the future.

'I am so pleased that you will have Philip to take care of you,' Laurent said. 'But you must visit us in Paris sometimes, Jenny. You will allow me to see Julia now and then?'

'Of course.' I kissed his cheek. 'You must visit us in Cornwall whenever you wish. Kate is my dearest friend – and I wish you both all the happiness in the world.'

And now Kate was leaving. She came downstairs to the parlour wearing a smart blue cloth travelling gown with a little fur-trimmed jacket and a dashing hat decorated with veiling and feathers.

'You look lovely in that dress, Kate.'

'Laurent chose it for me.'

'He always had good taste.'

'Yes, I know.' She kissed me goodbye and then hugged me, the sparkle of tears in her eyes. 'You know I would not leave you if I thought you needed me?'

'I know.' I smiled at her. She was my first real friend and I loved her dearly. 'I shall miss you, but Julia is getting stronger – and Nanny Simpkins has promised to come to us when we are settled in Cornwall. You should think of yourself now.'

'And you have Philip.' She looked long and hard into my face. 'You are happy now, aren't you, Jenny?'

'Yes . . . perfectly happy.'

'I am glad.'

'And you?' I asked. 'Do you love Laurent? Really love him?'

'I wasn't sure at first – I needed time to consider. But now I am sure. After I was so badly hurt, I did not think I would ever care for a man again.' She laughed at herself. 'What fools we women are!'

I laughed and hugged her. 'Be happy, dear Kate – and write to me often.'

'Of course. We shall meet sometimes. You must take care of yourself, dearest Jenny.'

After Kate had gone, I decided to visit Susanna. She could not come to me and it would be some time before we would see each other again. Besides, I needed to get out for a while; I had been shut up in the house too long.

I gave instructions that Julia was never to be left alone. One of the maids or her nurse would remain in the nursery at all times until I returned. She was better than she had been and, after her nurse had fed her, would sleep for some hours – though she was often still fretful throughout the night.

It was a cold, bright January day, but Susanna's house was only two streets away and I could walk there easily. Dressed warmly, with a fur tippet about my neck, I enjoyed the crisp bite of the air and the exercise.

I stopped to watch a brass band playing in the street. Children were marching behind, laughing with excitement. People were out shopping, laden with parcels, the streets crowded and busy. Suddenly, I was beginning to recover my spirits, to shake off the deep slough of despair that had hung over me for so long. It was so good to be alive!

Susanna was delighted to see me, kissing me as I deposited my gifts on the table beside her. I found her lying on a sofa piled with soft cushions in her dressing room. She was permitted to get out of bed now, though not yet strong enough to come downstairs. She rang for the nurse, who brought her two sweet daughters for me to see.

'They are beautiful,' I said, exclaiming over them. 'Henry was right, wasn't he? What are you going to call them?'

'Jennifer and Sarah,' she said, touching the face of the smaller twin. 'This is your namesake. I should like you to be her godmother when the time comes, Jenny.'

'I should like that. And you will be Julia's?' I asked.

'Yes, of course.' Her eyes went over me anxiously. 'You look thin, Jenny, and tired. 'How are you, really?'

'Much better . . . honestly.'

She nodded. 'And so you are going to marry Philip?' She looked very pleased with herself, as though it had all been her idea.

'Yes. He was generous enough to ask me again and I have accepted. I hope I shall be able to make him as happy as he deserves to be. He has been so good to me.'

'What nonsense!' she scolded teasingly. 'He loves you, Jenny – and I think you love him, don't you?'

'Yes, I do.'

'I could not be more delighted, my dear.'

'I should like you to come to the wedding.'

'Try keeping me away,' she declared. 'In another week I shall be on my feet again and ready for anything.'

'I think we shall marry at the beginning of March. It will give Philip a chance to arrange everything. He will have to let my present house and we want to marry in church . . . if possible.'

'You think there may be some awkwardness because of the child?' I nodded and she frowned. 'Philip will arrange it. Don't worry, Jenny. I know the church frowns on women who have had a child out of wedlock, but these things can be overcome. Philip will manage it if it's what you want, my dear.'

'Yes,' I said with a smile. 'I truly believe he will.'

I was thoughtful as I walked home. The sky had clouded over and it was almost dark, despite being only three o'clock in the afternoon. I saw a newspaper boy selling the late edition. I stopped to buy a paper from him, frowning as I read the headline – 'Twelve Retailers Prosecuted for Selling Beer Containing Arsenic' – and a little shudder ran through me. Marie could so easily have poisoned my child.

Before I left her house, Susanna had told me that her husband believed he had seen Marie in the street outside my house as he'd driven by in a hansom cab one morning.

'Outside my house?'

'Don't look so alarmed, Jenny,' she said. 'I thought I ought to mention it, but Henry wasn't absolutely sure it was her. He may have been mistaken. Besides, what harm could she possibly do to you or Julia? Your servants have been warned not to let her into the house, haven't they?'

'Yes. She is never left alone. In any case, I do not really think she would harm her. I was just surprised. I had thought she would go back to France immediately.'

As I hurried the last few steps to my house I had a sense of being watched and glanced over my shoulder. For a moment I thought I saw the outline of a woman's shape in the shadows at the far corner of the street, but then it had gone.

'Marie . . .' I called as an icy shiver trailed down my spine. 'Is it you? Are you there?'

There was no answer, of course. It was my imagination. Marie would not follow me – why should she? Marie would not stand in the street and stare up at my house. There was no need to be anxious . . . no need to fear for my child's safety.

Besides, we were leaving for Cornwall the next day. I would soon be with my grandmother – and Nanny Simpkins would be in charge of the nursery. There was nothing to worry about. Of course there wasn't!

I ran inside the house and straight up to the nursery. Julia's nurse had just finished feeding her and was about to put her back in her cot. Milly was clearing away a tray of tea. They had obviously been having a pleasant chat together over the teacups. Everything was normal, just as it should be.

And yet I had an uneasy feeling . . . a feeling that something terrible was going to happen. Perhaps Philip had been right after all – perhaps Marie was out there somewhere, watching and waiting.

The journey to Cornwall was uneventful. Julia's wet nurse accompanied us. She would stay for a few months until the child was weaned on to other foods and then return to her home in London.

It was a sadness to me that I was unable to feed my baby, but I knew it had happened to other women before me; it was not a failure on my part – and Julia's nurse had already weaned her own child but still had a flow of rich milk, on which my child was beginning to thrive.

Since Marie's departure, Milly had taken on the position of my personal maid. She was efficient and helpful, and I had decided to take her to Cornwall with me. She had never seen the sea before and was excited at the prospect. Philip's manservant was also travelling with us.

So there were five adults and two children in the first-class carriage that Philip had reserved for us. Julia's nurse could not be parted from her own son, nor would I have asked it of her.

'Anne's house will be overflowing,' Philip said to me with a wry smile, 'so I shall take rooms at the inn to be near you.'

'Will you be comfortable there?' I asked. 'Why don't you go home, Philip? I shall be safe enough at my grandmother's – and you can visit whenever you wish.'

His estate was about ten miles inland from Grandmother's home, near enough for him to come every day if he chose.

'I suppose I ought to give instructions at home – to make sure everything is in readiness for you and Julia.' He looked at me thoughtfully. 'As you say, you will be safe enough at Anne's house. And Nanny will be waiting for you at the Manor. I shall come back to you by the end of the week. And soon I shall take you home.' He smiled at me. 'I have often pictured you there, Jenny. It will be such a pleasure to have you there at last.'

'I am looking forward to seeing my new home.'

We should be settled at Allington Manor. Since leaving France I had moved from house to house and I was growing weary of it; I would be glad to be settled, to put down roots and make a home for us all.

Philip spent most of the journey telling me about his home, which had been built originally in the time of Queen Anne and was very old, very beautiful and had been in his family for centuries.

'I think you will love the house,' he told me. 'And the gardens. Some of the grounds were a little neglected towards the end of my grandfather's time, but I hope to restore them. I have a large library and the task of cataloguing all the books will be a lifetime's work – something we can share, Jenny.'

The more he talked, the more sure I became that I should be happy at his home. There were large grounds and perhaps I could find a place to create the garden of my dreams.

Before we knew it, we had arrived at the station of Breckon Ridge. We were a noisy, merry party as we got down from the train, reminding each other not to leave umbrellas, papers and books behind. Philip and his valet were busy sorting out all the various trunks and bags and arranging for transportation, and it was a few moments before I became aware of the eyes watching me.

Swinging round, I saw that Robbie's father was at the door of the station house, just staring at me with dark, intent eyes. He was wearing his uniform and I realised he must have returned to his job, despite all the gossip and speculation that he had been pensioned off after his son was taken away.

I sensed hostility in him towards me, though when Philip summoned him to help with the luggage, he touched his cap politely and appeared friendly.

'Back to stay with Mrs Ruston then, Miss Heron?'

'Yes,' I said, feeling a flicker of unease as I met his leering gaze. 'Yes, just for a while.'

Why was he staring at me in that way? It made me uncomfortable, and I knew that the time had come to discover the secret that lay between the covers of Mama's book. If it was this man who had raped my mother, it was best to have it out in the open at last.

No more secrets. No more lies.

'Come along, Jenny.'

Philip came to take my arm. He looked hard at the stationmaster, making him turn away.

I clung gratefully to his arm. He had arranged for two carriages to meet us – he and I went with Julia in the first, leaving the others to follow.

It had begun to rain, and I was reminded of the storm that had soaked me the first time I came to my grandmother's house. But this time I was travelling in Philip's carriage –

protected from the rain which had begun to sweep in from the sea. I looked across at the man who was so soon to be my husband and smiled.

'I am thankful to be out of London,' he said, raising my hand to kiss it. 'Within six weeks we shall be married and then I can look after you properly.'

'I'm so happy, Philip. I feel as if a dark cloud has been lifted from my life . . . that I can look forward to the future.'

'Nothing will harm you now,' he promised. 'I was anxious for you in London but you will be safe enough here . . .'

Grandmother was excited to see her great-granddaughter. She asked to hold her, and the joy in her face as Julia opened her eyes and looked at her was something I should never forget.

It was good to know that all the hurt and pain of the past had at last been put aside. A terrible thing had happened to my mother in this village, and, because of the horror it had created in her mind, she had never been able to return. Upstairs, the truth awaited me, but first I must allow my grandmother to meet her great-granddaughter.

'How beautiful Julia is,' Grandmother said. 'Very like your own dear mother was as a baby – but she has your hair, Jenny.'

'Oh, my poor daughter,' I cried, laughing. 'Do not say so, Grandmama! My hair has been the bane of my life. I can do nothing with it.'

'Your hair is lovely.' She turned to Philip, asking for his support. 'Jenny has lovely hair, hasn't she, Philip?'

'Jenny is beautiful all together,' he said, with a smile. 'I like the way her hair curls about her face. She should wear it loose instead of trying to confine it.'

'I should look like a gypsy,' I cried.

'Yes.' He nodded agreement. 'But it would suit you.'

I shook my head at him, my cheeks pink as I saw the warmth in his eyes. I had never been sure just why Philip had asked me to be his wife. I knew he was fond of me, that we got on well together and would be comfortable together . . . but did he love me passionately?

I had known passionate love. I cared for Philip very much – but was I in love with him the way I had been with Gérard?

The kisses he had given me so far had all been gentle, tender caresses that made no demands of me. But surely he would expect something very different from me when we were married?

'What are you thinking?' he asked when we were alone in the parlour a little later. 'I know you have something on your mind. I can always tell. Is something worrying you, Jenny?'

I shook my head. 'Nothing . . . I was only thinking that I am happy, Philip.'

'That's what I want you to be.' He ran a gentle finger down my cheek. 'Don't worry, Jenny. There's no hurry for anything. We have plenty of time . . . plenty of time.'

There was time for Philip and I to get to know one another, all the rest of our lives – but for me the time had come when I must face up to my past. I could no longer ignore what I knew was waiting for me, and I took the book of poems Mama had given me and ran my hand over its luxurious cover with regret. It seemed sacrilegious to destroy something so beautiful, but it had to be done.

I took a sharp paper knife and carefully slit the side of the cover, peeling it back a little at a time so that the letter inside should not be damaged. When I drew out the single sheet of paper my hand was trembling and my mouth felt dry.

What if Ned Watts was my father?

I unfolded the paper and began to read the words Mama had written there so many years ago, and then I gave a cry of distress.

'How could she lie to me?'

The truth was so shocking that I could hardly believe it. Clutching the letter in my hand, I went along the corridor to the door of my grandmother's bedroom and knocked. She opened it almost at once, her face white as she stared at me in alarm.

'What is wrong, Jenny?' she asked. 'Are you ill? Is something the matter with Julia?'

'Why did you lie to me?' I cried. 'Why did you not tell me the name of the man who raped my mother?'

Her hand crept to her throat, and I could see she was shaken. 'Oh, my dear,' she said. 'Please do not be angry with me. You were so upset – and I thought it did not matter. I was so ashamed . . .'

'Mama was raped by your husband,' I said. 'Max Ruston . . . Oh, how could he? She trusted him . . . liked him.'

Grandmother took my hand, drawing me into her room and closing the door behind us.

'It was my fault,' she said. 'As a child Adele adored Max. He made a great fuss of her, taking her on his knee, petting her – he loved her.'

'How could he have done what he did if he loved her?'

'He was always a womaniser,' Grandmother said, her face working with grief. 'I discovered him with one of the maids soon after we were married. I suppose I would have done better to leave him then, but it was so difficult for a woman to leave her husband in those days. Quite shocking. When Adele was young, it did not seem to matter – it was only after he became aware of her as a woman . . .' Grandmother sighed. 'I warned her to be careful of him, told her what kind of a man he was, and she changed towards him, taking care never to be alone with him – and that made him angry.'

'She says in her letter that he saw her with Laurent . . . that he was jealous and they quarrelled, then he forced himself on her. He hurt her terribly.'

'I know.' Grandmother wiped a tear from the corner of her eye. 'She would not tell me who had done such a terrible thing to her when I asked her – but when Max was dying, he confessed to me. He was in a great deal of pain, and his conscience would not let him rest. After he was dead, I found a letter to Adele amongst his things, and I asked Philip to take it to Paris. It was an abject apology. I believe that he repented of his sinful act towards her, and he wanted her to have some money to compensate for what he had done to her. She accepted the money, for your sake – it was to pay for your school fees, I believe – but she returned the letter unopened. It is still in his room with all his possessions. I have touched nothing since replacing it amongst his things.'

Grandmother went over to her chest of drawers, opened it and took out a key, which she placed in my hand. 'I have kept his rooms locked since he died. I hated him for what he did to Adele. But you have the right to know what kind of a man he was, Jenny. The key is yours if you wish to look through his things . . .'

'He was a gentleman . . . an educated man?'

'Yes, of course.' Grandmother was puzzled. 'Why do you ask?'

'Mama told me my father was an English gentleman,' I said, and returned the key to her. 'If that was the truth, it is all I need to know.'

'And you will try to forgive me for not telling you everything at once? It was to protect you, Jenny – but it was very wrong of me.'

'Lies are always wrong,' I replied. 'They distort things, cause needless distress. Mama told me half-truths, weaving a web of lies to protect me – and they have caused me such pain. Please, Grandmama, never lie to me again.'

'No, of course not – I promise.'

'Then of course I forgive you,' I said and kissed her.

I left her and went to the nursery, bending over Julia's cot to touch her face as she slept. She was so peaceful, so healthy and normal. I could laugh at my fears now.

'I shall never lie to you, my darling,' I whispered. 'You

will always know who your father was – and how much we loved each other.'

So at last the tangled web of lies was unravelled. I had tortured myself too long. Now at last I was free of the shadows that had hung over me . . . free to love again and to be happy.

Fourteen

The news was in all the daily papers. Her Majesty Queen Victoria was dead. She had died on the 23rd of January 1901 at Osbourne, the seaside home she loved; she was eighty-one years old and had been our queen for sixty-three years.

It was the end of an era and the people mourned her.

'It's a sad day,' Grandmother said to me as we drank tea together in the parlour. 'I know she had a long, full life but somehow one thought she would go on forever.'

I thought about the sunny morning when I had seen members of her family driving in the park and of what the woman I had met by chance had said to me that day – 'We shan't see her like again . . . she was an example to all of us.'

Her words were echoed over and over again in the national newspapers and the whole country was in mourning for a much-loved queen.

It was mid-February now and mild for the time of year. The snowdrops and aconites were out in Grandmother's tiny garden, heralding the arrival of an early spring. In another two weeks I should be married.

I had already met Nanny Simpkins; she was an upright woman in her early sixties with white hair, bright eyes and a no-nonsense manner about her. I believed that my child would be safe in her care and I was beginning to feel so much better.

Nanny Simpkins had been delighted with Julia, assuring me that she was doing very well for a premature baby and putting on just the right amount of weight.

'There is nothing to worry about, madam,' she had told me. 'Julia will be perfectly well in my charge.'

Philip had been right to ask her to come and take charge of the nursery. I need have no fears for my daughter now that she was with me.

The days passed pleasantly. I divided my time between Julia and my grandmother, though I looked forward to the future when I would go with Philip to his home. I thought often of being his wife, of the years to come, but for the moment I was content to be with my grandmother.

I had forgiven her for her small lie, and I had come to terms with the past. Max Ruston had done a terrible, wicked thing when he raped a girl he had loved. He had regretted his evil act, and no doubt he had suffered for his sins, but nothing could change what he had done – or the tragic consequences of that act. My mother had never been able to forget or forgive, and, although I believed I could at last put the past behind me, I did not think I should ever want to know more about him than I did now.

And so I spent my days in content – sewing, reading, walking to the village. I began to meet local people who had known Mama as a girl, and had liked her. I gathered their stories as though they were pearls to be treasured.

I was sitting in Grandmother's small parlour when Vera came in that morning. She had been down to the village shop to fetch the papers and letters as she usually did, and I could see by her face that she had something to tell me.

'What is it, Vera?' I asked. 'What have you heard?'

She sat down and I noticed that her hands were trembling.

'They were talking – there was another of those attacks . . . like before.' Her face had gone pale – she looked shocked, distressed. 'But there can't have been . . . How can it have happened again? They locked that boy up and he . . .'

'He killed himself. Yes, I know,' I said. 'He could not bear the thought of being locked away for the rest of his life. You say another girl has been attacked?'

'Yes.' Vera looked at me. 'She was brutally beaten and . . . raped. The odd thing was that the man was supposed to have been wearing Robbie's old coat . . . You don't suppose it was . . . ?' She shook her head. 'No, of course not. It couldn't be . . . could it?'

'Are you thinking what I'm thinking?' She stared at me in silence as I paused to let my words sink in. 'The coat was always too big for Robbie. It hung on him like a sack and probably belonged to his father in the first place.'

'You mean it was him – Ned Watts – all the time? Not Robbie . . . but his father?'

Vera looked horrified as I nodded. She gave a little cry of distress and pressed her fingers to her mouth.

'But that means . . . oh, no! That poor, poor boy . . .' Her eyes filled with tears of pity. 'And I said they should lock him up for good. What a wicked woman I am!'

'No, of course you aren't,' I said. 'It wasn't your fault, Vera. Most people thought as you did.'

'*You* didn't,' she said. 'You saw a man out in the garden – you thought it was him . . . Robbie's father. If we had only listened to you, Jenny . . .'

'I wasn't sure. I thought it might have been the station-master out there that night, but I could not be certain. Even now we have no proof, Vera, unless he is caught in the act of harming someone.'

'It's wicked,' she said. 'Wicked. Someone should do something about it.'

'Philip will be here tomorrow afternoon,' I said. 'We can tell him . . . ask him what he thinks we ought to do.'

I stood staring out at the garden before I went to bed that

night, remembering the way the stationmaster had looked at me the last time I had seen him. Had it been him who stood staring up at my window that night? Was he responsible for the latest attack on a village girl?

I had wondered if he might be my father, but now I knew that it was not so – yet somehow I still felt that these attacks had been precipitated by my arrival in the village. Both of the more serious attacks had happened when I was staying here. I had the oddest feeling that they had something to do with me . . . or the past. What was it the stationmaster had said to me once? '*I remember your mother . . . oh, yes, I remember her right enough.*'

I turned away from the window, pulling the curtains tightly before I undressed. It was foolish to imagine that I was being watched, but the feeling had been growing stronger day by day. Sometimes, recently, as I'd walked back from the village, I had felt I was being observed in a secretive way. I'd sensed some malevolent force near me.

No, no, I was being foolish. No one was out there. I was perfectly safe here and so was my child.

I was up early the next morning. I had found it difficult to sleep. For the first time in weeks I had dreamed of Gérard. He had come to me as I stood in the garden – my special garden.

'Be careful, Jenny,' he had warned. 'The danger is close . . . very close. Danger for you . . . for *you* . . .'

What danger? Surely there could be no danger for me here in my grandmother's house? My child had been in danger for a while, but Marie had gone and any danger that might have threatened us was surely past.

I was a little confused, for I saw no reason for my dream. I was well again and my child was thriving. Philip had been right when he said that perhaps what Julia needed was more fresh air and less coddling. We were both so much better down here in the sweet clean Cornish air.

So what was there to fear? I laughed at myself, dismissing my dream as mere foolishness.

I decided to go for a walk on the beach that morning. There was a fresh wind blowing in from the sea but it was not cold. I needed a long walk to blow the cobwebs from my mind.

I watched the foam-crested waves racing towards the shore, crashing around the spurs of jutting rock. The tang of salt was on my lips, and the pebbles were still wet where they had been washed by the tide. Overhead seabirds whirled and screamed their mournful cries, adding to the sense of fear that just would not leave me.

It was silly to be anxious. Philip would be here soon. My dream was just foolishness. Nothing terrible threatened me. These horrible attacks on young girls could have nothing to do with me.

I spent more than an hour walking on the beach, then, as I turned back towards the steep steps that led up to the garden of Grandmother's house, I saw a woman standing at the top of the cliff looking down at me. I knew her at once and a chill ran down my spine.

Marie . . . it was Marie!

'Marie!' I called up to her, but my words were blown away with the wind. 'Marie . . . wait for me. I am coming up. I want to talk to you . . . to apologise.'

I began to climb hastily. The steps were deeply cut and I could no longer see the top of the cliff. Would she be there when I reached the top? Why had she come here? What was on her mind? Had she come to harm Julia?

I was breathing hard, in a blind panic, my pulses racing. I climbed as quickly as I could. She must wait – I had to speak to her. I had to tell her I was sorry . . . to avoid the tragedy that I was suddenly certain was waiting to happen.

It was our habit to put Julia's pram in the garden for an hour or so if the day was fine. Was it there now? Had Marie touched my child? Had she harmed her? All the old fears crowded in on me, terrifying me.

When I finally reached the top of the cliff I was panting and out of breath. Marie had gone – there was no sign of her. Where was she? Had she gone into the garden or along the narrow path that ran at the edge of the steep cliff?

'Marie . . . Marie!' I called, looking about me frantically. 'Where are you? Oh, where are you?'

'She's gone,' a man's voice said behind me. 'Saw me coming and went off, she did.'

I knew that voice!

I whirled round to find myself staring at the stationmaster. I gasped and my heart began to beat wildly as the fear gripped me. He was wearing the coat that had hung so ridiculously on Robbie, and was staring at me in a way that made icy chills run down my spine.

'What are you doing up here?' I gasped, fighting to recover my breath after the long climb. 'Why did Marie run away? What did you do to her?'

'I never touched her,' he muttered, his eyes glittering. He looked sullen, angry. I sensed a deep resentment in him. 'She weren't the one I were after . . .'

'What do you mean?' My heart was still beating wildly and I felt a shaft of sheer panic. I had no doubt that this was the man who had been attacking young women in the village – and, in a flash of blinding revelation, I realised I was to be his next victim. 'Don't you dare come near me. I'm warning you – you will be in a great deal of trouble if—'

'You're just like her,' he said, ignoring my threat. His nose was running from the cold; he wiped it on the sleeve of his jacket. 'I knew you the first time I set eyes on you – you're her bastard and now you've got a little bastard of your own. Whores, the pair of you!'

'How dare you!'

'I saw her with that Frenchie . . . lying with him in the sand she were . . . kissing him, lettin' him do things to her . . .'

'They were in love,' I said. 'They loved each other all their lives.'

237

'She were beautiful, too, just like you – enough to send a man crazy with wantin' she were. I loved her once,' he went on, a strange, angry look on his face. 'Asked her to walk out with me . . . I were young then and not bad-looking. I didn't have no money, of course, but she used to smile at me as she walked by. Knew I fancied her she did . . . led me on she did . . . Then laughed when I told her I wanted to wed her.'

'You . . . loved my mother?' I stared at him in bewilderment. 'Adele Heron . . . refused your offer of marriage? She laughed at you?'

Suddenly I understood his hatred for my mother – and for me. I remembered the haughty look I had given him that day at the station, and understood why he had been so angry. He thought I had been looking down on him – as my mother had. How the sins of the past come back to haunt us!

'She had the smile of an angel,' he went on as if I hadn't spoken, 'but she were a devil in her heart. I weren't the only one she led on – not by a long chalk. He had her, that Frenchie. I reckon he was the one what had her, but there might have been others.' His eyes honed in on my face. 'I would have wed her even after he went off and left her, but she scorned me, laughed at me . . . I weren't never good enough for her.'

There was both anger and hatred in his eyes. I was shocked by the force of feeling in him. He must have carried his grievance inside him for years, letting it fester and build out of all proportion.

My mother had not meant to hurt him: she laughed at everyone. It was natural for her to be friendly. She had not meant to flirt with him. She had probably felt shocked and horrified at his approach, and so she had laughed. And because of that he had nursed his grievance for years until it finally burst out in a violent act of rape.

'Was that why it started?' I asked. I was filled with a sick horror. 'Was that why you started to frighten the girls – because you wanted revenge for what she did to you?'

238

'That were Robbie, the daft lad,' he said, a sly grin on his lips. 'It only happened when he'd had a few drinks too many. I was careful not to let him have much money but sometimes he'd get a few shillin's and he'd drink too much cider . . . then he'd play tricks on the girls. He never did them no harm – it weren't in him, the daft bugger. Too soft for his own good he were, always bringing injured creatures into the house.'

'But he didn't rape that girl, did he? He didn't attack that girl – the one they put him away for. He couldn't have, because—'

'He's dead and better off out of it,' Ned Watts said harshly. 'His mother should 'ave died afore she gave birth to him, not after. I should 'ave strangled him at birth. He were all right while she were here to look after him, but I 'ad me job. I couldn't watch him all the time. I knew he'd be in trouble one of these days.'

'But it was you who attacked those last girls, wasn't it? Not Robbie . . . *you.*'

He nodded, his eyes narrowing as he looked at me. 'It were after I saw you and got to thinkin',' he said in a hoarse voice. 'You ain't just like her but there's somethin' about the way you look at a man turns his insides to water . . . and you're *her* daughter. It were you I wanted that night I saw you, standing there with nothing on but your shift . . . but I couldn't get at you and then after you looked at me as if I were dirt that day, I would have come after you. I sent Robbie up to frighten you. I thought you might come down to him, talk to him the way you did sometimes, but the ladder broke and the daft lad ran off . . . It were you I were after, but the other one were there . . .'

I felt sick. It *had* been him standing outside my window that night, watching me. I hadn't realised how revealing my nightclothes were in the light of my lamp. He probably believed I had done it to tempt him. And then I'd made him angry the day I went shopping with Grandmother. He had used his own son to get at me, thinking I would come out to question the boy, but Robbie was frightened and ran away – and I had sat drinking hot milk in the kitchen while Ned Watts went in search of another victim. It was me he had wanted to rape . . . me he had wanted to take his revenge on – for what he imagined was my mother's disdainful treatment of him all those years ago.

'Those poor girls – they did you no harm . . .' I felt sick, dizzy. 'Why did you hurt them?'

'Bitches, both of them,' he muttered, his eyes glittering feverishly now. 'Whores . . . all women are whores and bitches.'

'My mother . . . she shouldn't have laughed at you,' I said. 'I'm sorry she hurt you – but you shouldn't have done what you did to those girls. It was wrong. You are responsible for what happened to Robbie. It's because of what you did—'

'I dare say I'll rot in Hell,' he said and a trickle of saliva ran down his chin. 'Burn for me sins. Mebbe I deserve it – but before I go I'll 'ave me revenge . . .'

He took a step towards me. I gave a little cry of fear and stepped back. He came nearer. I could go no further or I should be too close to the edge of the cliff – one false step and I could go tumbling over that edge to the rocks below. I held out a shaking hand to ward him off.

'Come one step nearer and I shall scream.'

'Won't do you no good if you do, not out here. No one is goin' to hear you.' His eyes narrowed. I saw hatred and lust in his face and felt the vomit rise in my throat. 'I've got you now, my little beauty and—'

I screamed in terror. He made a lunge at me, but before he could grab me a whirlwind of flying skirts and wild hair came rushing at him from behind. I saw a flash of something silver and he shouted in pain as the knife was plunged into his shoulder. He then turned to grapple with the avenging fury who had attacked him.

I stumbled, gasping in terror, moving away from the edge of the cliff as they began to struggle for possession of the knife. At first I was too frightened, too confused to realise what was happening, then I saw the woman's wild, tormented face and I knew.

'Marie,' I whispered. 'Oh, my God, Marie . . . Marie . . .'

She did not hear me. Her face was white with anger, her eyes strangely blind, as if she saw nothing but the man who had attacked me. She was like a madwoman, a screaming, vengeful virago intent on murder.

'I'll kill you,' she screamed, plunging the knife into his chest, arm and neck again and again. 'You touched her, meant to harm her. I'll kill you . . .'

He was grunting in pain, fighting with her, beating at her with his fists. Marie was so strong – much stronger than any normal woman. He had his hands around her throat now. He was trying to strangle her but she fought like a mad thing. It was a titanic struggle . . . terrible and yet magnificent. I watched them, horrified as they slithered and slipped on the bare rock at the edge of the cliff.

And then I screamed as they suddenly went tumbling over it, still locked together, falling into space . . . down . . . down . . . down to the ragged spurs of black rock at the bottom.

I screamed over and over again, not daring to move. I was rooted to the spot, terrified, shocked, sick – unable to believe what I had just witnessed.

'Oh, no . . . no . . . no . . .'

And then all at once Philip was there. He looked at me and then down at the rocks below, his face going white when he saw the broken bodies of the man and woman, still locked together in death.

'My God!' he said. 'What happened? What happened, Jenny?'

'I can't . . .' I was trembling, crying, too stunned to speak. 'Please . . . take me away . . . take me inside . . .'

'Of course. Of course, my darling.' He put his protective arms around me, holding me close. 'Forgive me. I thought you would be safe here. If anything had happened to you . . .'

I clung to him, sobbing as he led me into the house.

It was some time later before I was calm enough to give him the details of what had happened. He was shocked. Everyone was shocked. No one could quite take it in . . . no one could believe that I had come so close to death. It was too horrible, too tragic.

'Marie saved my life,' I said when I could think clearly again. 'I saw her waiting for me at the top of the cliff and I called up to her – but when I got there she had disappeared.'

'But why was she carrying a knife?' Philip asked with a frown. 'Was she planning to attack you herself? What was she doing there – why had she followed you from London?'

'I don't know.' I shook my head. 'Perhaps the knife was to defend herself – against you or anyone else who tried to stop her talking to me. She just wanted to talk to me, Philip. To make me believe that she wasn't trying to harm Julia. She must have thought someone might try to stop her.'

She couldn't have planned to kill me. I wouldn't believe it – not Marie. Not Marie . . .

'Perhaps . . .' said Philip, and I could see doubt in his eyes. 'She must have been half out of her mind – on the verge of a complete mental breakdown. We shall never know for sure.'

'She saved me,' I said, tears beginning to run down my cheeks. 'If he had . . . You would have been too late, Philip. If Marie hadn't attacked him when she did . . . She died for me. She gave her own life to save mine, Philip. Whatever else she did, she saved me.'

'If anything had happened to you . . .' He looked terrible, his face ashen, his mouth white with shock. 'I couldn't have stood it, Jenny. I couldn't bear to lose you.'

I heard the sob he tried to suppress and was surprised. 'Do I mean that much to you?'

'Of course you do,' he said, and his voice was harsh with emotion. 'I love you, Jenny. I love you more than I can tell you. Surely you know that?'

'I . . . wasn't sure,' I said softly. 'I knew you cared . . . that you liked being with me but—'

I got no further. Philip reached out and took me into his arms fiercely, crushing me against him, his mouth demanding and passionate as he kissed me.

'You are my life,' he said hoarsely. 'If you had died, I should have wanted to die, too.'

I felt the shudder run through him and smiled as I put my hand up to touch his cheek.

'I didn't,' I said. 'I'm here with you, Philip.'

'And I shall never leave you alone again,' he said. 'I'm taking you back to my home. You can stay there until we are married. I don't give a damn what the gossips make of it. I want you under *my* roof, where I can look after you myself.'

'I am quite safe here now, my dearest,' I whispered, smiling up at him. 'But I should like to come home with you – and I don't mind what anyone says either . . .'

'Oh, Jenny, Jenny . . . my little gypsy,' he said and bent to kiss me again. 'I loved you from the first moment I saw you in Paris. I never thought then that I had a chance of making you mine – but I loved you. I knew that there would never be another woman for me.'

'Oh, Philip,' I said, laying my head against his chest. 'Take me home, my darling . . . take me home.'

Fifteen

Philip's house was so beautiful, beyond anything I might have expected. Built of soft, buff-coloured stone, it was bathed in winter sunshine the first time I saw it. Not a huge, stately mansion, but a rambling, pretty house with a sloping thatched roof and leaded windows.

'Oh, Philip,' I said. 'I love it. I've never seen such a pretty house.'

'I'm glad you like it,' he replied and smiled down at me. 'Do you think you can be happy here, my darling?'

'Oh, yes,' I breathed. 'Oh yes, I can be happy here.'

When he led me inside I saw that there were many fine pieces of classical furniture, set out not in a formal way – as Laurent's house had been – but more comfortably. Everything was polished and clean, but there were gloves and a riding crop on the hall table, bowls of flowers that had scattered petals on the tables, invitations tucked behind mirrors . . . and books everywhere.

It was to his precious library that Philip took me first. He was like an eager child, showing me the books – so many books that it would indeed take a lifetime to sort them out.

'I've found several rare volumes,' he told me, his eyes alight with enthusiasm. 'Look at this, Jenny – it's a Book of Hours . . .'

Together we exclaimed over the glorious illustrations and the glowing colours.

'My great-great-grandfather was a collector,' Philip told me. 'I think he bought everything he could get his hands on.

A Cornish Rose

There are so many rare editions here . . . everything from Byron to Chaucer.'

I smiled at his enthusiasm. I could see that Philip would spend a great many happy hours in his library.

The day of our wedding was fine and bright, though the breeze was cold as it blew in from the sea. I wore a gown of lemon silk and flowers in my hair, which was loose and flowing down my back.

I thought I looked like a gypsy, but Philip said I was beautiful.

The church service was private and attended by only our closest friends and loved ones – including Laurent and Kate, who had come over specially. Afterwards, we held a large reception at Philip's house to which all his neighbours were invited. I knew that they all must know I had a child but, perhaps because my new husband was a well-loved, popular man, I saw no censure in their eyes. I had been accepted for Philip's sake.

When at last everyone had gone, Philip took my hand and led me upstairs to our bedroom. He stood gazing down at me for a long time, then he reached out to pick the flowers from my hair one by one.

'You are so beautiful, my Jenny,' he whispered. 'So lovely I am almost afraid to touch you . . . afraid that I shall disappoint or hurt you.'

I realised that he was afraid he would not match up to my memories of Gérard and I was touched by his humility. I reached up to kiss his mouth.

'You could never disappoint me, Philip,' I said. 'Don't be afraid, my love. I want you to love me. I want to be yours . . . truly yours.'

'Oh, Jenny,' he said hoarsely, and then reached out to take me in his arms. 'I love you so much . . . so very much.'

I lay looking down at my husband as he slept, a smile of

content on his beloved face. How much I loved him! We had been married just two days and I had discovered such joy in our loving.

I had thought it impossible to find as much pleasure as I had had with Gérard. I had hoped at best for contentment, but Philip had given me so much more. There was a maturity and a depth to his loving that had never been there between Gérard and me – something strong and good that came from the very nature of the man.

It was such a beautiful morning. Philip was still sleeping as I slipped from our bed, pulled a velvet robe over my nightgown and went downstairs into the garden.

I had already explored some of the grounds, but they were large and we had been too busy for me to have seen everything. I had noticed what looked like a wall of rose hedges and I was curious as to what lay behind it. There was plenty of space for me to create my garden here, but I was still looking for something . . . a special corner that would be mine alone.

I am not sure what drew me to the rose hedges, except that they seemed rather private and secluded. The dew was sparkling on the grass that morning and the spider webs hung with diamonds as I found the rose hedges and discovered that they formed a kind of avenue.

What lay beyond that secret way?

I had a feeling of excitement, of anticipation as I made my way through the narrow, overgrown path – and then, all at once I was there.

I could hardly believe my senses. It was the garden I had seen so often in my dreams. Neglected, forgotten, abandoned . . . waiting for me to bring it back to its former glory.

My garden! I could not believe it. Immediately, I felt a sense of peace, of belonging.

'Goodbye,' I heard the voice as a whisper on the wind. 'You are safe now, my little bird . . . safe and happy.'

'Gérard . . .' My throat caught with emotion and tears stung my eyes. I felt the touch of a kiss on my cheek and I knew Gérard was with me . . . then all at once he had gone. 'Goodbye, my dearest . . .'

I was alone but not alone. I could hear the sound of children's laughter. I saw them running – two little boys playing with their older sister. I saw their shadows, smelt the sweet perfume of roses and lilies on a summer's day. Then I saw him walking towards me – the man with whom I should spend my life.

'Jenny . . .' Philip's voice was anxious and I knew that he was real. I was no longer seeing ghosts, past or future. 'I woke and you were not there. I was worried.'

I went to him, my hands outstretched in welcome.

'Philip,' I said. 'What is this place? Who made this garden?'

'It was my grandmother's,' he said, slightly puzzled. 'She loved to come here. When she died my grandfather ordered that it be left to go wild. He could not bear to come here without her.'

'Please . . .' I said, gazing up at him. 'Let me make it mine. Please, Philip. I want to restore it . . . to make it beautiful again.'

'Of course,' he said. 'You can do anything you want. You have no need to ask. Everything I have is yours – I want only to make you happy.' His face was strained and anxious. 'You are happy, Jenny? You don't regret—'

I hushed him with a kiss.

'I regret nothing,' I said. 'I love you, Philip. I shall always love you.' I clasped his hand tightly. 'The past is gone . . . let it go.'

Epilogue

My daughter Julia was married this afternoon. It was a perfect day. The sun shone and the church was filled with the perfume of white lilies and roses from my garden.

Julia walked down the aisle on her father's arm looking serene and beautiful in white lace and satin. I sat with Kate and my two sons, Pip and Lawrence, sitting on either side of me, watching as she took her vows.

Julia has lived her life in sunshine, surrounded by the love of her family. She knows nothing of the dark shadows that hung over me at the time of her birth, nor will she ever. There is no need to burden her with the fears that haunted me for too long.

She knows that I was in love with Gérard de Arnay, that he was my lover and that she was conceived out of wedlock. She also knows that I came to love Philip very much, and that he loves her as if she were his own daughter.

She has no need to wonder about her birth, or to search for a dark secret at the heart of a web of lies. She visited her grandfather in Paris a few weeks before he died, and he left money in trust for her in this country. She loved Laurent, and grieved for him when he died – but her grief is behind her now.

She is very much in love. A beautiful, serene bride.

When I watched my daughter walk to meet her husband on her wedding day, the thought uppermost in my mind was that I hoped she would be as happy in her marriage as I have been in mine.